PUCK:
ALPHA ONE
SECURITY

BOOK 4

JASINDA WILDER

PUCK:
ALPHA ONE
SECURITY

99 PROBLEMS

NINETY-NINE PROBLEMS, BUT A BITCH AIN'T *one*—the Jay-Z line went through my head. Despite everything it was kinda funny because one bitch wasn't my problem; there were *two* of them. And don't get your panties in a knot. I mean "bitch" as a term of endearment—I liked those two girls, Lola and Temple, which was why I was here in the first fucking place.

Significantly higher up the problem list was the fact that I was in the mostly empty baggage compartment of a privately owned 727, and we were way, way up there, meaning it was cold as fuck in here—pressurized and liveable, but fucking freezing.

Another problem was I had no weapons and, furthermore, I had no plan for what to do when we got wherever the hell we were going—that lack of knowledge was yet another problem on the list.

Additionally, Harris and the gang, as far as I knew, had no idea what was going on, although I knew they would find out eventually. Which meant, for the moment, I was on my own . . .

In the cargo hold of an airliner flying at cruising altitude.

Without a weapon.

Responsible for the lives of two beautiful women, who happened to be the girlfriends of my two closest brothers-in-arms.

Between the injury and my lame attempt to cauterize the wound with my cigar, my finger hurt like a bitch.

On top of it all, literally, were the twenty-some armed men a few feet above me in the passenger cabin.

Good times.

Going in my favor, though, were two facts: I was a stone-cold, hard-ass motherfucker, and I was *really* pissed off.

Also going in my favor was my background in both the military and FBI—I was patient, I was used to long periods of hurry up and wait. I could hunker down in the most uncomfortable situations and stay in a state of readiness for hours. Which was what I had in front of me at the moment . . . I was cold, I was in pain, I was pissed off, I had female friends needing rescue, and I had no clue where we were going or how long it would take to get there, and I had no idea what I was going to do once we arrived.

So I did what any self-respecting grunt and cop would: I snoozed.

A snooze was a specific thing for cops and Army grunts: you ain't sleeping, but you were also not quite awake. You were in-between, relaxing, resting, eyes closed, brain off, muscles loose, but not quite un-conscious; you were ready to spring into action at the sound of a CO's bark or the crackle of the radio. Personally, I have perfected the snooze. I could let myself sink into a state that was *just* this side of totally asleep and then the instant my senses told me it was go-time, I was in motion without so much as a yawn. It was a great way to juice up your batteries between firefights and also great for passing long periods of boredom on a stakeout. Or, in this particular case, both.

As I snoozed I thought back over the past couple of days. What a shit show. That bastard Cain and his men ambushed us and, long story short, his goons swooped in and captured the women and me and put us on this plane. What a jackass—and a pussy, too: hurting women and kids was pathetic. He would live to regret it if I had anything to do with it. Not to mention the fact that my chest still hurt like hell from taking bullets in my vest during the firefight. As I mentioned, one of the bullets ripped off the top off the middle finger on my left hand and that *really* pissed me off. That was my "fuck you" finger. I'd managed to cauterize it a bit with the end of a cigar, but the wound would not close completely. When I finally got my hands on Cain, the bastard was going to pay.

I needed to rest more than I needed to lose my shit over my finger, so I closed my eyes and the next thing I knew my snooze had lasted what felt like six hours or so, which meant we were most likely headed to Europe. The runway had been north-south oriented, and the aircraft had taken off into the north and then banked wide and slow to the right. Hard to tell without visual cues, but the angle and duration of the turn made me feel like we'd turned east or northeast, and from then on travel had been straight as an arrow. Six hours or so from Arkansas in a north easterly direction in a 727 traveling at cruising speed . . . the UK maybe, or Spain or France.

My estimation of the time I'd been snoozing was just that—an estimation. I didn't wear a watch because there was no point, I'd lost my burner phone at some point during the chase, and I didn't own a day-to-day personal cell. If we were on a mission, I just bought a burner to use for the duration of the mission, but if we're between ops, I didn't carry a cell. Time was a construct, and I didn't like being accessible all the damn time. I liked my personal time and personal space way too much to let any ol' dick call me and gab at me all fucking day.

Point was, I didn't know the exact time, or how long we'd been flying. It was just that we ain't in Kansas anymore, Toto.

What kicked me out of my snooze was a sharp banking turn, signaling the pilot was orienting himself with a runway. That was followed by the *thunk-cachunk-grrrrrrrr-thunk* of the landing gear being lowered. A moment later my stomach lurched as we descended, and then the bark and bump and skid of touchdown. Then I began to feel a bit of panic. Just because I was a stone cold hard-ass motherfuck-er didn't mean I was devoid of emotions. I got squir-relly before a big op, and if folks were shootin' at me I got pissy like anybody else. And when I was facing shit like I was facing then, I got a bit panicky.

I could take on plenty of assholes with fists and feet and forehead—I'd been a barroom brawler and bare-knuckled boxer from the time I was knee high to a tadpole—but twenty assholes with guns . . . I didn't like those odds.

So . . . now what?

Play it by ear, I guess.

But fuck, fuck, and double motherfuck, I wished to hell I *at least* had my Beretta.

I felt the aircraft brake and pivot as we taxied, and I took stock again of the small amount of bag-gage in the hold. A dozen suitcases, all containing nothing but clothes and clothes and clothes and more clothes—all female and of widely varying sizes, but all scanty and skimpy, hooker getups and runway shit. Another suitcase with shoes, another with all kinds of makeup. A cooler full of food, which I raided when I first snuck in here. There were no weapons, and nothing I could even use as a weapon.

And the presence of all the girl gear had my wheels turning. Why would a bunch of mercs and thugs have brought evening gowns and booty shorts and mascara? Well . . . seeing as they kidnapped two fine-ass women, I guessed we were headed to a people market, wherein Cain sold women like sides of beef.

Now here's something to know about Puck Lawson: I did *not* take kindly to the sale of human flesh. People were people, and people ain't for sale. If a woman made the choice to sell her body, that was her choice, and I got no issue with that—better not, since my mama was a hooker. But that was different. She was doing that herself, to survive, to make ends meet, because she liked sex, whatever the case might be. But if she hadn't chosen to pursue that occupation, then that shit was slavery, and as far as I knew slavery was ended in this country awhile back. So if Lola and Temple were en route to being sold into the sex trade, then some folks were about to get their shit *wrecked*.

You wanna see the really ugly side of an already

ugly motherfucker? Try and sell someone when I was around.

The 727 came to a halt, and I positioned myself to the side of the cargo door. I heard the rattling rumble of a diesel engine, and the whining of the aircraft jets spooling down, another soft *thunk*—the stair lift was being positioned outside. Voices, male, gruff, speaking . . . Czech? Ukrainian? Not sure, exactly, since I didn't have Thresh or Anselm's polyglot skills. Then female voices, several of them, all frightened, angry, speaking English and Russian and some Asian dialect and half a dozen other languages. All the female voices were abruptly silenced when a handgun went off and a male voice shouted, "*SHUT UP!*"

Yeah, that dude was gonna be first to die if I had anything to say about it.

I knew orders were being given—I could only tell from the tone of voice since the orders were in whatever language those dickknobs spoke. Silence for a moment, and then I heard the clatter and thunk of the cargo door opening.

A male head popped in, followed by the rest of the body—average height, average build, brown hair, kinda ugly, and carrying an AK on his back by a strap. He passed right by me without seeing me, somehow, and made straight for the pile of luggage strapped down in the middle of the hold. He was about two hundred feet away and was busy trying to sort the luggage; it was black as hell in there and I could barely see him.

As the second dude walked past me, I tiptoed up behind him, wrapped my arm around his throat and gripped my wrist in a chokehold. Fucker didn't know self-defense, apparently, because all he did was gurgle and thrash, surprised and, well, choked to death. When I was sure he wasn't going to pull out some Judo shit, I loosened my hold so he could answer a question.

"English?" I growled in his ear over the noise outside and the sound of the engine slowing down.

"*Da! Da!*"

"Where are the girls being taken?"

He wiggled, and I squeezed until he quit.

"Market," he rasped.

"Which market? Where?"

"Don't—don't know!"

I squeezed again, hard enough to impress upon him the understanding that I could end him with a flex and a twist. "Talk, bitch, or you're dead."

"I don't know!" He gurgled this a little too loud, and I clamped down until he thrashed and struggled. "Promise, promise—I only load baggage and guard door."

"The assholes in charge—they know everyone by name and face?"

"*Nyet.* But they only speak Russian or . . . *Ukrainets.* From Ukraine, *da*?"

"How many?"

"How many where?"

I heard a diesel engine cough into life, and assumed that meant time was short.

"Doesn't really matter how many, does it?" I asked, but the question was meant rhetorically.

And besides, I didn't give him a chance to answer. I squeezed until he thrashed, and kept squeezing until his kicking slowed, and then I set him down, stripped him of his AK, and checked him for useful shit. He had a cheap plastic lighter, some shitty Russian cigarettes, a spare mag for the AK, a beaten, old, and scuffed-to-hell Makarov 9mm with a mag for that. A decent handful of cash in American dollars, Euros, and Rubles, a passport, and a small black folding knife.

Enough to get me started.

I hauled the body to the very back of the cargo hold and hoped to hell nobody looked in there, or knew who had been sent in to get the bags.

I heard a voice shouting something, in what sounded like Russian, getting closer, so I stuffed the cigarettes, cash, lighter, magazines, and knife in my BDU pockets, slung the AK around my back, and shoved the pistol behind my waistband at the small of my back. And then started slinging suitcases toward the cargo door.

My plan was stupid, but it was all I could think of: pretend to be one of them for as long as I could and then start shooting, or whichever course of action seemed best at that particular moment. Right now, though, I threw suitcases. A pair of hands grabbed them as they reached the door; he didn't glance in, thankfully. If he had, he'd have seen the dead guy, which probably would have ended the game before it started.

I started to wish I could speak more than just English. Thresh and some of the other A1S guys spoke more than one language, but that just wasn't my skill set. I could ping a nail with a 9mm round from damn near a hundred yards, I could read blood splatter as easily as "Run, Spot, Run," I could hold my own in a firefight, fistfight, or knifefight, and I could analyze ballistics and trajectories like a road map. I just couldn't speak anything except plain old English, and even that I often mangled. Fine. Whatever. Wasn't usually a problem. Right now, though? I had a feeling it was going to be a major fuckin' problem.

I tossed the last suitcase at the opening and followed it over, hopping out of the baggage hold after it. A monster tub of lard with platinum blond hair, wearing a maroon track suit with three white stripes down the sleeves and pant legs, was waiting by the back end of an aging Mercedes party bus, the kind of thing that was bigger than a van but shorter than a tour bus, usually used for bachelorette parties and winery tours. He tossed in two suitcases, and then glanced at me as I hopped down.

"*Gde Anton*?" he said, peering at the cargo hold doorway.

I shrugged, grabbed a suitcase and tossed it in the back. My heart was hammering, but I kept up the pretense, helping the big fat bruiser load the luggage into the van. He was easily six six, and probably weighed three hundred or three fifty, but it was all flab; he was gasping and sweating just from tossing a few suitcases.

My plan was just to bluff my way through, shrug and grunt and act dumb, and hope an opportunity presented itself. When the luggage was loaded, Tubby McTracksuit climbed up and behind the wheel. I climbed up into the van after him, and the guy shot me a quizzical look but didn't object, so I took the nearest seat, shifting the AK around front as I sat down. I scanned the van, and my heart sank. I saw not only Lola and Temple, but Layla and Kyrie too, plus another eighteen or twenty other girls. What the fuck? How did the A1S girls end up here?

All the women were between sixteen-ish and forty-ish, ranging from the plain side of pretty to drop-dead gorgeous, and they were of all builds and ethnicities. And they all looked terrified. Most of them had tear tracks dried on their cheeks, and a few looked dazed and numb. Fuckers had all four of our women? They had *Kyrie*? Motherfuckers weren't smart, then. Taking Kyrie meant they'd pissed off Valentine Roth, and that was *not* a good move. They had Layla, which meant Harris was pissed off, and they had Lola and Temple, which meant Thresh and Duke were pissed off. Four of the deadliest men on the planet, with nearly endless resources at their disposal—and you snatched their women? Pretty fuckin' stupid.

It would have been comical, except that even for those guys time was of the essence. I only hoped they knew where we were, and they got here in time.

All four of the women saw me and recognized me, but I shot them a hard stare and shook my head as subtly as I could. None of them visibly reacted.

Tubby McTracksuit twisted in his seat and whacked me on the arm. "*Gde Anton*?"

I shrugged again and tried to look like I couldn't give any less of a shit.

He honked the horn, waited a moment, and then honked again. "*Yebat yego*," he muttered and shoved the vehicle into gear.

It couldn't be this easy, could it? Nah. Probably not. Something was going to go wrong. It was just a matter of what, how bad, and when.

To review: I wished to fuck I had a cell phone, and I wished to fuck I spoke Russian. But as Grandpappy Lawson used to say, if wishes were fishes, I'd stink like fucking fish.

I stuffed one of the dead Russian's cigarettes into my mouth and lit it with his lighter, and puffed a cloud of smoke at the ceiling, letting my eyes wander idly over the other passengers. I kept my expression neutral as I skipped over the women I knew. There was quite a broad spectrum represented here: Asians, blacks, Indians, Caucasians . . . and all of them were mighty fine looking women.

My gaze stopped, pretty much of its own accord, on a woman sitting two rows away from me across the aisle. She wasn't the type of girl I hit on at a bar, let's just start there. For one thing, she was probably taller than me, which normally didn't work out too well. For another, she seemed . . . prim. Sweet. Aristocratic. She was sitting all upright and proper like we were at a black-tie dinner or some shit, her shoulders straight, her head high, knees together, hands on her lap, and her expression was closed, tight, and cold. I respected that, the fact that she could retain her decorum under these circumstances, probably knowing what her fate would be. Plus, she was just . . . delicate looking. Gorgeous as hell, but delicate. I didn't mean frail, just . . . shit. I didn't fucking know what I meant.

Maybe five ten or five eleven, tall for a woman, and an inch or two taller than my five nine. Long, thick, wavy, shimmery locks of glossy mahogany brown hair—a shade that wasn't quite auburn, but still had hints of red. It hung loose around her slender face and thin shoulders, so thick, so much hair . . . *I want to wrap that gorgeous hair around my fist and fuck her brains out from behind*—that was the thought running through my head, and my dick responded in kind, stirring in my pants just thinking about it. Made me an asshole, but hey, I never claimed to be anything else.

Her face, though . . . she was truly, stunningly, classically beautiful. High, sharp cheekbones, cute as a button little nose, a wide mouth with plump lips—she could rival Julia Roberts in terms of mouth hotness. She was sitting across the aisle from me and on the outside, so I could see she had legs for goddamn days, sheathed in a sensible black knee-length skirt, power suit style. She had on a long-sleeved forest green blouse, buttoned to a hot but still modest second button, enough to show a hint of cleavage but not enough to make mouths water. The skirt and blouse were rumpled, the worse for wear, yet she still looked put-together, in control, and hot as fuck. Her knees were pressed together, her feet tucked on an angle underneath her seat, and I could see a hint of sensible black heels. Her skin was creamy smooth and naturally golden tanned and was everything sweet and luscious.

She caught me staring, and her eyes met mine—hers were storm-cloud gray and utterly fearless. Scratch that, I saw a hint of nervousness, but she met my stare boldly, and didn't look away. I couldn't help it: I winked at her, shot her a brief, cocky grin. She rolled her eyes and looked away, barely suppressing a hiss of anger.

I glanced at Layla and saw she was trying not to laugh, having watched the exchange, both my blatant perusal of the girl and her reaction to my wink and smile. Layla knew me as well as anyone, and if anyone was going to keep calm in this situation, it was Layla Harris. That bitch had ice in her veins, and I knew for a fact she could hold down her end of a gun battle. I honestly felt a bit of relief, knowing I had Layla with me, because I knew I could rely on her to help me wreck shit when the time came to put down the hurt.

I'd let the cigarette dangle from my mouth, not really smoking it, more letting it sit there for show, to look the part. Then I took a drag, held it in my mouth as if inhaling, and spewed out the smoke. Knocked the ash free and rolled my shoulders, fiddled with the AK as if bored, glancing at the driver. He seemed oblivious, navigating us through some rundown suburban neighborhoods like you'd see outside any airport anywhere in the world, fading paint on aging buildings, trees lining the streets, and the occasional billboard—I wasn't much on languages, but at least I could tell we were in a country that used Cyrillic, Russia probably. The sky was as gray as lead and heavy, the buildings around us low, squat, ugly blocks in every direction.

I kept watching, shifting now and again as Tubby drove for what seemed like at least thirty minutes, if not longer. Some of the women started dozing, despite themselves.

Not Layla, and not sexy Miss Ringlets, though. They were both wide-awake, alert, watching.

Ringlets especially. She tried to keep her gaze out the window, but it kept sliding back to me, and I wondered what she was thinking.

SPARKIN'

H<small>E *WINKED* AT ME. FOR REAL? WHO EVEN WINKS</small> anymore? What was the wink supposed to mean? I felt his eyes on me, and it was fairly obvious what those jackasses were planning, but still. A wink? It wasn't the kind of wink that said *I'm about to rape you*, though. It was . . . almost friendly. Playful. What the hell?

I also noticed the way he glanced at the four women sitting together across the aisle from me. I wasn't sure who knew whom, but it seemed some of them knew each other, and Mr. Short, Buff, Bald, and Bearded seemed to know the four women, although he did a passable impression of not recognizing them.

Can't fool me, though.

I also noticed that the body language of all four

of those women seemed to relax ever so slightly when they saw Beardy.

Another odd detail: Beardy had a messed up finger. Recent, from the looks of it, the middle finger of his left hand was gone from the middle knuckle, the stump looking scabbed and burned and messy, still oozing nastiness, although he seemed somewhat oblivious to it.

The more I looked at Beardy, the more out of place he seemed. He was wearing a black T-shirt with the sleeves cut off to create a muscle shirt, and the logo on the front was a bunch of angry red lines creating what was probably supposed to be lettering—a heavy metal band T-shirt. His pants were the kind of surplus military gear you could get from any surplus store anywhere in the States . . . but that was what was odd about it—did they have Army/Navy surplus stores in eastern Europe? He also had a full sleeve of tattoos on his right arm from shoulder to wrist, and a lot of the images were . . . uniquely Western, just put it that way. A pair of dice and playing cards, revolvers with the barrels crossed, a 1940s-style pinup girl, Clint Eastwood as Dirty Harry, handcuffs, an M-16 with a US Army helmet hanging on it—a symbol for knowing someone killed in action . . . all über-masculine Americana tattoo images. A little out of place for a Russian gangster.

My street-sense was tingling.

Beardy caught me staring, then, and shot me

another wink. I glared back at him as his eyes blatantly skimmed down my body, checking me out. Not much to see, buddy—you and your thug asshole buddies snatched me as I was leaving work, which meant they'd gotten conservative Colbie, the version of me who wore business-formal skirt suits at an office-appropriate knee-length and blouses that showed little to no cleavage. Had they snatched me an hour or so later, from my home, I'd probably be a lot less conservatively dressed. But I supposed I was glad for that. Conservative Colbie wore her skirt suits like armor; once I zipped that skirt up and buttoned the blouse, I put on my take-no-shit mentality. It was this mindset that had taken me from homeless drug-addicted orphan teenager to Harvard Business School graduate with a double minor in Chinese and Russian.

I knew the score here—I was on my way to being sold into the sex trade. But these jackasses really had no idea who they were dealing with, or what I'd been through, and what I was prepared to do in the name of self-preservation. I'd survived heroin addiction; I'd survived on the streets of New York as a teenage girl alone; I'd fought my way into Harvard on loans, grants, and scholarships, then graduated *summa cum laude*. I did all that on my own, no handouts, no ass kissing, no favors. After all that, I'd landed myself a job at one of the top import-export firms in the country.

And these assholes thought they could just nab

me off the streets and sell me like a bag of dope? I did *not* think so.

I didn't know how, but I was getting my ass back to New York, and if I had to break some heads back-alley-brawl style, I wouldn't even feel bad.

Beardy, though. He was interesting. At first I'd just dismissed him as another gangbanger and hadn't given him another thought. Then he'd shot me the wink and the smirk, and I'd noticed the tattoos and the looks the four women were giving him, and I took another look at him. And I realized he wasn't exactly bad looking. Sure, he had that crazy god-damn beard, but it wasn't a hobo beard, it was well groomed, brushed, maintained, shaped. It was a well-loved beard. Big, bushy, long as hell, but it suited him. Framed a strong jaw and an expressive mouth. The end hung to mid-chest. And his eyes, man, those eyes of his were . . . complicated. Dark brown, like chocolate and coffee, sharp and bright with intelligence, wary, alert, and piercing. Yet when he shot me that stupid wink, if I were a writer, I'd have said his eyes twinkled. He wasn't a tall guy, but he was massive de-spite that. His arms alone gave my waist a run for its money in terms of width and breadth, and his chest and shoulders were equally as massive. It wasn't fat, either—I saw the tendons and cords of muscle shift-ing and tensing as he moved, saw the bulge of his bi-cep when he reached up to scratch his scalp. He was brawny and powerful, and I found myself wondering about him, unable to stop stealing glances at him.

Bad timing for curiosity, though. I mean, kind of a dumb idea, wasn't it? Getting hot for my kidnapper?

You would've thought I'd be more afraid, but I was in survival mode, which meant whatever feared I might have felt was pushed deep down. I'd have a nice little girly fit later, when I was safe and alone, but for now, I knew I had to keep it together. It was a false calm, but better than hysterics. I'd seen some of the other girls break down and indulge in bouts of tears, dissolving into sobbing puddles of fear and exhaustion, which only served to piss off the gangsters.

Speaking of which, there had been a lot of guards on that plane, at least twenty that I'd counted; yet there were only the two on this bus—the driver and Beardy. Where were the rest? Why send so many of them only to leave us guarded by a single pair?

The bus pulled up to a stoplight, and that was when I got at least one answer to my questions. I heard a crackle of static from a walkie-talkie, and a male voice said, in Russian, "*Chekov, are you there?*"

Ah, that explained it: the rest of the guards were in other vehicles ahead and/or behind this one.

The driver pulled a handset from the pocket of his tracksuit and answered in Russian. "*Yes, what is it?*"

"*Anton is missing. Have you seen him? Is he with you?*"

"*No, he's not,*" the driver, Chekov, answered. "*He's*

not with you?"

"*No. He was supposed to unload the bags.*"

"*Someone else unloaded the bags,*" the driver said. "*A new guy.*"

"*A new guy? There is no one new.*"

The driver twisted in his seat and shot an odd look at Beardy, then returned to face forward as the light turned.

I watched Beardy during this exchange, and he gave no impression of understanding what was being said; he scratched his nose with an index finger and then wiggled the stump of his missing middle finger, as if testing the pain level.

"*If there is no one new, and Anton is missing, then who is this guy on the bus with me?*" the driver asked.

"*Good question. Find out.*"

The driver slid the walkie-talkie back into his tracksuit jacket pocket and then reached into the other pocket and withdrew a huge silver handgun. He checked the mirrors and pulled off the road into a mostly empty parking lot outside a partially demolished building, shoving the shifter into Park.

Beardy finally seemed to realize something was up, glancing out the window as if curious as to why we'd stopped. He eyed the driver, who tried to surreptitiously pull back the slide of his handgun, but the noise as the slide clicked back into place was distinctive and unmistakeable. Beardy glanced at me as he pulled a small black handgun from his waistband then cut a glance at the driver and back to me, wiggling the gun; it was a question—*does he have a gun out*? I nodded, a tiny movement of my head.

The driver twisted in his seat to look at Beardy. "What did you say your name was?" he asked, in heavily accented English.

"Puck," Beardy said, and then instantly realized what had just happened. "Shit."

The following few seconds were a blur of noise and movement taking place too fast for me to track. As soon as the word "shit" left Puck's mouth, he lifted his gun and shot the driver, a single deafening concussive *BANG*! Red spattered against the windshield, a hole appearing in the glass, spider webs spreading. Screams filled the bus. Puck was out of his seat the moment his gun went off, yanked the handle that opened the driver's door, snatched up the shiny silver pistol, patted the driver's pockets, and tugged out two magazines. Puck then grabbed the body by the shoulders and, with a grunt of effort, heaved the corpse out the door. The dead driver flopped to the ground, his head crunching wetly on the pavement, his feet still inside the bus. Puck leapt into the driver's seat, jerked the shifter into drive, and floored the gas pedal. The bus growled, and we were all thrown back in our seats as the vehicle accelerated, and I heard a nasty thump as the wheels rolled over the body.

The road we were on was mostly abandoned; a single sedan passed us, and upon seeing the body flop out of the van, their tires squealed, and they peeled away. I got the impression that this might not have been an uncommon occurrence in this area.

So now we were moving. The only problem? Blood coated the inside of the windshield, making it impossible for him to see.

"Well that was dumb," Puck said, sounding irritated. "This is not going as I'd hoped."

"What the fuck are you doing here, Puck?" one of the women asked; she was medium height with dark skin and a springy mass of curly black hair, and she was so curvy she made me stare, and I'm as straight as they come. I'm . . . svelte, let's call it. Not stick-thin, and I've got a decent rack and nice tight ass, but nothing like that woman had.

"Getting you out of here." He wiped at the windshield with his hand, but only smeared it and made the visibility worse.

"Well you're sucking at it so far," the woman said. "I'm gonna give you a C on this rescue attempt, so far."

"I'd rather you give me those double Ds," Puck said, shooting her a grin.

She smacked his shoulder hard. "You're a pig." She whipped off her T-shirt to reveal a pink tank top with purple bra straps peeking out from underneath. "Here, asshole," she said, handing him her shirt.

Puck took the shirt and wiped at the blood, folded it and wiped again, and finally made a little progress, clearing a patch through which he could see. "Thanks, Layla."

I could see the driver's side mirror, and the reflection of a big black SUV in it. As I watched, a passenger window lowered and a figure leaned out, a machine gun in his hands.

"Umm." I raised my hand. "Puck, I'd check your mirrors."

He glanced at me in the rearview mirror, and then checked his side view mirror. "Shit. I was hoping you girls being in here would stop them from doing anything too crazy."

The woman, Layla, held on to the driver's seatback and crouched next to Puck. "Can I hang out the side of the bus and shoot at them like in the movies? I've always wanted to try that."

"I don't think so. You drive, I shoot."

Layla grabbed his bicep and shook it, pleading with him. "Come on, Puck. Please? Just a couple shots? You know I can hit them."

Puck snorted. "Bitch, please. Harris would have my ass if I let you do that." He glanced at her. "'Sides, that shit is a lot harder than it looks."

I watched them bicker, amused, and wondered what Layla would do, being called a bitch. Me, I would have slapped him hard enough to show him who the real bitch was.

"Oh, don't be a wet blanket, Puck. I won't tell him if you won't."

The way Puck hesitated made it seem like he was actually considering it. He wouldn't, would he? No way.

Puck handed her his pistol. "Don't try to hit their tires, that's Hollywood bullshit, and it never works. Either go for the engine block or the driver. And when they start shooting back, get your juicy ass back in the bus."

Layla took the pistol, held it by the barrel, and whacked Puck on the top of the head with the butt. "I'm married to your boss, Puck Lawson! You can't talk to me that way."

"You can stop a man from touching, but you can't stop him from looking . . . or appreciating." He rubbed the top of his head, and then ducked involuntarily when the clattering *crackcrackcrackcrackcrack* of an AK-47 blasted the air behind us, and the rear window shattered.

"EVERYONE ON THE FLOOR!" Puck shouted. "Layla, start shooting."

I hit the floor, too, and then thought better of it; I wasn't a hider. I crawled forward as Layla levered open the bi-fold bus door, held onto the handle mounted on the inside of the frame, leaned out, and aimed the pistol one handed at the vehicle in pursuit of us. I focused on Puck but heard the *BANG!* . . . *BANG!* . . . *BANG!* as she fired.

I tapped Puck on the leg. "Hey."

He glanced down at me. "Hey there, gorgeous.

You have the advantage with me, I'm afraid—you know my name, but I don't know yours."

I ignored his statement and pointed at the shattered rear window. "Go shoot at them."

"You'll drive?" he asked. I nodded, and he slid off the chair while keeping one hand on the wheel and his foot on the accelerator. "Keep it straight and hold steady on the gas until Layla is back inside."

I slid behind him to take his place at the wheel, but the tight quarters meant I had to press up against his back, sliding my thighs under his butt so I could get my foot on the gas pedal. As soon as I was sitting and had the wheel and my foot on the gas, Puck sat down on my lap and twisted so he could look at me. His eyes twinkled again: merry, amused, glittering with intelligence and humor—and lust, as he blatantly looked down my shirt.

"Umm." I pushed at him, but it was like trying to push over the Rockerfeller building. "Get off, asshole."

He slid off me and pivoted in a crouch. "Oh, I intend to. You and me both, sweet thing." His eyes met mine, and he winked. "Gotta tell me your name first, though."

"Does that shit actually work for you?" I asked, giving him my best die-*you-asshole* glare.

He shrugged. "Yeah, usually. Telling a woman exactly what I intend to do, and how well, and how often . . . yeah, it works pretty damn well."

"It's not gonna work on me, though." I jerked my

thumb at the rear window. "Go shoot someone."

"Shooting people is my second favorite activity." He winked at me again and hauled the AK-47 around and held it in both hands as he moved forward in a crouch.

"And stop winking at me!" I shouted. "Nobody winks anymore! It's stupid."

I heard a snicker from Layla, who had pulled herself back inside the bus. "What?" I snapped. "What's so funny?"

She held out her fist for me to bump. "You— you're funny. I like you. We can be friends."

I tapped my fist against hers. "Good to know I have your approval." I gestured at Puck. "Is he always like this?"

Layla nodded. "Worse, usually. You're meeting Puck when he's focused on work. Just wait till he has time to *really* hit on you."

"Work? This is . . . work?" I frowned. "And if he hits on me, I'll hit back, just sayin'."

"Careful, he might like it."

I couldn't help a little snicker from escaping. "Dammit, you're right." I grinned at her. "Colbie Danvers."

"Layla Harris."

While Layla and I were talking, Puck was shooting, the AK-47 barking intermittently, and then after a moment the sound of shooting stopped. I glanced in the rearview just in time to see the SUV behind us rotate sideways, the windshield riddled. It skidded sideways, then a tire caught and it rolled, metal crunching and glass shattering. I returned my attention to the road ahead, a four-lane thoroughfare that could have been in a neighborhood outside New York City, except for the fact that the street signs were all in Cyrillic.

There was a lot of sniffling and whispering and clinging happening among the other women in the bus, with the notable exception of Layla, the other three women, and myself. Hope blossomed—we'd gotten rid of our pursuers, which hopefully meant we were home free—I glanced in the rearview mirror again and felt my stomach clench. The SUV was visible in the distance, overturned and smoking . . . but there were two more on our tail, their windows opened.

I heard gunfire, felt thunks and clunks as bullets smashed into the back of the bus, and then the windshield in front of me spiderwebbed even more as several holes smashed through it. More thunks, smacks, dings. And then a *POP!* and the steering wheel jerked to the right as the back right tire blew, and the bus swerved across the centerline.

"They popped a tire!" I shouted. "Hold on!"

I fought for control, jamming the brakes and trying to wrestle the huge vehicle back into the correct lane before oncoming traffic smashed into us.

"Swing around!" Puck shouted. "Pop a

U-turn—wheel it over hard and floor it!"

I didn't follow orders well, never had and never would. But for some reason, when Puck barked that order at me, I listened without thinking twice. I let off the brakes, hauled the wheel hand-over-hand all the way to the right and floored it. The bus slewed around awkwardly, tipping dangerously, the diesel engine roaring in protest. The front tires hopped the curb, and I had to let off the accelerator momentarily to avoid plowing into a tree. The instant the nose of the bus was clear, I floored it again and heard the cracking chatter of Puck's AK-47, drowning out the screams and crying of the other women. Layla was bracing herself in the door opening again, feet against the doorframe, one hand on the handle, the other hand extending the pistol. The lead SUV in pursuit swept past us, tires screeching as it tried to pull off one of those cool-looking brake turns. It didn't quite manage the maneuver, though, spinning around too far—which provided Layla a perfect opportunity to crack off a trio of fast shots. Her aim was damn near perfect, it looked like, holes peppering the passenger side window and turning the driver's side opposite red—the SUV bolted forward, out of control, and smashed into a wall surrounding a construction site.

"Goddamn, Layla!" Puck crowed. "That there was some good shootin', Tex!"

Layla threw herself backward into the bus and put her back to the side of my chair, reaching up with one hand to push forward the lever that closed the door. Another burst of firing from Puck—I checked the mirror and saw that the last SUV had been incapacitated, the engine smoking, the windows along the entire length of the vehicle riddled with holes, gore visible on the opposite side of the interior.

The flat tire was flapping, the rim scraping and grinding, pulling at our momentum and making the steering wheel wobble and shudder.

"Can't keep this thing on the road much longer," I said, as Puck moved back toward the front.

"No shit." He scratched his scalp with a fingertip as he searched the road ahead. I heard sirens, somewhere in the distance. "We gotta make ourselves scarce."

"Sounds like the police are on their way." I glanced at him. "Couldn't we just pull over and wait for them?"

Puck stared at me like I was crazy. "Number one, these guys probably own the cops. Number two, even if the cops were honest, we just killed a bunch of people, and even if was in self-defense, that's still a bunch of questions I don't have any easy answers for, and number three, we're in a foreign country which we entered illegally with no documentation, and number four, I don't speak fucking Russian."

"Well, yeah, that much is obvious. The driver was talking about you right before he pulled over. They figured out that you'd tried to replace some guy named Anton."

Puck eyed me. "You speak Russian?"

I shrugged. "Yeah. And Mandarin."

From the other side of Puck, Layla piped up. "Her name is Colbie Danvers."

"Because I can't introduce myself," I remarked, shooting her a glare.

Layla just shrugged. "Just introducing my friends to each other."

Puck looked from Layla to me. "Wait, you two know each other?"

"Nope, we just met," Layla said. "But we're kindred spirits."

I rolled my eyes. "Yeah, that's us, Anne Shirley and Diana Berry." When both Puck and Layla just stared at me, I shook my head in disgust. "*Anne of Green Gables*?"

I was still driving, trying to keep the bus mostly straight as I searched our surroundings for somewhere to pull over.

"Never read it," Puck said. "Not really my thing."

"What, reading?" I snorted. "Color me shocked."

"Actually, Puck has a PhD," Layla said. "Pull in there." She pointed at a road that was somewhere between a side street and an alley—a narrow, crumbling lane between rows of buildings.

I filed away that little tidbit about Puck as I pulled into the alley, passing what looked like an auto garage on one side and an abandoned ware-house on the other. Beyond the abandoned ware-house was a rickety, toppling wooden fence sepa-rating the alley from a row of dilapidated houses. I drove slowly down the alley, the flat tire *flap—flap—flapping*, and the rim grating against the ground. A bit farther down, the wooden fence gave way to an abandoned lot, overgrown with shrubs and trees, the ground covered in the ruins of a building long-since torn down, now nothing but crumbled cinder-blocks and rusted rebar, the lot now used as a local dumping ground, overflowing with trash. Opposite was another fence, this one green metal and shoul-der-height, topped with coils of barbed wire, tin roofing visible above it. After about a hundred yards, the alley dead-ended at a flat gray metal gate.

I halted the bus a dozen feet from the gate and glanced at Puck. "Now what?"

Puck opened the door and exited the bus, let-ting out a sigh. "No fuckin' idea. This whole running from bad guys thing ain't exactly my area of exper-tise—usually it's the other away around."

He trotted off, the AK-47 slung around behind his back, pistol in one hand.

Layla went out after him, and so I followed—a few seconds later the other women who seemed to be part of this particular group joined us.

Two of the other women were blondes and the third was a woman with dark skin and black hair—she could have been a sister to Layla, based on looks alone.

Layla pointed at the first blond woman. "This is my best friend, Kyrie St. Claire. The other gorgeous blond lady you might recognize . . . she's Temple Kennedy. The one with the curly black hair and killer body is Lola Reed. Everybody, this is Colbie Danvers."

I said hi to everyone, my mind racing. Kyrie St. Claire . . . the name rang a bell. There'd been a recent article in *People* or one of those celebrity gossip magazines about the reclusive billionaire playboy, Valentine Roth—apparently he'd gotten married and had a baby . . . the woman in the photographs had been named Kyrie St. Claire. Then there was Temple Kennedy, star of a reality TV show and the daughter of a famous actress and equally famous rock star.

"How do you ladies all know each other?" I asked.

Layla answered. "Well, Kyrie and I have been friends for years. She's married to Valentine Roth, and I'm married to Roth's head of security, Nick Harris. Lola and Temple are both involved with employees of my husband, which makes them kind of like sisters to Kyrie and me."

"Welcome to the Alpha One Security Sisterhood, Colbie," Kyrie added.

Kyrie was on the short side but stunning all the same. Her hair was golden, her eyes blue, and her voice soft and unassuming; she didn't seem any more fazed by recent events than Layla did . . . none of these women did, for that matter.

"The what?" I blinked at Kyrie as I tried to process her words.

Kyrie gestured at Puck, who was standing beside me. "You and Puck . . . it seemed like you guys were—"

I held up my hands palms out. "Um . . . no."

Puck returned then. "So this is a good spot to hide out for a couple minutes," he said. "Away from the freeway and other main roads, trees and abandoned buildings for cover. Should give us a chance to figure out a plan." He eyed me and then Layla. "Did I miss something?"

Layla smirked. "I was just welcoming Colbie to the Alpha One Security fam, since she and you seem to hit it off pretty well."

"And I said nobody is hitting anything off," I put in.

Puck just grinned at me and winked yet again. "Not yet, at least."

"How about not ever?" I snapped.

Puck sidled closer, and the closer he got the more on edge I became. I could feel his proximity so keenly it set the fine hairs on the back of my neck on end, and then he got closer yet and I could smell him. He was a little more than an inch shorter than me, but somehow seemed able to make it feel like he was surrounding me, staring down at me with his chocolate brown eyes. I wasn't breathing, I realized, and sucked in a breath.

What the hell? What was he doing to me? Why was I reacting to him like this? Men didn't affect me. No man had ever affected me like this; no man had ever made me forget to breathe, made me feel small and delicate and yet somehow safe. He was dangerous, I knew that, I'd seen him kill only moments ago—dangerous men were a known quantity to me. The only way to survive on the streets was to join a gang, so I was well-versed in the language of macho, swaggering, alpha males, well-acquainted with guys who could and would shoot you as soon as shake your hand. Puck was different; he had that same machismo, the same cockiness and swagger, the same hardened, lethal air, but Puck was something new, a kind of man I'd never encountered before.

I was searching his eyes, trying to figure him out, trying to figure out my own reaction to him—when he reached up, his hand moving slowly, deliberately, and his palm cupped around my waist, his fingers dimpling in my back just above the waistband of my skirt. He tugged me up against him, and my breath caught. He was a hard mass of muscle, immoveable and powerful and masculine, his eyes glittering and bright, his lips quirked in a sly smirk. And goddamn, that beard. I'd never been a fan of big beards, but somehow, on Puck, it was just . . . perfect.

I can bury my fingers in the thick black mass of his

beard and yank him in for a kiss—

Gah—what? Who put that ridiculous thought in my head? Sorcery, I tell you.

His hand was huge and strong, his fingers spread across my back, the span so wide his thumb brushed near my shoulder blades while his pinky was teasing flesh in the tiny gap where my blouse had risen above my skirt. The touch of his hand was making me crazy. There was shirt material between his hand and my skin—except his pinky—and yet I felt his touch like fire.

And I stopped breathing again.

"You feel that too, don't you?" he murmured.

I stepped backward out of his touch. "Nope."

I'd momentarily forgotten there were other people around us—Layla, Kyrie, Temple, and Lola, not to mention a bus full of women. And sirens howling somewhere.

"Ha, yeah, welcome to the sisterhood," Layla said. "You can fight it all you want, but you're just delaying the inevitable."

I pivoted to face her. "The hell are you talking about?"

She pointed at Puck and then me. "You two. That. Y'all were *sparkin'.*"

I snorted. "Yeah, good one." I tried to pretend I wasn't blushing, that I didn't still feel his hand on my back even though I'd put several feet between us. "You're crazy."

"Sparks, Colbie." Puck winked fucking *again*, this time exaggeratedly, broadly, just to piss me off. "There were *sparks*. No sense fighting the inevitable."

I pointed at the bus. "Are you people forgetting about the dead people and the police and—I don't know—the fact that we were all kidnapped and were about to be sold into prostitution?"

"Oh, I doubt they would have paid us," Layla said. "I think Cain is more the slavery type than the prostitution ring type."

"If what Duke and I went through was anything to go on," Temple said, "then yeah, I'd say Layla's right."

Everyone knew what Temple Kennedy looked like—you saw her on magazine covers and billboards all the time, even if you didn't watch her show—she was tall and sleek with just the right amount of curves, perfect blond hair and blue eyes. She and Kyrie both had the same coloring but they were equally stunning in different ways.

I stared at them both. "Is there really a difference? Forced to be a prostitute or sold as a sex slave . . . seems like the same thing from where I'm standing." I gestured at the bus. "And again, can we maybe stick to the salient facts? Such as, for example, them?"

The bus windows were full of faces; the women inside were watching us intently. Waiting. None of them seemed inclined to want to leave the relative safety of the bus. Not that I blamed them.

"We can't just leave them," Puck said, "but it's going to be hard enough for me to get the five of you out of here, much less another dozen women, most of whom probably don't speak English."

"You don't need to include me," I said. "I can take care of myself."

Puck pointed at Layla with a thumb. "You saw what she did. Pretty sure she can take care of herself, too. That ain't the point." He stabbed his chest with the same thumb. "Getting these four women back to my friends and my boss and my boss's boss in one piece is my job, and I take my job very fucking seriously."

"I'm sure you do. I'm just saying, I can rescue myself, but thanks anyway."

Puck laughed. "You're missin' the point, Legs. I *want* to rescue you. I'm hoping you'll find yourself extra thankful, if you know what I mean."

"Legs? Really?" I glared at him. "Next you'll refer to me as Tits, or Ass, am I right?"

"Nah, that'd just be rude."

"You are unbelievable." I gaped at him and then turned to Layla. "How the hell do you deal with this asshole?"

She just laughed and shrugged. "Puck is just . . . Puck."

Lola spoke up for the first time. "What was it you said on the plane, when we first met, Puck?"

Puck grinned. "I'm like whiskey—I'm an acquired taste."

"Not exactly how you said it the first time," Lola said, an eyebrow quirking up.

Lola was exotically gorgeous, with dark caramel skin and springy black hair in a crazy explosion around her shoulders, tall and strong looking, with tits and ass even Layla couldn't quite match.

God, those women were all incredible—it would've been easy to feel insecure around four women each more beautiful than the last.

"How'd I say it on the plane?" Puck mused. "Oh yeah . . . I'm whiskey, bitch!"

I groaned in aggravation. "You're all acting like this is business as usual!" I gestured again at the windshield, blood-smeared and bullet-riddled. "That's not normal. I thought I was pretty good at staying calm, but I'm starting to freak out just a little."

Puck moved toward me, feathered his hands into my hair, and his fingers found the back of my neck near the base of my skull, where my tension tended to gather in painful knots. His strong fingers kneaded gently but firmly, and the tension loosened.

"Colbie, babe—just breathe." His smile was reassuring and calm. "We got this. You're in good company."

I rolled my head and shrugged my shoulders, not liking that I liked the way he was massaging me. "Don't touch me. And don't call me babe—I'm not your babe. I'm not your anything."

But yet I couldn't quite make myself stop him

from massaging my neck. Damn me.

He chuckled. "You're a prickly one, ain'tcha, princess?"

"If you're such a big shot, then how are you going to get us out of here?" I rolled my eyes and huffed, and then the huff turned into an involuntary breath of relief as he shifted his touch and found the worst knot and managed to knead it away. "Do you even have a plan?" I asked, my eyes sliding closed as he worked the tension out of my neck.

"Get everyone somewhere safe, find a way to contact the boys . . ." his next words were whispered in my ear, "and then get you naked and make you come at least a dozen times."

I shivered. "Bullshit."

"Which part?"

"You couldn't make me come a dozen times even I did let you get me naked, to which, by the way—no."

"I said *at least* a dozen. Bet you a thousand bucks I can."

Damn him. Damn him. And damn me—doubly, for being so affected by him and for being a sucker for a bet; I offset my income during college playing poker . . . and not always honestly. Street habits died hard, what could I say? If you could count cards and bluff as easily as breathing, and had tens of thousands of dollars in college debt, yeah, you were gonna cheat at poker. And sometimes, you let yourself get roped into high stakes games simply because you had a really hard time turning down a bet.

"At least twelve times? In what span of time?"

Puck's laugh was low and dark with lust. "Like to gamble, do you?"

"No," I said, the denial automatic. "Well, maybe. Yes."

Another chuckle. "A thousand bucks says I can."

I groaned. "I'm not taking your wager, Puck Lawson."

"Yes you are."

"No, I'm not."

The sirens were all around us now.

Someone cleared her throat. "Sorry to interrupt, you two," I heard Layla say, "but we kinda need to get going soon."

Puck backed away from me, and I breathed a sigh that was equal parts relief and disappointment.

"Time to move," Puck said. "We need a cell phone so I can get hold of the boys. Layla, you stay here, watch the rest of these ladies. Colbie, you come with me since you can actually talk to people around here."

"Do we have any money?" I asked.

Puck dug into his pocket and came up with a handful of wadded up bills in various sizes and colors. "I took this off Anton." He fished a small roll of hundreds out of a different pocket. "Plus my backup cash. There's a thousand here if we need it."

I took the stolen currency from him and sorted

through it. "Two thousand in rubles, two hundred in Euros, and about a hundred in dollars." I did some quick mental conversions. "According to the rates as of yesterday, this is about . . . three hundred forty dollars total, not including your personal stash."

Puck stared at me. "You can do currency conversions in your head?"

I shrugged. "I'm in imports and exports, so knowing the conversion rates is part of the job."

"And you speak Russian and Chinese?"

I nodded. "I specialize in Russian and Chinese high-end imports."

He seemed impressed. "Nice. Smart chicks make me horny."

I lifted an eyebrow at him. "I'm starting to wonder what *doesn't* make you horny."

He laughed. "You have a point. There isn't much. Nuns . . . I'm not a fan of nuns, except the fake ones in porn. Centipedes also freak me out. Um . . . the IRS—they piss me off to no end. Pretty much everything else makes me horny." He let his eyes rake down my body blatantly. "A hot, smart, educated woman with a wicked sharp tongue? You got me rockin' a chubby, and I don't even know what color your bra is yet."

"Blue," I blurted. Now why the hell did I tell him that? He didn't need to know. "Let's get moving."

Puck's eyes shot to my chest, as if he could see through my shirt, but then he quickly shifted his gaze up to my eyes, his expression serious. "So. Which way, you think?"

I frowned at him. "How the hell should I know?"

He shrugged. "Thought maybe you'd seen a sign or something that might point us toward a gas station or liquor store."

"Yeah, I was a little too preoccupied to read any of the signs," I said drolly.

"You've got a point, I guess." Puck ejected the clip from the butt of his pistol, checked the contents, and stuffed it into his waistband behind his back—the whole series of movements was swift and practiced. He set off, glancing at me with a confident grin. "Well, I guess we just do our best lost tourist impression and hope for the best."

I laughed. "Really, really, really lost tourists."

"Don't see many other choices," Puck said.

He had a point there.

3

DANGER HACKLES

THIS CHICK WAS BOSS. FOR REAL. FLUENT IN three languages, knew the currency conversion rates off the top of her head, stayed cool as cucumber when shit got gnarly, sassy and snappy and didn't take any shit, and was fucking breathtakingly gorgeous.

I had to have her.

Worse, I wanted to know more about her.

Worst of all . . . I wanted her to *like* me.

I was pro level at not giving a shit what anybody thought about me—which was the main reason I got fired from the FBI, and why I never made it past E-4 in the Army. Yet something about this Colbie Danvers chick had me trippin', had me wondering what I could do to impress her, and I didn't just mean with my godlike powers of cunnilingus. This wasn't like me. Not like me at fucking all. Fumbling attempts at impressing a hot chick? Yeah, until I met Colbie, I thought that was something I'd left behind in goddamn grade school.

I might not have the ability to crook my finger and have every bitch in the bar begging for a turn on her knees—like Duke and Thresh—but I could score a honey for the night without much effort. Confidence bordering on—and sometimes crossing over into—arrogance, charisma, boldness, and 20 inch biceps would get you pretty far, even if you weren't a goddamn pretty boy like Duke, or a titan like Thresh. Not that I was ugly, I just wasn't on the same level as those boys. Regardless, I haven't had to work for it in years, was what I was saying.

Colbie, however . . . she gave off the impression that I was gonna have to fight hard for every last inch I got with her. Which was fine—I loved a good fight, never backed down from a challenge, and never refused a bet.

And you better believe I didn't miss the gleam in her eye when I dangled a wager in front of her.

For the moment, though, I needed to keep my focus more on the job at hand and less on how fucking phenomenal Colbie's ass looked. That skirt, man. All business, no frills, nothing sexy at all, but god*damn*, it showcased that ass: tight, round, firm, yet still had a nice little jiggle when she walked. And those legs? Mmm-mmm-*mmm*. Long, long, long legs, legs for days, lithe legs, firm, toned, smooth legs. The kinda legs a guy pictured wrapped around his waist when he was rubbing one out in the shower . . . only better.

The job, Puck, the job. Focus on the job.

I shook my head like a dog shaking water off its coat, trying to dislodge Colbie's ass from the center of my thoughts. In fact—I lengthened my stride so I was beside her, so I couldn't stare at her ass. Of course, now the challenge was to keep myself from stealing glances down her shirt to see if she really was wearing a blue bra, and if so, what kind—full coverage, push-up, demi . . . shelf? Yeah, you bet I knew bras, brah—I loved everything to do with tits. Whether they were naked, shown off in lingerie, pushed up by Victoria's Secret, or just hanging loose behind a thin T-shirt, I just plain old loved tits. So yeah, I knew about bras.

And judging by the glimpses I was getting of Colbie's rack, I guessed she had a C cup, maybe 32 or 34 around. And she was probably wearing full cover-age, because the all-business skirt and button-down shirt combo felt like she dressed to be taken seriously for her skills in the office rather than her body stats. Of course, sometimes those girls in the business at-tire surprised you—take that pencil skirt and but-ton-down off and suddenly she was rocking a few scraps of lace and a come-hither grin.

Not sure about Colbie, whether she'd wear sen-sible, comfortable underwear to work, or something sexy to make herself feel good even if no one saw it.

For that matter, what if she was attached? Didn't seem like it, judging by her reactions to me: interested, but wary. Attracted, but didn't want to be.

Goddamn it. Distracted again.

I growled in irritation, tore my eyes off her cleavage, and walked even faster so she was behind me.

I tried to focus on my surroundings. I had the .45 I'd taken off the driver and the two spare mags, and Layla had the Makarov and the mags for that. Sadly, I'd left the AK in the bus because I was relatively certain I couldn't walk around with an assault rifle in plain view, even in Russia or wherever the fuck we were.

We were in a pretty rundown area, not a whole lot of much to be found except for trees and billboards and the occasional warehouse or whatever. We started walking away from the sound of the sirens and hoped we'd eventually find something useful, because what else were we going to do? We had no idea where we were, and none of us had a cell phone, so it wasn't like we could pull up Google Maps or some shit. We hadn't seen another soul, either, except for the occasional car or semi truck.

We'd left Layla in charge of the rest of the group, safely hidden in the alley where we'd parked the bloody, shot-up van. Colbie and I found the nearest main road and followed it, hoping to find a liquor store or gas station. It was mid-morning, a bright, sunny day with only the occasional passing cloud to occlude the sunlight.

I scraped at my scalp with my hand and winced and shook my hand when I accidentally bumped my finger-stump. "Shit. I really need to get this mother-fucker cauterized better." I dug in my pockets for the lighter and the knife. "You squeamish, Colbie?"

She snorted. "You blew a guy's head off right in front of me, and then I got behind the wheel with the blood still running down the inside of the windshield."

I bobbled my head side to side. "You have a point."

I held the knife in my uninjured hand and the lighter in the other, flicked the wheel to get the flame spurting, and held the flat of the knife blade in the flame.

Colbie touched my wrist. "Can I suggest you wait a second?" She pointed ahead at what appeared to be the local version of a convenience store. "If you're going to do that, I'd suggest a bottle of vodka and something to bite down on."

I eyed her, folding the blade away. "And you say this why?"

She lifted one shoulder in an elegant movement. "Call it common sense."

"What I call is bullshit on that answer."

She sighed. "Because I've seen it done, if you must know. I don't give a shit how tough you are, it hurts like a bitch. Also, you need vodka or something to clean it." She gestured at my finger. "What you have going on there is an infection just waiting to happen. What did you do, try to burn it closed?"

"Yeah, sort of."

She made a disgusted face. "That was pretty dumb."

I frowned at her. "Why?"

"Do you know nothing about basic emergency wound care?" She indicated my finger again. "The ash is going infect you. Like, if you don't get an infection I'll be shocked."

"Yes, I do know a little about basic triage," I said as we stood outside the front of the store. "I did a tour in Iraq and eight years in the FBI. I was just short on other options."

But I decided she had a point as I pulled open the glass door, which sent a string of bells jangling. The glass was reinforced by iron bars, and the interior of the store was identical to any liquor store in any shabby end of town anywhere I'd ever been—everything packed in so tight there was barely room to move, lots of shelves stacked two deep with bottles of cheap liquor, and a counter at the end of the store with two-inch-thick bulletproof glass on the other side, all the high-end liquor and cigarettes behind the counter along with the bored-looking cashier.

"Give me some of those rubles," Colbie said.

After I handed her a stack of notes, she grabbed a pint of vodka from the top shelf nearest us and took it to the counter, where she struck up a conversation in Russian with the cashier—a middle-aged man with silver-streaked brown hair and weathered, craggy features, cigarette dangling from the corner of his lips. After a brief flurry of exchanges, Colbie turned to me with a frustrated expression on her face.

"Good news and bad news. Bad news, it turns out we're in Kiev, Ukraine." She lifted the rubles. "Which means none of this currency does us any good unless we can get it exchanged somewhere, which is unlikely seeing as we have no passports."

"And the good news?"

"Pretty much everyone in Ukraine speaks Russian, so I can still communicate easily."

"But he won't accept any of the money?" I asked.

Colbie eyed me, the oozing stump of my finger, and then turned to the cashier. She jabbered something in Russian, gesturing at me, and then grabbed my injured hand to show the cashier. The cashier shook his head, and Colbie responded with what seemed to be to be a plea.

"I need more money," she murmured to me. "I think he'll accept the cash we have, but it's gonna cost extra."

"Did you tell him it was a sex injury?" I quipped, peeling off more rubles, and a couple twenty-Euro notes for good measure.

She snorted. "No, I didn't say what happened, and he hasn't asked." She tilted her head at the window.

"Don't know if you've noticed this or not, but the neighborhood we're in isn't exactly the nicest. Don't think folks around here ask too many questions."

"Yeah, I noticed . . . that was actually a joke."

She and the cashier went back and forth a few more times, and then the cashier finally nodded. Colbie slid the rubles and the Euro notes under the glass, and then the cashier tossed a cell phone onto the counter, a cheap-looking model of a brand I'd never heard of before, encased in thick plastic packaging.

"Hey." I poked Colbie in the ribs. "Ask him if he's got any cigars."

Colbie eyed me. "For real?"

I shrugged. "I never joke about cigars, guns, or sex."

She rolled her eyes at me. "You just asked if I'd told the cashier your missing finger was a sex injury."

"Oh yeah. So I don't joke about cigars or guns, and I only joke about sex with a woman I'm really, really interested in having sex with."

"Oddly specific," Colbie said. "And I'm not sure being only *really really* interested is going to cut it, if you're talking about me. I'm pretty picky."

I laughed. "Ah, I see. Well then, I'm really, really, really, *really* interested in having sex with you." I gestured at the cashier, who was ignoring us to watch a small TV on the counter. "Ask about the cigars, babe. Please."

She shook her head but asked anyway; the

cashier passed a packet of three cheap but serviceable cigars through the slot, and Colbie passed a ruble note through, but the man just grunted in dismissal and waved us off. Taking back the cash and handing me the cigars, she took the vodka and the cell phone and we left the liquor store, headed back the way we'd came, making for the alley where the rest of the group waited for us.

Once again, I found myself walking beside Colbie and having the devil's own time trying to keep my eyes off her cleavage, which was distracting and irritating, because I'm not typically easily distracted.

I increased my pace so I was a step ahead of Colbie.

"What's the matter, Puck? Don't like walking next to me?" Colbie asked, opening her stride to match mine.

"No." I forced myself to keep my gaze scanning around me, watching for signs of Cain's assholes coming for us. "You're distracting."

"Distracting? What am I doing to distract you?"

I couldn't help glancing at her and noticing the way she wrinkled her nose in confusion. It was cute. Normally, if something was *cute*, I avoided it like the plague. Cute was anathema. Kids, kittens, girls young and innocent enough to be considered cute . . . I stayed the hell away—far, far away. I liked Harleys, dive bars, tattoo parlors, and the kind of chicks who liked to get down for a couple hours and then found the door their own damn selves . . . the kind of woman who wrinkled her nose and made me go *awwwww* . . .? No. NOPE. Nooooo way, José.

Yet there was Colbie, sixteen different kinds of sexy, alluring, hot, and gorgeous, yet also cute as a fucking button with that nose wrinkle and tilted head.

Motherfucker—this was bad.

"You're existing, that's what you're doing to distract me." I decided to play it like I always played it—shoot from the hip, blunt as a hammer, no filter. "I keep wondering if you're really wearing a blue bra, and if so, what kind, and how can I get you to show it to me—and then how can I get you out of it? And I wonder whether you're the type of chick who wears plain and comfortable underwear to work, or the kind who wears fancy lingerie because you like feeling sexy. And I also can't handle walking behind you because I'll stare at your ass the whole time, and if I walk beside you, I'll stare at your tits, and I shouldn't be staring at you at all, because if the events of the last seventy-two hours are anything to go by, this shit is just getting started, and I have to be on my A-game or we're all dead. Or, more likely, I'm dead and you're all being sold into Cain's network."

She was quiet for several paces, obviously chewing on what I'd said. "First, it's not my fault I distract you—lack of focus is on you, not me. Second, my bra really is blue." She pulled the edges of her shirt open a bit to show a sliver of sapphire blue satin. "And it's nothing fancy, just a regular bra. Third, I'm the first type, for the most part—I pick underwear based on fit and comfort more than style, although I do have a few sets of fancy stuff, but I don't wear them very much, and for sure not to work. What are we on, number four? Fourth, it's also not my fault if you can't stop staring at me—see also item number one. Fifth, what happened in the last seventy-two hours to make you feel like this is just getting started? Addendum to item number five: if three trucks full of dead guys is this shit just getting started, then maybe I should be a little more afraid than I currently feel. Sixth, who the hell is Cain? And seventh, how would one lose a finger during sex?"

I laughed. "Um . . . that last one is a good question—S&M gone wrong?"

We'd arrived at the alley by that point, just in time for Layla to overhear that last exchange. "Do I want to know?"

I shook my head. "No, probably not."

She eyed the vodka. "Not really the time to start pounding vodka, Puck."

I moved away from the rest of the women, sat down in a corner where the brick wall of the liquor store met a tall, leaning sheet-metal fence. There was a stick on the ground, a couple inches long and the same thickness as my finger, missing all its bark; I set that in my teeth and clamped down on it as I heated up the knife blade.

"Shit, Puck." Layla crouched near me. "Want me to do that?"

I shook my head. "No."

"You sure?"

I nodded. "I'm sure." My words were muffled by the stick.

I really wasn't looking forward to this, but I had no idea when I'd be able to get medical attention, and if this thing kept bleeding like it was, I'd start to get light headed; I already was a little and feeling kind of nauseous. Probably an infection, like Colbie had predicted. But fuck it, right? Gotta do what I gotta do. I twisted open the vodka and took a shot, then poured some onto my finger—which stung like a bitch as the alcohol hit the mess.

I heated the knife blade until it was glowing red, and then folded my fingers in so I was flipping the bird with my sad, messy little stump. Setting the lighter down, I hesitated a second, two, three . . . sucked in a few deep breaths and held the last one as I lowered the flat of the red-hot blade to the wound.

There was the hissing sound of searing meat, and the sickly sweet smell of cooking flesh, and I bit down on the stick between my teeth so hard I felt and heard the wood crunch and give, and I screamed out loud. I was a tough motherfucker, okay? I'd been shot, I'd been stabbed, I'd been beaten and left for dead, all sorts of shit. Cauterizing that finger? Fucking hurt like a motherfucking bitch. I held the knife on for a few seconds, then pulled it away, gasping, groaning, sweating, stomach heaving—checked it, saw it was still oozing a bit, and held the hot blade against my finger again. I repeated this three more times, checking for fresh blood each time, until the wound was totally cauterized.

"Fuck, fuck, fuck, fuck, fuck," I snarled, spitting out the stick and tossing the still-hot knife onto the ground beside me.

I examined the finger; the wound was gnarly, all red and seared brownish, but it wasn't bleeding anymore, so I called it done. Well . . . almost. I dumped some more vodka onto the closed wound, biting down on the stick and growling through the burn. Finally, fucking finally, I was as done as I could get.

This time, I took two long swallows of vodka.

"Fuck." I capped the vodka and levered myself to my feet, woozy from the pain. "That was exciting. Let's do it again!"

Colbie eyed me as I blinked through the dizziness and the lingering waves of pain. "You gonna make it, tough guy?"

"I dunno. I might need a little mouth to mouth," I drawled. "I'm feeling a bit faint."

"Nice try, but no." She picked up the knife from the ground, opened it, and sliced open the package containing the cell phone. "How did you lose the finger, for real?"

I gestured at the crowd of women, most of whom

were crowded around us, sitting, standing, some chatting to others who shared a language, most just staring blankly and trying to keep their shit together. "Long story. Short version is, I was with Lola and Temple, taking them to my cabin to hide out—"

"Hide out from what?"

"From Cain—I'll explain him in a minute. The bad guys, the same group who snatched you, found us at my cabin, I'm still not sure how. There was a fun little shootout, during which I lost the upper half of my favorite finger, and then they snatched Lola and Temple, and I took off in pursuit. Fortunately for me, they used a small, local airfield, which meant while they were looking the other way, I managed to sneak into the baggage compartment of the jet y'all were on." I wiggled my stump, and then hissed because moving it hurt.

"While I waited for them to load the bags and get ready for take off and whatever, I realized my finger was still bleeding pretty heavily. I was on my own, alone, with women I've sworn on my life to protect no matter what. They were held captive on the plane, and it was about to take off. I didn't have any supplies I could use as a tourniquet, there was no chance of medical attention, and I had to be ready to run as soon as the opportunity showed itself. Couldn't let those assholes get away with my buddies' girls, right? So I lit my cigar, got it glowing as hot as I could and did my best to sear that fucker closed so I'd at least stop it from bleeding quite as much.

"Yeah, I knew it was stupid, and yeah, I knew it was probably going to give me a really sweet infection, but what the fuck was I supposed to do? I was losing a lot of blood, and I couldn't just say fuck it and let Lola and Temple and everybody sort themselves out, could I?"

Colbie just blinked at me for a couple seconds. "That's the short version?"

"What, you wanted the unabridged?"

Layla pointed at me. "You keep an eye out for a minute, yeah? I'm gonna take a look around. We've been here awhile, and I've got a bad feeling." She trotted off, pistol in both hands, heading for the opening of the alley.

As Layla walked away I shot a look at Temple, an idea had just occurred to me. "Now that I've had a second to think about shit, how *did* they find us at my cabin? Literally half a dozen people in the whole fucking world know where that place is, and all of them are with A1S."

Temple frowned. "I've been wondering that myself. They kept just . . . showing up, no matter where we went. Duke assumed they were after him, that they had put a tracer bug sort of thing in him while he was unconscious."

I groaned. "That was the assumption, wasn't it? The tracker was in Duke, and the whole thing was part of Cain's vengeance plan." I rubbed my face with both hands. "Shit, shit, shit. This complicates things."

Colbie raised a hand. "Wait, I'm confused. Who's tracking who?"

I pointed at Temple. "We assumed Cain's guys had put a tracker in Duke when they snatched him out of Denver. But they already had Duke when they showed up at my cabin in Arkansas, which was a secure location that's nearly impossible to find if you don't know exactly where you're going. Yet those fuckers just showed up for a party within minutes of our arrival there. Point here is we all assumed wrong, the reason they snatched Temple was because she was with Duke at the time and Cain doesn't like loose ends."

Colbie nodded, understanding dawning. "But the fact that there was an entire airliner full of kidnapped women changes that theory."

"He decided to kill several birds with one stone," I said. "He had Duke, he had a good-lookin', high profile celebrity . . . why not grab you and Kyrie while he's at it, right? What better way to really rattle Harris's cage than to literally hurt everyone connected to him?"

"Who the hell is Cain?" Colbie demanded. "You still haven't answered that question."

"A bad guy. If it's illegal and unpleasant, he deals in it. Drugs, guns, prostitution and human trafficking, smuggling, extortion . . . you name it, he has a hand in it somewhere on the globe. Nasty fucker.

Once again, I'm just giving you Sparks Notes version, here."

"Layla's husband, Harris, my boss—we provide personal security for Valentine Roth, which is why Kyrie is involved. We also hire our services out as . . . arbiters of hazardous situations, you might say, as well as routine celebrity security. One of the jobs we contracted for was to go after a kid who had gotten kidnapped for ransom, the daughter of Jon Lonigan and Callie MacPhereson. We did the job, brought the kid back, but the mission went sideways. See, Cain and Harris have what you might call a standing grudge, and Cain was the guy who had kidnapped the kid. Well, when he cottoned on to the fact that Harris was coming after the Lonigan kid, he decided to use the opportunity to get even. The rescue op turned into an ambush, which did *not* go well for Cain's crew. We decimated those sloppy fuckers like shooting fish in a barrel. On top of it all, we got the kid, *and* kept the ransom cash, *and* killed a bunch of Cain's mercs. This turn of events pissed him off but good, understandably enough."

I ripped open the package of cigars with my teeth, tugged one free, bit the end off and spat it out, lit it, and puffed till it was chugging nicely.

"God, this cigar is shitty." I spat out a shred of tobacco and shrugged. "Still, a shitty cigar is better than no cigar."

"Glad you're happy." Colbie rolled a hand in

circles. "So . . . what? Cain was pissed off . . . and then what?"

"For a solid year, we all thought that was that, hoped he'd let it go. Then all of a sudden, we all started having our days go to hell all at the same time. Thresh picked up a tail, which turned into a gunfight down in the Everglades. Duke vanished right around the same time, and I picked up a tail of my own. I don't take kindly to being followed, so I left the dumb fuck in a dumpster in Las Vegas, missing most of his head. Right about that same time, I got a call from Thresh and then Harris and then Lear all within about sixty seconds, so I met up with Harris and the boys just in time to see the end of a truly epic gun battle courtesy of Duke and Cain." I gestured at the group of women. "Which brings us to Duke being snatched by Cain's guys all over again, and Lola and Temple getting run off with, and our presence here in merry ol' Kiev."

Colbie frowned. "And your newest theory is that the tracker was in Temple the whole time?"

I nodded and shrugged at the same time. "Pretty much the only thing that fits."

"Maybe this is a stupid question, but . . . did the tracker ever get removed?" Colbie asked.

I glanced at Temple, who paled.

"Oh my god," she breathed. "So they can still track me? Right now? Here?"

"Well fuck," I growled, clamping the cigar between my molars, "that complicates things somewhat."

Just then we heard two shots close together—
BANGBANG!—and then a brief pause, and two more
quick shots—*BANGBANG!*

"Shit," I growled. "That's probably Layla having
fun without me."

I took off like a rocket toward the alley's mouth,
skidding to a halt as I hit the road. Glancing to my
right, I discovered Layla standing beside a non-
descript white panel van. A man's body was on the
ground at her feet, his lower half still partially inside
the passenger seat of the van. As I arrived, she was
hauling him out and dragging him toward the alley.
I jogged toward her and grabbed the dead guy's leg,
and we carried him into the alley and deposited him
behind a dumpster.

"Thanks," Layla said. "Found these assholes
watching the alley." She gestured at the van. "Still gotta get rid of the driver."

Layla had been smart about the way she'd taken
the two guys out. One in the passenger seat, one in
the driver's seat—she'd taken out the passenger first,
so the blood spray and mess hit the driver rather than
bathing the whole interior of the van, and then she'd
shot the driver second, so the mess from him went
mostly out the open window. A car passed, slowed
down, the occupants rubbernecking as they sidled
past, eyeing the van and the blood on the sidewalk
and the obviously dead dude in the driver's seat. They
took one look at me and my handgun and Layla and

her weapon, both right out in the open, and the driver floored it, tires barking as they peeled out and vanished down the road.

Layla and I hauled the second corpse into the alley and tossed him on top of the other one, behind the dumpster and out of immediate view from the main road.

Layla indicated the van. "Figured the van might be a good way to move around less conspicuously," she said.

"Good thinking." I hopped behind the wheel and started the engine. We drove the short distance to our hideout, and I pulled into the alley.

Layla hopped out and opened the rear doors to hustle in the crowd of uneasy, bored, and scared women, making sure Lola, Kyrie, Temple, and Colbie were nearest the front. Once everyone was loaded into the open space—squashed and crowded and uncomfortable, by the looks of it, but out of view, I pulled away from the alley, where we'd been sitting for too long anyway. Not having any idea where to go, I just kind of drove at random while Colbie fiddled with the phone, setting it up.

Finally, she handed it to me. "It's ready. Call whoever you have to call."

One of the few advantages of not being reliant on a cell phone is that I still memorize phone numbers; I dialed Harris. It rang exactly twice before he answered.

"Puck. Thank fuck."

I pulled the phone away from my ear and glared at it. "How the hell'd you know it was me?"

"Because there are exactly eight people on the planet who have this phone number: Roth, Kyrie, Layla, Duke, Thresh, Anselm, Lear . . . and you." He paused, and I heard a number of familiar voices in the background. "All of those people are currently sitting around me except Kyrie, Layla, and you, and Cain's soon-to-be dead fuckers have the girls, so I assumed it was you."

"Well, boss, I got good news and I got bad news."

"Hit me," Harris said.

I held out the phone toward Kyrie and Layla. "Say hi to Harris, girls."

Layla took the phone from me. "BABY!" she shrieked. "I swear to Christ, Nicholas Harris, if you don't get your ass over here and take me home, I won't suck your cock for an entire month . . . yes, I'm fine, they barely touched me . . . I think Puck said Kiev . . . I love you too, Nicky baby. Okay, yeah—Valentine, hi—okay, yeah. Here she is."

Kyrie took the phone from Layla. "Hey, honey. I'm fine too." She sniffled hard. "How's—how's my baby girl? Sasha and Alexei are both with her? Good. No, they just . . . it happened so fast, I couldn't do anything. You know I like you to stay out of things, but this time, honey, I think you need to get personally involved. Whoever this Cain asshole is, he needs to pay. My daughter saw me get *kidnapped.*" Kyrie's voice, normally warm and even and soft, went hard and cold and sharp as a razor. "He *pays*, Valentine."

She handed the phone off to me, and I took it. "Mr. Roth?" I asked.

I heard his distinct voice on the other side, vaguely English, deep, smooth, cultured. "Mr. Lawson. You have the situation in hand, I hope?"

"Getting there, sir. You have my personal guarantee of Kyrie's safety, that much I can say."

"What will you need?"

I thought for a moment. "Well, sir, the situation is a little complicated, tactically speaking. It's not just Kyrie and Layla—"

"Miss Kennedy and Dr. Reed," he cut in, "yes, I've been informed."

"Right, but there's more."

"More what, Mr. Lawson?"

"People, sir. Women."

A significant, pregnant pause. "Explain, please." There was a muffled sound, and then his voice more distant. "You're on speakerphone, Mr. Lawson."

"Jesus, dude, call me Puck. Mr. Lawson was my old man, and he's twenty years dead." I cleared my throat. "This is deeper and more complicated than we originally thought, boys. It's not just about that Lonigan op that went sideways. Never really was, I don't think. Cain is heavily involved in human trafficking. Might even be his primary stream of income, if this situation I'm in now is any indication."

"Puck, brother, glad to hear your voice, man," I heard Duke say.

"Hey, pretty boy. Listen, it was never you they were tracking, it was Temple."

"Yeah, I figured that out."

"Well thanks for sharing, dick."

Duke laughed. "You were already AWOL by the time I figured it out. When Cain's mercs nabbed me at Harris's compound, they took me to . . . a stock pen, you might say, but for people. I woke up in a room full of women, all young, all pretty, and all destined for a trading block over in your current neck of the woods."

"Yeah, that's the situation, buddy. I chased Temple and Lola for a good hundred miles and ended up in the belly of a 727, which just happened to be full of exactly what you just mentioned, a bunch of pretty young things from all over the globe. We landed in Kiev, I busted some skulls, and got the women away. That's the short of it. The less fun part is that Temple is still being tracked, or at least that is the assumption I'm working under. I've got our four girls plus another dozen or so. Tricky part is, I'm short on resources. Two pistols with one spare mag for each, a handful of cash, no IDs, a bunch of women in tow, most of whom don't speak a lick of English, and we're in the shitty end of motherfucking Kiev. So if any of you smart bitches have good ideas for me, I'm all ears."

Anselm cut in, then in his quiet, German-accented voice. "I have an idea, I think. I have a connection in that part of the world who may be able to help you." He paused a moment, then continued. "He operates . . . in somewhat of a gray area of the laws, if you take my meaning. I have done some work with him in the past, and in this situation I think he might be willing to help. Rather eagerly so, unless I am very greatly mistaken."

"Meaning what?" I asked.

Anselm let out a slow breath. "I know very little about him, only what I needed to know for the operation we cooperated on. It was a human trafficking sting, a venture that joined intelligence and law enforcement operatives from many E-U countries. My . . . associate, shall we call him . . . was the inside man, an undercover agent. It was personal for him, however-er. He was searching for his sister, who had been sold into prostitution. We found her—well, *he* found her, during the sting. It was not a pleasant situation."

"He got made?" I ventured.

"*Ja.* Very bad for her." Anselm's accent seemed thicker, which I took to mean he'd been there and had seen the messy fallout. I could imagine it all too well, having been in on several such stings myself during my time with the FBI. "So, I will contact my associate, provide him with this mobile number, and he will call you."

"Sounds good," I said. "And hey, Anselm?"

"*Ja?*"

"Is your buddy as scary as you?"

Anselm's answering laugh sent goosebumps down my spine. "*Mein freund*, in comparison to Ivar, I am only a cute little puppy dog."

"Well, doesn't that just make me feel all warm and fuzzy inside," I joked. "Just do me one favor when you talk to him, will you?"

"*Was ist?*"

"Make sure Ivar knows I'm one of the good guys, huh?"

Anselm laughed again, less creepily this time. "Not a problem."

I heard Thresh's deep, rumbling bass voice. "Yo, Puck. Lola there?"

I handed the phone to Lola, who smiled her appreciation at me. "Thresh, sweetheart, hi."

I turned away for that conversation, and Temple's with Duke.

After the conversations were finished, I slipped the phone into my pocket. I drove in a random pattern for another thirty minutes or so, circling the same block a few times, and then another one, killing time and hoping to stay off anyone's radar.

"Um, Puck?" This was Lola. "Maybe not the best timing, but I kind of have to pee. Is there anywhere we can stop?"

"We might as well find somewhere to stock up on some snacks and shit anyway," I said. "And I'm sure you're not the only one who needs to piss."

I kept my eyes open as I navigated around the suburban neighbourhood, and it wasn't long before I found a decent-looking gas station with a full quick mart. I pulled in and parked in as inconspicuous a spot as I could find, and the women all took turns heading inside for a potty break. Colbie, after her turn inside, came back with several white plastic bags full of bottles of water and some Ukrainian-brand granola/protein bars, some not exactly fresh but still edible fruit, and a bunch of pre-made gas station sandwiches. Most of the women seemed content to sit in the van out of sight and eat, while Layla and I stood outside the vehicle, keeping watch while we refuelled our bellies—the van's tank was still full, thankfully.

I finished my sandwich and a banana, downed a bottle of water, and headed inside to hit the bathroom myself. I exited the quick mart and quickly walked back to the van, pausing to wipe my hands on my pants, since the gas station's men's room had been out of paper towel.

The gas station was situated on a corner of a major thoroughfare and a smaller side street, with an alley running parallel to the side street behind the gas station and the other business next to it. I glanced up at the alley as I climbed into the van . . .

Just in time to see a white panel van—identical to the one we were in—slowly drive down the alley, two men in the front seat, both of whom watched us with hard, cold eyes. My skin crawled, and my danger hackles prickled.

What? You'd never heard of danger hackles? That creepy, crawly, ants-on-the-back-of-your-neck sensation you got when you knew something ain't right, you just weren't sure exactly what? I called them the danger hackles.

And mine were crawling like I had a whole anthill milling around up there.

I glanced at Layla, who already had the Makarov out, held low against her thigh. "Saw them, did you?" I asked.

She nodded. "I saw 'em. I'll stay here in the van, watch the girls. You go on the offensive."

I grinned at her. "You're a woman after my own heart, Layla."

She playfully nudged my shoulder. "Don't waste time flirting with me, stupid—the bad guys aren't going to kick their own asses."

I checked the mag in the pistol—full—and then the spare in my pocket, also full. I pulled the slide, rolled my cigar to the other side of my mouth and puffed a few pulls.

"Keep 'em low, keep 'em quiet," I said.

Colbie eyed me. "What can I do to help?"

"Gimme a good luck kiss?" I suggested.

She rolled her eyes. "How about no."

"Then for now just hang tight and be pretty."

The look she gave me then was scathing and withering, but I caught a hint of a smile trying to sneak out from behind the mask. Her voice betrayed nothing but ire, however. "I'm more than just a pretty face and a tight ass, Puck. I can handle myself."

"Listen, princess. I get that, I really do. Problem at the moment, however, is that I don't know what we're facing, and we've only got two guns. I know from experience that Layla can handle a gun, which is why I'm giving her the other gun and leaving her in charge here. I don't know your skills, and that's not a criticism, it's just a fact. So try not to take it personal, okay? Right now, my job is to keep you safe, and I'm not doing that if I take you unarmed into a situation with unknown variables." I met her gaze and hoped she saw I meant it. "I may be an incorrigible horndog and manwhore, but I'm not a sexist."

She just rolled her eyes again and turned away. "Whatever, Puck. Go do your killer commando bullshit."

I turned and trotted away, but not before I heard Colbie muttering to Layla. "Is he seriously like that *all* the time?"

Layla's answer warmed me from head to toe.

"Colbie, honey, lemme give you a piece of advice when it comes to dealing with Puck: don't ever underestimate him. He puts up this bad boy, trash-talking, brash and bold, take no shit and give no shit façade, but there's more to him underneath all that." She snickered. "You just gotta put up with a lot of flirting and pickup lines to get to it."

It's always nice to know friends got your back.

4

STORY SWAP

I WAS WELL AWARE I WAS GIVING PUCK MIXED signals. The reason for those mixed signals was that I was feeling pretty damned mixed about the guy. On one hand, I admired his toughness and tenacity— the street kid in me appreciated that in him. And on the other hand, he was everything I hated in men— charming, arrogant, and self-assured. Don't get me wrong, timid men were boring, but men like Puck? They didn't stick around long, and that was something I'd had enough of in my life. More than enough. Too much. He was attractive, and he knew it. He affected me, and he knew it. And I hated both of those facts. So the back and forth. I wanted him, I didn't want to want him.

Sitting in the opening of the van's rear doors

beside Layla and Kyrie, I watched as he trotted away, cigar clamped between his teeth, and I wondered what I was going to do about him.

"You should give him a chance," Layla said.

I shot her a surprised look. "Did I say that out loud?"

She blinked at me. "Say what out loud?"

I felt myself blush. "Nothing."

"You were thinking about him, weren't you? Trying to figure him out?"

I shrugged. "More . . . trying to figure out what I am supposed to do."

Layla's wink and grin was . . . salacious. "Do about him, with him, or to him?"

"Yes," I said, unable to hold back a smile.

Layla laughed. "That's Puck for you."

There was a gunshot. A silence, then two more gunshots in quick succession, another longer pause, and a fourth and final gunshot. I felt my heart rate ramp up, felt the bizarre twinge of worry.

Layla just laughed again, and I realized she'd been watching me. "Don't worry. If Puck was on the losing end, there'd have been a hell of a lot more shooting."

"It only takes one," I said.

"Not when it's Puck we're talking about."

"You think a lot of him, don't you?"

She lifted a shoulder. "Yeah, I guess. He's an asshole, he's vulgar, he's a horny fuckboy, he's rude, he's blunt . . . but he's also intensely loyal, insanely smart, a great friend, and really, really funny. I'm close to all of the guys who work for my husband, but I think Puck and I just . . . get each other the best."

"Good for you." I tried to sound convincing. "But he's not my type."

Layla snickered. "Honey, Puck isn't anyone's type. You don't go looking for guys like Puck. They find you, and somehow, you're never quite able to walk away after that."

I eyed her. "Speaking from experience?"

She bobbed her head side to side. "You could say that."

"How'd you meet your husband?"

Layla hesitated. "That's . . . a complicated story to tell," she answered.

Kyrie moved up to stand between Layla and me. "Not really," she said. "Her husband worked for my husband."

"Oh *really*," Layla drawled, laughing sarcastically. "Is that what we're saying, now?"

Kyrie blushed. "Fine. It's a little more complicated than that."

Layla snorted. "I'll say. Valentine . . . purchased Kyrie. The idea was she'd work off her debts the old-fashioned away, shall we say, but that sort of went sideways. As in, they fell in love. Of course, Valentine had enemies who wanted to get at him. There was some kidnapping, a lot of people shooting at other people, some more kidnapping—of me, this time.

Nick was sent to rescue me, and in the process I kind of fell onto his dick and from there fell in love with the rest of him."

I blinked a few times. "Um. Hold on, there's a lot to . . . unpack, in that."

It was Kyrie's turn to snort. "I'll say."

I stared at one woman and then the other. "Valentine Roth . . . *bought* you?" I asked Kyrie. "So you fucked him to pay your way free? And then his enemies kidnapped you, then Layla, and then . . ." I blinked again. "You don't live boring lives, do you?"

Kyrie shook her head. "No, we certainly don't. Well, I do, now. But Layla doesn't. And I think you might be getting the wrong idea about Valentine and me. It really is impossible to explain without sounding stupid, though. Let's just say I was placed in a position where I had very few other options but to do whatever Valentine wanted. Which, it turned out . . . was me. That turned into something more between us, and eventually it stopped being about money or sex and started being about *us*."

"That's the Sparks Notes version, I take it?"

Kyrie nodded. "That's . . . the abridged Sparks Notes version."

I blew out a breath. "You people are complicated."

"You have no idea," Layla said. She glanced past me at the alley down which Puck had vanished. "Oh, here he comes."

He was approaching at a leisurely stroll, pistol

in his hand held low at his thigh, chewing on his cigar, which was still lit, still in the same place between his left molars. He had a handful of white paper napkins in his other hand and was wiping at his face . . . red with blood spray. His cargo pocket bulged with weight—pistols taken from the newly dead, I assumed.

He stopped near Layla, Kyrie, and me. "That was easier than I expected. Cain must be sending his C team after us for now."

Puck shoved the gun behind his waistband at the small of his back and climbed back behind the wheel of "our" van. Layla and Kyrie tucked their legs into the van, which left the shotgun seat open; obviously they were conspiring to keep me near Puck as much possible. I went along with it, taking the passenger seat. Once we were all safely inside the van, Puck backed out of the gas station and headed down the alley he'd only just vacated.

He shot me a cocky grin as I buckled in, eyeing the blood etched into the wrinkles of his neck and around the corners of his eyes. "Don't worry, babe, none of it's mine."

I rolled my eyes at him. "Forgive me if I don't weep into my apron from relief."

Puck's grin was amused. "Oh, don't tell me you weren't at least a little worried."

I shook my head. "Nope."

"She was totally worried," Layla said, suddenly

crouched directly behind the two front seats.

I glared at her. "Whose side are you on, anyway?"

She just laughed. "The side of getting you two alone so you can get busy."

Puck high-fived her. "I like that side. That's my favorite side."

"By all means," I said, sweeping my hand in a sarcastic gesture toward the panel van as we passed it, parked on the side of the road. "Let's get in the back of that van and get it on."

Puck made a face, finally removing the cigar, staring at the end, which was now cold. "Oh, I don't think you want to do that. It's . . . a little messy in there." He jerked a thumb at another alley as we passed it, pinching off the cherry of his cigar and stuffing the stub into the cargo pocket of his pants.. "That's a likely looking alley, though."

"Oh yeah, up against the wall in a dirty alley," I mocked. "You really know how to show a girl a good time."

Puck leaned close, whispering. "Honey, when I show you a good time, you won't just forget *where* you are, you'll forget *who* you are."

I felt his breath on my ear, felt the sizzle of his proximity, the heat and the promise in his words; somehow, I found myself believing him. Not that I'd let him know that, of course.

"You think so, do you?" I said, arching an eyebrow at him.

"I know so."

"Better be a hell of an orgasm, then."

Puck laughed. "*An* orgasm? Colbie, Colbie, Colbie. You don't get it, do you?"

"Get what?" I looked at him, irritated at his confident, arrogant, knowing smirk.

"*An* orgasm won't make you forget shit." He leaned toward me again as we stopped at a traffic light, and I inclined my ear to him, expecting another whisper. What I got was his teeth, sinking into my earlobe, his breath hot, his lips grazing my ear. "So many orgasms you lose count? That might do the trick, though."

I fought the urge to gasp. His teeth on my ear . . . stupid. Cliché. But dammit, why did it affect me so badly? Why did I have goosebumps all up and down my arms? Why was my heart racing?

"Bullshit," I breathed. "You can't make me lose count."

"Oh no?"

I shook my head. "Before it was a dozen times, now it's so many I lose count? Yeah, right. What's next? So many orgasms I propose to you on the spot?"

"You doubt me."

I shrugged. "I find it hard to believe."

He frowned at me thoughtfully. "When was the last time you had more than two orgasms in a row?"

I went several seconds without answering. Glanced back, making sure Layla and Kyrie and the others were otherwise occupied in their own conversations.

Puck's gaze was sharp. "You never have, have you?"

"Sure I have," I lied.

Puck laughed. "You lie, Danvers."

I kept my voice low. "Fine, you're right. What's your point?"

Another few moments in silence. "Wait . . ." Puck grabbed my arm and stared hard at me before turning back to the road. "You're not—" His inquisitive sideways stare was meaningful.

I stared back at him for a moment, trying to fill in the gap. And then the penny dropped. "Am I . . . what? A virgin? God, no. Jesus, Puck."

He blew out a breath of relief. "Thank fuck. Virgins are a lot of work."

"And you know this from experience, do you?"

He shrugged. "Once, which was enough."

"I'm not sure what to think about that. It seems to be a pattern with you."

"I am who I am. I've been around, yeah. But I'm always up front about the way things are, and I'm not going to apologize for being who I am, or the way I am."

"So a virgin agreed to a one-night stand with you?"

"Something like that."

"Explain."

He eyed me. "Why?"

"I'm curious."

"About me sleeping with a virgin?"

"Yes."

He bobbed his head side to side. "I don't really like to talk about the women I've been with, especially to other women." He cocked an eyebrow at me. "It never goes well, I've learned."

"I'm just curious. It's not going to change my opinion of you."

He laughed, but it was somewhat mirthless. "Something tells me that your opinion of me isn't very high anyway."

"Not true."

"Tell me why you want to know."

I thought for a moment. "I'm genuinely curious. You're an interesting person. And I remember being a virgin. For most girls, it's a pretty big deal, and I don't see how a girl would be willing to give that to a random stranger in a one-night stand, especially going in knowing exactly what it was. So . . . I'm curious."

Puck sighed. "Fine, I'll tell you. But you have to share something of an equally personal and revealing nature."

"Personal and revealing?" I asked.

He nodded. "I'd tell you anything you want to know about nearly anyone else I've been with." He held up a hand and ticked off his fingers as he listed. "There was Miss Hewitt, my first, when I was thirteen.

Substitute gym teacher, stone-cold fox, and yeah, she got fired for it. Molly Clancy, my first girlfriend, fourteen. Or maybe it's the one-night stands you're interested in . . . Amy, last month. Met her at a bar, went to her place, left the next morning having gotten zero minutes of sleep. Clara, a few nights before Amy, same story. Hannah and Georgia, roommates. Yes, at the same time. I left them passed out in Hannah's bed. Passed out, I emphasize, from what you might term a surplus of orgasms. Sherry, Eileen, Tory, Kendra . . . same story. Those girls were all different nights, by the way. Want to know specifics about them?"

"None of that is personal or revealing."

He shrugged. "Not particularly. I sleep around. I pick up barflies. I'm not a pickup artist, I don't have a line I use or some funny little gimmick."

"How do you get them to go to bed with you then?"

"I buy them a drink. Engage them in conversation, and I listen to them." He winked at me. "And then I promise them three orgasms to every one of mine."

"And that works?"

He nodded. "Oh yeah. Most women are undersexed, I think. Under-pleasured. Don't know the meaning of a truly good time in bed with a man who knows what he's doing. I may not look like Channing Tatum or Brad Pitt, but I like to think I've got a certain . . . aura about me, know what I mean? Promise a woman she'll come more times in one night than she ever has, she'll go with you out of curiosity, if nothing else."

"And you think that's how you'll get me naked, huh?"

He grinned. "I'm hoping."

"Dream on, Bullwinkle."

"Oooh, a classic cartoon reference. Now you're talking my language."

I couldn't help a grin. "You like cartoons?"

"Hell yeah! The classics, though. Looney Tunes, Rocky and Bullwinkle, Mickey Mouse, The Flintstones, The Jetsons, Transformers. I'll even include the 1990s Batman animated series, but I usually stick to pre-1990."

I couldn't help a thrill of excitement. "Cartoons are my secret indulgence. I have all the Looney Tunes on boxed set, like literally every single one ever made." I felt a blush creep over my cheeks. "I have a sacred ritual. Every Saturday and Sunday morning, I eat a huge bowl of cereal and I watch cartoons in my underwear."

"Chuck, Fritz, or Tex?" he asked.

I sighed. "How am I supposed to pick?"

He grinned. "Good answer. Why? Why cartoons?"

I hesitated. "That would probably count as my personal and revealing anecdote."

"We're back to that?" He ran his fingers through

his beard. "I thought I had successfully diverted us away from that. Damn."

I couldn't help a laugh. "Nice try, but no."

He snapped his fingers and then pointed at me. "You're good, Miss Danvers, I'll give you that." A few moments in silence.

"Okay, we'll do this in two stages," Puck said. "Stage one, we trade heavy personal shit. You tell me why you like cartoons, why you have a sacred weekend ritual—and don't think I missed the fact that you watch them in your underwear. I have this image of you in superhero boy briefs and nothing else, eating cereal out of a mixing bowl, watching Bugs Bunny. Don't ruin it for me with the truth."

"And in turn you'll tell me what?"

"I'll let you choose between three options: how my dad died, what my tattoos mean, the tragic story of how my first and only serious girlfriend died."

"Molly Clancy?"

He shook his head. "That was innocent hormonal teenage infatuation. We walked from our neighborhood to the mall twice a week and had fumbling, awkward sex in her parents' basement."

I thought hard. "And the second stage?"

"What I suggested—I'll tell you about how I ended up being a virgin's first, and in turn, you have to tell me something of equal value."

"And what would you consider equal value?"

He bobbed his head to one side. "That's up to

you, but it has to be sexual in nature."

I nodded. "Okay. Fine. You're on."

He gestured to me. "Ladies first."

I laughed. "Oh no. This whole trade personal stories thing is your idea, so you go first." I glanced out the window. "Where are we going, anyway?" I asked.

"I was just thinking about that." He gestured behind us with his head. "I'm going to try to find somewhere we can wait for Anselm's guy to call me. We can't just drive around forever."

Somehow, Puck's hand found its way near mine, and I stared at him then back down our hands, which had somehow managed to get all tangled up, resting on the cracked vinyl armrest of my seat.

I stared meaningfully at our hands. "Um. Puck?"

He gazed at me, a study of innocence. "Colbie?"

"Why are you holding my hand?"

"Because I want to. Because I've been walking next to you thinking about holding your hand, and it's wigging me the fuck out. Makes me feel like I'm twelve instead of thirty-seven." He squeezed my hand. "So I'm holding your hand. Because I want to."

I eyed him. "You're thirty-seven?"

He nodded. "Yes ma'am. Thirty eight as of November third."

"You seem younger."

He grinned. "I'll take that as a compliment."

"It was one." I glanced down at our hands, still joined. "Why does it make you nervous?"

"Because I like you. You make me nervous, just in general, and I don't know why. Because I like you, I suspect. You're different. You're playing a hell of a game of hard to get, and that turns me on, and I'm not totally sure I'm gonna win this game, and that would be a first, which also scares the hell out of me. But mainly because I've never wanted anyone as badly as I want you."

"We've known each other for a matter of, what, two hours?"

"And here we are holding hands."

I nodded. "I'll concede that point. I've never held hands with a guy on the first date before, let alone within hours of meeting him."

"See? There's a thing. Sparks, or whatever you wanna call it."

I poked him in the shoulder. "The trade, Puck. Stop trying to divert the conversation."

He laughed. "Can't get anything by you, can I?" Puck turned back to me. "So, heavy shit first. Which of three options do you want to hear about?"

"The tats."

He blew out a breath. "Shit. You're good, Colbie." He reached up, touched his shoulder where the tattoos began. "This"—he indicated a classic car—"is a 1939 Ford Coupe. My old man owned one when I was a kid. It was his pride and joy, his baby. He named it Evelyn." His voice took on a gruff, scratchy drawl. "'You and Evelyn, Pucky. You're it, you're all I got.' I'm not sure who he loved more, me or that Ford. So the tattoo of the car is in memoriam of Pops."

"What happened to him?" I asked.

Puck didn't answer immediately. "That's the danger of telling you about the tats—each one has a meaning and memory."

"Thus the reason I asked about them—I'll learn more about you."

He nodded. "Pops was murdered. It was . . . ugly." Puck paused, tugging on the end of his beard with his free hand. "He was a gambler. A good one, most of the time. Only, one night he got involved in a game where the stakes went a little too high for his blood, but he wouldn't back out, wouldn't fold. Knew he could win, because Pops was that good. Only, the guys he was playing against didn't play fair. They cheated, and my old man . . . he didn't take that shit lying down. Didn't go well. They roughed him up, forced him to take them to our house. I was there, saw them coming. I hid. Watched them rough him so he'd tell them where he kept his valuables. He didn't fucking have shit, of course, but that didn't stop them from trying. So he gave them the keys to Evelyn, the only thing he had of value. They took the keys and shot him."

I squeezed his hand. "Jesus, Puck."

"I was seventeen. Just graduated high school. He was gonna give me Evelyn as a graduation present."

"What happened? Did the police ever find them?"

He was quiet for a little too long. "Nope. But I did."

My blood ran cold. "You did."

He nodded. "Found them, all four of them. And Evelyn. Seventeen . . . and I was *pissed*. Never really been completely stable, you know? Growing up with a hard drinking gambler dad as my only parent, no mom, no real supervision? It wasn't a recipe for a nice, well-adjusted kid, let's just put it that way. So yeah, I found the fuckers, and I killed them. My dad had guns, and I grew up shooting. It was . . . easier than it should have been. And in that part of Arkansas, a few gunshots wasn't going to worry anyone, so nobody called the police. Put the bodies in Evelyn, drove it to a spot I knew, an old quarry turned into a lake. Sent it over the edge, just like in the movies. Only, unlike in the movies, as far as I know, nobody ever found 'em."

"Jesus."

"And that was that. I bought myself a one-way bus ticket to Los Angeles, as far from Arkansas as I could get, joined the Army, and never looked back."

"You killed four men at seventeen years old."

He eyed me carefully, warily. "Might be worth mentioning that literally nobody else knows that story. Not Harris, not Layla, not Duke or Thresh, or anyone."

I let out a slow breath. "Wow. Um. I'm . . . I don't know how I feel."

"Scared of me now?" He sounded . . . resigned.

I squeezed his hand. "My heavy personal shit isn't much nicer, and I'm still holding your hand, so you tell me." I touched the tattoo of the 1939 Ford. "That's a lot of story for one tattoo."

He nodded. "The rest are the same."

I examined his shoulder and arm—the M16 with the helmet on it seemed pretty straightforward, and something I guessed he wouldn't want to talk about just yet, so I traced the outlines of the cards and dice, the revolvers, and the pinup girl.

"What about these?" I asked.

Puck grinned. "You've got a nose for the interesting stuff, don't you?" He lifted his arm to look at the tats. "So, the interesting thing is, those three tats are connected."

"How so?"

"I did a tour in Iraq as a grunt, followed by a few months worth of guard duty in Germany to finish out my enlistment period, and then I shipped back to the States. Of course, when I enlisted, I was a seventeen-year-old kid with no family who was also on the run from a quadruple homicide. Didn't exactly have a home to go to, you know? I knew the cabin was still mine, but it was in the middle of nowhere, literally, no electricity, no plumbing, nothing. So I hit stateside with no clue what to do or where to go. I'd spent four years as a grunt, most of that boots on the ground in Iraq doing CP—combat patrol. No real education beyond high school, no real skills other than shooting, marching, and pumping iron. The only other thing I knew how to do with any real skill was play cards. I learned how gamble sitting on my old man's lap. He'd bring me to card games, and I'd watch him play. I knew the card suits and poker hands before I could walk. So I found a card game. Made enough money gambling to set myself up with a life, for a bit."

I frowned. "So that explains the cards and dice, but how does that connect to the pinup girl and the revolvers?"

He laughed. "Well, I ended up in what you might call an underground version of the world series of poker. All totally illegal, of course, but hey, it was good money. The whole thing was flashy and as blinged out as you might expect from high-dollar, cash-only, underground poker players. Fancy cars, velvet covered tables, bottles of Cristal and Hennessy, all that shit. And real live pinup girls. Instead of strippers or topless chicks or something tacky like that, they hired these girls as waitresses and had them get hair and makeup done to look like old school pinup girls, complete with vintage bathing suits." Puck hesitated a moment or two. "I got involved with one of them. Raquel, her name was. At first it was . . . you know, just physical. But I kept going back for more, and she seemed interested in more, so we never really talked about it, but we . . . got together, I guess. I dunno what you want to call it. I ended up living with her. She was . . . Raquel was . . ." He hesitated again, this time hunting for the right words. "Not what you'd call a classy sort of lady, but she was the sweetest damn thing. She modeled some, mostly scantily clad or not at all, did some exotic dancing, some escort work—strictly non-sexual, she insisted. And she had the pin-up girl thing going—she had a whole website for her work as a pinup girl. It was good business, I guess."

"You keep using past tense," I pointed out.

He nodded. "Because she's dead. First and only serious girlfriend, remember?" Puck tugged on his beard again. "She was always bugging me about do-ing something with my life besides playing poker. She'd yammer on until she was blue in the face about how I was so smart and had potential and if she were as smart as I was she'd be doing something besides modeling and dancing. I tuned her out, figured she was full of shit. I'd barely graduated high school, and I only did that much because Pops fuckin' made me. School was bullshit, and all I knew was gambling and guns." He touched the crossed revolvers. "I got this to piss off Raquel, along with the other two, the cards and dice, and the pinup girl. The pinup was for her, but it was also like, guns, gambling, and girls is all I'm good for."

"What happened to Raquel?"

Puck sighed and tugged on his beard hard enough that it looked painful. "She got hit by a taxi. Shouldn't have been a big deal, just a broken leg and some contusions or whatever. But she—she picked up an infection. The hospital bungled it all to hell, and she died. Fucking freak thing, you know? Staph infection or one of those flesh-eating things, can't remember what it's called. You generally only get them in hospitals. She got it, and they didn't handle it right, and she fucking died. She was twenty-three. Prime of her life, gorgeous, had her whole life ahead of her."

"Did the hospital get in trouble?"

Puck shook his head. "Nah. We weren't married, and she'd run away from home when she was just a kid. Nobody to sue them. They told me she'd died, that there wasn't anything to do, and I should just . . . fuckin'—go home. So I went home. Got her buried. I was the only one at her funeral."

"Jesus, Puck."

He laughed. "Running theme, I'm noticing, you saying 'Jesus, Puck.'" He squeezed my hand. "Twelve years ago, now. Old pain. It's fine."

"Does it hurt less, now?"

He shrugged. "Not really." He touched the tattoos in question. "So that's those three. The guns were just to piss her off, and because I thought they looked cool. The cards and the pinup were about how I made my living and about Raquel, the only good thing I'd ever really had in my life up to that point."

"What about your dad?"

"That's complicated." He waved a hand. "Short story is he was a drunk, and he wasn't always nice. I knew he loved me, but when he was at the bottom of a bottle, he turned into . . . someone else. He was angry. Life had dealt him a shitty hand. Ma died when I was baby, he got laid off, all sorts of shit. But he was all I had, and he was . . . he was Pops. Like I said, it's complicated."

I examined his tattoos. "I'm scared to ask about any others."

He touched the M16 and helmet. "You can probably guess about this one . . . a buddy killed in action. Dirty Harry is there because that movie is the shit, and I love Clint Eastwood. The handcuffs . . ." he laughed, "that one's got a funny story attached to it."

"Tell me."

He lifted an eyebrow. "It ain't exactly a PG story, babe."

I lifted an eyebrow back at him. "Does it seem like that's bugged me so far?"

He conceded with a shrug. "Guess not. So after Raquel died, I figured the best way I could honor her memory was to do what she always wanted me to do, make something of myself. I enrolled in Santa Monica College—which I paid for gambling, by the way—because a counselor told me I could transfer to UCLA as long as I put two years in and kept a C plus average. So I did two years at Santa Monica, and then transferred to UCLA. I enrolled in a criminal justice class at Santa Monica, but only because it filled my requirements. Turned out I enjoyed it, and that sort of piqued my interest in forensics, so I ended up studying that at UCLA. But then right as I got my bachelors, a recruiter from the FBI talked me into a career in law enforcement. I thought that was funny as shit, all things considered. I mean, I paid for my degrees with illegal gambling, and there were four bodies at the bottom of quarry because of me."

"Seems pretty PG to me, so far," I said.

He chuckled. "That's all just background. So I ended up in the FBI, did my time at Quantico, made agent, got put into the forensics department. I spent a good year and half, almost two, not really dating or seeing anyone during my time at Santa Monica, not even hooking up. I was focused on school, and losing Raquel was still kind of raw, you know? Once I got into UCLA, I started hooking up again, and at that point, I kept it basic, you know? Well, I had to work my way up, in the Bureau. Just because I had a bachelors in forensics didn't mean I was going to get the good cases right away, or be a forensics lab tech or whatever. I had to put in my time. Lots of legwork, boring cases, all that bullshit.

"One case was investigating this woman suspected of being a madam. Nobody could pin anything on her, but there was lots of circumstantial evidence that she was running a multi-state ring of hookers."

"Oh dear."

He laughed again. "You have no idea. Well, I was sent to hunt down some leads. I found the woman, the main suspect, started an interview . . ." He sighed and shook his head. "She seduced me. I mean, it wasn't hard, but I should have known better. Anyway, I let her seduce me, and we . . . well . . . she liked some interesting stuff, let's just say that. I ended up hand-cuffed naked to a hotel room bed, and she was gone in a puff of smoke. Eventually someone went looking for me, found me, uncuffed me, and I got reamed out, disciplined, all sorts of fun shit. Well, I went out with some guys from the Bureau one night, told them the story over drinks, and ended up getting that tat to commemorate the occasion."

I couldn't help laughing. "You let the suspect of an investigation seduce you?"

He nodded. "And handcuff me to the bed with my own cuffs. She knew exactly why I was there and figured she had my number pretty well pegged. Correctly, as it turned out."

"Was it worth it?" I asked.

Puck laughed. "Hell yeah! She was older and ex-perienced, and holy hell, did I learn some amazing new tricks from that woman."

I frowned. "By older, you mean what?"

He tipped his head to one side. "I was twenty . . . seven? Twenty-eight? And she was at least mid-for-ties, if not closer to fifty."

I laughed again. "Jesus, Puck."

He nodded. "That's me." He cut a glance at me. "So. Your turn."

I sighed. "Really? You end on a funny note, and

now I've gotta dredge up all my old shit?"

He nodded. "That's the agreement."

I sighed again. "Fine. So I had a totally boring, normal, two-parent, suburban life until I was sixteen. Mom was a dental technician, and Dad was the manager of a car dealership. I had an older sister, Danielle. I was a dancer, I was in the math club at school, had a perfect GPA, a cute boyfriend, my own car, I was popular." I swallowed hard. "My dad's parents were both dead, and my mom was the only child of elderly parents. Which meant I had one set of grandparents, who were in their eighties when I was sixteen. I had one uncle, my dad's brother, and his wife, but they lived three states away, and my dad wasn't close to them."

"Not liking how this is sounding, babe."

I nodded. "You can probably guess. My mom and dad were taking my sister to a fine arts camp for the summer—she was a painter, a really talented one. Well, a guy wasn't paying attention, crossed the centerline, and crashed into my parents' car head-on, doing sixty in a forty-five. Mom and Dad were killed instantly, and my sister died on the way to the hospital. My grandparents couldn't take me. They were in an assisted living place, my grandmother had dementia, and my grandfather could barely walk. Which left my aunt and uncle, Tammy and Craig. I knew them, but not well. They'd come over for Christmas every few years, but we just weren't close to them. They didn't have kids. Tammy couldn't, I guess, and they decided against adoption. I dunno much about any of that." I spent a few moments in silence, staring out the window at the passing buildings, trying to put my thoughts in order. "At first, living with them was okay. They were nice enough, pretty much just let me do my own thing, since I was almost seventeen. Senior year of high school, new school, new state, parents dead, sister dead, no friends, didn't know anybody . . . it was rough, as you might imagine."

"That fucking sucks, Colbie, I'm sorry."

I offered him a small smile. "That's just background, Puck."

He winced. "Shit."

I nodded. "Yeah. So I'd been living with Craig and Tammy for . . . six months, eight months, something like that. I came home from school one day, and Tammy was gone somewhere. Shopping, drinking with friends, I don't know. Craig was home. Got laid off, I guess, and got wasted. He was stumbling around the house, shirt open, pants undone. Saw me . . . made a pass at me."

"What? Are you fucking kidding me?"

I sighed. "I wish, Puck. I tried to squeeze past him, brush it off as just . . . a drunk thing. He . . . um—yeah. You know."

"No." Puck's voice was hard. "Hell no."

I nodded. "Yep. On the stairs." I swallowed hard again. "I went to the police, filed a report, had the whole rape kit thing done. Tammy visited me in the hospital . . ." I trailed off, finding it hard to finish.

"And blamed it on you," Puck filled in.

"Got it in one." I ran my hands through my hair, an agitated gesture. "So I had nowhere to go. Seventeen, an orphan, two months shy of my diploma, no work experience, nowhere to live, and no one to trust. I checked out of the hospital with the clothes on my back, not a cent to my name, not even a backpack."

"Fucking hell." Puck squeezed my hand, and this time he didn't let up. "What'd you do?"

"I was homeless. I lived in a homeless shelter, showered in the gym showers before school started, stole some clothes from a Goodwill store, got free lunch and breakfast at school . . . it worked out. I graduated high school with a 3.9 GPA. The second I had my diploma, I started hitchhiking north. I don't know why, I just figured New York was the place to be for a homeless girl."

"Damn. 3.9 GPA and you were fucking homeless?"

I shrugged. "I'd done well in school, and then when the accident happened, all I had to focus on was school. It was all I had, so I dug in hard, I guess."

"How'd you go from homeless to where you are now?" Puck asked.

"That's . . . not an easy story to tell, nor a short one."

"Sparks Notes?"

I shook my head. "Wouldn't do it justice."

"Come on, Colbie, you gotta give me something."

"You told me a lot, so I kinda have to, don't I?"

Puck blew a raspberry. "You don't *have* to tell me shit, Colbie. But I'm interested."

"I got hooked on heroin." I blurted it out, a dirty secret known only to me, till now.

"What? How?"

"I got a job as a parking lot attendant. Had a spot in a homeless community, under an overpass, near some people who'd look out for me at night. Thought I could save money, you know? Get an apartment, make ends meet, figure things out. Build a life. Well . . . I made friends with some people, a couple girls who were in a gang. They looked out for me, protected me, got me a better job at a Footlocker . . . and they also pressured me into trying heroin. It was the thing, you know? What they did. They sold it, as distributors for another guy. And I got hooked. It nearly killed me. I OD'd once, got arrested a few times, started living for the next hit, that whole cliché."

"Goddamn." His gaze was sharp as it swiveled to mine. "How'd you get clean?"

"A counselor at a homeless facility. After the OD, I went there because I knew my friends in the gang wouldn't help me get clean, and if I went back to them, I'd keep shooting up. The counselor, Miss Lewis . . . she took an interest in me. Somehow, she found out that I'd done well in high school, and as a way to keep me busy, convinced me to study for the SAT. So I lived in the homeless shelter and studied at the library, took the SAT, aced it." I smiled at the memory. "Miss Lewis then convinced me to apply to a bunch of universities, just for fun, she said. What if, you know? Like, what did I have to lose? So I applied to like twenty universities, Ivy League places and state colleges all over the country. And then Miss Lewis talked me into applying for grants and scholarships, had me write a million essays about why I wanted to go to college and whatever. For me, it was about not being homeless anymore, it was about the idea of a future. When I OD'd, I realized that . . . I had two paths in front of me—death or jail with my friends from the gang, or something else, a path that led to a future, a path that led to me being something, being someone . . . worthwhile."

"So you got into a college?"

I grinned. "I got into Harvard. And I got a scholarship, not a full ride, but a pretty big one. And Miss Lewis showed me how to take out school loans, and I got a job to cover the rest."

Puck stared at me. "Harvard?" He sounded suitably impressed. "You went to Harvard?"

I nodded, still grinning. "Sure did. Got a masters from the Harvard Business School with a double minor in Chinese and Russian."

"After being a homeless heroin addict."

"Damn straight," I said, with no small amount of pride in my voice; I figure I've earned the right to be proud of that.

He shook his head. "Colbie, that is impressive as hell. For real. You deserve major fuckin' props for that shit."

"Wanna know how I supplemented my spending cash when I was at Harvard?" I asked.

"How?"

"Poker."

Puck gaped at me. "The hell you say."

I shrugged, and then winked at him. "I've always had a head for numbers. Some friends from my dorm talked me into playing poker one day, and I discovered I had a talent for it." I hesitated, because this was another little thing nobody knew. "And, um, I also figured out that I could keep track of who had which cards. Made it easy to make sure I won."

Puck's eyes narrowed as he cut a glance at me. "You count cards?"

I bobbled my head side to side. "Yeah?"

He was quiet for a minute. "Hmm. Did you cheat a lot?"

I shook my head. "That's how you get caught, doing it all the time. The trick to getting away with it is to make sure you lose frequently enough that no one suspects you. If you win every hand, they'll figure it out pretty quick. I only really counted the cards when the stakes were high enough that I couldn't afford to lose."

"So if we played poker . . ."

I laughed. "It would depend on the stakes. I don't gamble anymore, but—"

"Bullshit," Puck interrupted.

"What?"

"I said, bullshit. You don't just stop, not when you play poker the way we do."

"I'm not a gambling addict, Puck," I said, feeling defensive and a little angry.

He raised both hands. "Neither am I. But there's no rush in the world like a high-stakes poker game."

I sighed. "True enough. I still play now and again. Some of the guys at work play every Friday, and I'll cash in sometimes. They're my friends and co-workers though, so I don't take too much of their money. I don't play high-stakes games anymore." I shrugged. "No need, and the risk isn't worth the reward. In college, I played for spending cash. I had a job that helped pay for books and offset the cost of tuition and whatever, but I put all of it into keeping my debt down. Poker was so I'd have money for the club and new shoes and whatever. If I lost too much, it wouldn't ruin me. Nowadays, I have rent and bills, and if I gamble away my paycheck, I'm fucked. Even counting cards, you can still lose, and those high-stakes games are closely watched, especially in New York. And besides, that's how you piss off the wrong people, cheating at high-stakes poker in New York City."

Puck laughed. "Ain't that the truth."

The rundown urban sprawl had become a fairly nice-looking downtown area with the occasional five- or six-story apartment building, shops, cafes, and restaurants.

Layla poked her head between the front seats. "The troops are getting restless back here, Puck. We need to stretch our legs if possible."

"I was just thinking it was about time to stop." He pointed at a park on our right and pulled the van to a stop at the curb beside it. "How about this?"

The park wasn't much more than an open area with some trees and benches and an aging, rusting playset covered in graffiti, but it was back from the main road quite a way and had lots of trees to shield us from prying eyes, at least a little bit. There were buildings on three sides, so the only place anyone could approach us was from the street, which Puck was positioned to keep watch on.

We unloaded from the van and spread out into the park. The group of rescued women naturally split off into pairs and groups according to shared language, and Lola, Kyrie, Temple, and Layla clustered together on one bench, discussing something that involved a lot of giggles and glances at Puck and me, alone together on our own bench.

Puck looked over at the group of gossips, and then at me. "Wonder what them biddies are gigglin' about? I'll give you three guesses, and the first two don't count."

I snorted. "No kidding." I sighed at them. "They seem so relaxed about this whole thing. It's taking everything I've got to stay calm, and they're sitting there giggling like schoolgirls."

"This is old news for them. And, like you, they're probably doing a lot of pretending they're less affected than they might really be, deep down." He shifted so he was a little closer to me, his thigh brushing up against mine; I didn't move away from his touch. "Does that bug you? That my friends are talking about us?"

I shrugged. "Not really. What are they saying, you think?"

He dug his cigar out of his pocket, blew lint off the ash end and a loose thread off the mouth end, lit it, puffing until it was trickling thick gray tendrils. "Probably whether we'll shack up, when, and if it'll stick."

"What do you mean, if it'll stick?"

He blew a cloud of smoke away from me. "These bother you?" he asked, lifting the cigar in gesture.

I shook my head negative. "Nah. Cigars and cigarettes are kind of unavoidable when you play poker with a bunch of serious poker bros."

"You smoke?"

I shook my head. "Nope. I did, for a while. While I was trying to kick heroin, I sort of replaced the smack with Newports."

He chuckled. "Oh man, Newports. I *almost* miss those fuckers."

"You smoked Newports?"

He nodded. "In the Army. The whole 'smoke 'em if you got 'em' thing was usually the only break you got. My buddy Dante was the one who got me into Newports."

I gauged his suddenly closed expression, the quietness of his voice. "Something tells me Dante is the reason for the M16 and helmet tattoo."

He nodded again, staring down between his feet. "IED."

"I'm sorry."

"Me too. And thanks, Colbie."

"Most people, when you say you're sorry for their loss, they say something like *what are you sorry for*."

He leaned back against the bench, eyeing the cherry of his cigar. "I've always thought that was a bullshit answer. Disingenuous at best, off-puttingly dickish at worst." He put the cigar to his lips and his cheeks hollowed, and then he blew out a series of concentrically smaller smoke rings, shooting one ring through the next. "Folks tell you're they're sorry when you're talking about someone you lost, they're just expressing sympathy, not offering an apology. That shit is obvious enough, right? So why be a dick about it? Just say thanks for the sympathy and move on."

I bumped his knee with mine. "You never

answered what you meant about Layla and the others wondering if it'll stick between us."

He let his head hang backward with a groaning chuckle. "You really don't let shit go, do you?"

"Nope. I'm a bulldog about getting what I want."

He sat up again, extending his arm along the back of the bench, behind me; his arm wasn't touching me, so it didn't precisely count as being *around me*, but it was close enough that my heart pitter-pattered, which was stupid and ridiculous. "Well, you see, the company I work for, Alpha One Security, or as we call it, A-One-S—we started out as six confirmed bachelors. Then Harris and Layla hooked up during that Brazil snafu and just sort of stayed together. Then Thresh went and snagged himself Lola, and now it seems Duke has somehow managed to score himself a fuckin' celebrity girlfriend, because of course that pretty fuck would end up dating a hot famous chick. So the going theory is that by the time shit finally settles down, all of us will be paired off. And those girls are figuring I'm next, with you."

"And what are you thinking?"

He let out a long breath and tapped his cigar to knock loose a chunk of ash. "I don't know yet. A bit soon to be putting labels on our shit when I ain't even kissed you yet."

"You know what I can't figure out?"

He eyed me. "Whassat?"

"Sometimes you talk exactly like a man with a

PhD, and sometimes you talk like a foul-mouthed redneck."

Puck's laugh was a loud, genuine bark of amusement. "That's 'cuz I'm one hundred percent both, sweetheart."

"Oh. I guess that would explain it."

He grinned at me around his cigar. "That's me, Puck Lawson, a remarkably well-educated redneck with a potty mouth."

"Is your given name really Puck?" I asked.

I wasn't ready to ask him why he'd said he hadn't kissed me *yet*—mostly because I knew the answer, and I wasn't ready for him to kiss me—and I also wasn't ready to know how he'd managed to bang a virgin, nor was I ready to share any part of my sexual history with him.

He grinned. "Colbie-baby, the answer to that is something I have never revealed to anyone. Nor will I."

I frowned. "Why?"

A shrug. "Personal choice. Puck's my name, and that's all anyone needs to know."

"Does the military know your given name?"

Puck's grin was mischievous, his eyes twinkling. "Handy part of working with one of the world's most skilled hackers is that he can take care of pesky things like records."

I tilted my head. "Who do you know that's a hacker?"

"One of the guys on the team. His name is Lear Winter."

"And he can erase military records?"

Puck snorted. "He wanted a job with NSA when he graduated from MIT, so he hacked into the director's private computer and left his résumé."

"Holy shit." I eyed Puck. "So if I wanted my vagrancy and possession arrests to go away . . ."

"Shit, I could do that," Puck said. "Those give you problems at work?"

I shrugged. "It has in the past, yes. I love my current job, but I would like to advance, and having a police record is troublesome, as you might imagine. I can usually explain the arrests, but it's annoying. You live homeless as long as I did, you're pretty much going to get arrested for vagrancy at least once."

Puck chewed on his cigar as he eyed me. "I can take care of that for you when we get back to the States."

"Really?'

He nodded. "Easy as pie." He smirked at me. "It'll cost you, though."

I sighed and rolled my eyes. "Figures." I gave him a sarcastic, sidelong stare. "Let me guess—you'll want a blow job or something."

Puck's expression seemed genuinely disconcerted as he dropped the cigar butt on the ground and crushed it with his boot heel. "What kind of douchebag do I seem like? Jesus. No, I was gonna say a date."

He was irritated, but then he turned his serious, heated gaze on me. "When I get a blow job outta you, it'll be done of your own volition, because you wanted to give it to me."

I felt a little faint, a little irritated at his presumptuousness, and a lot turned on. "Oh." I sounded breathy and stupid, so I tried again. "Oh *really*." There, that was better—sarcastic, caustic, disbelieving.

He leaned close, and his nose brushed the side of my neck, and then his lips brushed my ear—I shivered, and felt my nipples harden. "Yes, really. You'll *beg* to put those beautiful lips of yours around my cock."

"I have *never* begged anyone for fucking anything in my life," I hiss. "And I'm not about to start, not even for you, Puck Lawson."

His laugh was a low rumble. "You'll beg, Colbie." His teeth nipped my earlobe, and I gasped. "And I'll oblige you willingly."

"What makes you so sure?" I managed to sound fairly in control of my voice, so kudos to me for that little victory.

"Because all I'm doing is talking, and you've got headlights poking through your shirt and bra." His voice dropped to a whisper. "I bet you've got beautiful nipples, Colbie. Thick and plump and pink, with nice big dark areolae. Don't you?"

I glanced down and saw that he was right: my nipples were prominently on display. "Maybe they're small and flat and ugly, with no areolae at all," I whispered back.

I flinched and my gasp was squeaky and breathy when he pinched my nipple, a quick, sharp bite of sudden stinging pleasure that I felt in my pussy even with two layers of fabric between my flesh and his finger and thumb.

He laughed. "No way. You're too responsive."

"Stop, Puck," I breathed. "Everyone's watching."

"Who cares?"

I leaned away from him. "I care."

He let me put a little distance between us. "Now imagine what I'll make you feel when I get you alone and in private."

I was breathing a little heavily, my thighs were pressed together, my nipples were throbbing and erect, and my pussy was aching and wet. He'd gotten me this hot and bothered in public with a few words and one quick pinch. Jesus, maybe he was right about everything he said he could do.

5

SHITSHOW

HOLY. SHIT.
　　This chick.

This *chick*, man. She didn't give an inch. She gave nothing away for free. She was into me, I could tell that much, don't get me wrong, but god*damn* . . . she was *not* making that shit easy.

I *liked* it. I liked it a lot. If I wanted to make her gasp, I'd have to work for it. If I wanted to see her writhe and squirm because she was so turned on she couldn't help it, but didn't want to be turned on by me, then I'd have to fuckin' put an effort into it.

Getting a kiss from her was going to require patience and skill and honesty and all the game I had; getting her naked and riding my cock? Ohh man . . . that might very well be the greatest challenge of my life.

Challenge accepted.

I felt a vibration in my pocket and a second later heard an electronic ring; I dug the phone out of my pocket and accepted the call. "Hello?"

"Puck Lawson?" The voice on the other end was quiet and almost soft, but icy.

"That's me."

"I am Ivar Krieg. We have a friend in common."

"Anselm, yeah. Thanks for calling, man."

"*Ja, es nichts.* You are in Kiev, *ja*?"

"Yeah."

"Do you know where, precisely?"

I glanced at Colbie. "Can you figure out our cross streets?"

She nodded. "Yeah. One sec."

I went back to Ivar. "Hold on a minute and I can tell you."

"Okay."

Colbie trotted from the bench to the nearest intersection, and my eyes never left her—primarily to keep an eye on her and to make sure nothing untoward happened in the hundred-some feet from the bench to the corner, but also because her ass was phenomenal and because a woman running in heels was an incredible sight performing an incredible feat, if you asked me. She trotted back and I relayed the cross streets to Ivar.

"Ah. I know exactly where you are. How many

of you are there, and are you safe there for the immediate future?" His English was impeccable, even smoother than Anselm's.

"We're at the park not far from the intersection. We're safe for now, but Cain's boys have a way of showing up unannounced. If they do show up, we're gonna have to make tracks and fast," I said. "There're nineteen of us."

"*Scheisse*," Ivar hissed. "That is a lot of people."

"Don't I know it, brother." I heard a diesel engine roar and tracked the sound, but it was a city bus groaning and swaying to the next stop. "How much did Anselm tell you?"

"Enough. That you have stolen from Cain his human trafficking merchandise, and that you require assistance in Kiev."

"One of the girls has a tracer in her, we're relatively certain, so you can safely assume that wherever we go, they won't be far behind."

"I know someone who can neutralize that easily, although she operates out of Prague." Ivar hesitated, thinking. "Twenty people, one chipped . . . are you armed?"

"Minimal. Two nines, a forty-five, and a forty, mag and a spare for each."

"Not so much, considering. You will need more." His cadence quickened, taking on the authority of someone who gave orders and was used to them being followed. "Remain where you are if at all possible—it is a good spot. If you receive company, dispose of them if possible. To attempt to elude them with so many extra bodies around is impossible. Can you split up if necessary?"

"Affirmative. Thirteen of the nineteen are unknowns. They were on the plane and I wasn't gonna just leave 'em there. There are six of us who I cannot and will not separate from."

"The thirteen, they are locals?"

"Negative. Assorted nationalities. Most are not native English speakers, and none of them are locals from what I can tell."

"And you know nothing of their places of origin?"

"Most of them I can't communicate with, so no. If you can have 'em dumped at a consulate or something, they can become someone else's problem."

"*Nein*, I have a better idea. I know someone who specializes in placing victims of trafficking in safe houses where they can be reunited with family if possible, or given a new life, if not."

"Yeah, Anselm mentioned that human trafficking is a bit of a . . . ah, sore spot for you."

"I have made it my personal mission to hunt down and end human traffickers. It is a vendetta for me. And this man, this Cain . . . he is a personal enemy of mine in particular. It was he, I believe, who was responsible for my sister's kidnapping, enslavement, and death. I have sworn a blood oath that I will put a bullet in his skull."

"Well, Ivar, you know what they say—the enemy of my enemy is my friend, and I wouldn't mind putting a hole or seven in that piece 'o shit my own self."

Ivar's laugh was an icy rattle. "I believe we understand each other very well, *Herr* Lawson."

"Indeed we do, Mr. Krieg, indeed we do."

"I am in the air as we speak. Your man Harris was able to secure a flight for me from Berlin."

"ETA?" I asked.

"Less than two hours until landing, and perhaps twenty minutes after that to your location. I have ground transport arranged already in Kiev."

"Sounds good. See you in a couple hours then, Ivar."

"*Jawohl.* I look forward to our meeting."

He clicked off, and I replaced the phone in my pocket. "Well, he seems like he'll work out just fine," I said to Colbie.

"Nice guy?"

I chuckled. "I hope not."

Colbie frowned. "I don't follow."

"I don't need a *nice* guy, I need a *competent* guy. I need the kind of guy who can get hold of untraceable firearms. I need a guy who can dispose of corpses. I need a guy who knows what to do with a bunch of scared, innocent women who all speak different languages, kidnapped from who the fuck knows where." I withdrew one of the pistols I'd taken from the guys in the panel van and set it on my leg between us. "Any guy who meets those criteria probably ain't a nice guy, know what I'm sayin'?"

Colbie eyed the pistol. "I see what you're saying." Her gaze went to me. "So . . . are you a nice guy?"

I snorted. "Not by a long shot. Wasn't even a nice kid, and only got meaner as I grew up." I smirked at her. "Nice is really fuckin' overrated, you ask me." Sliding the pistol toward her, I met her eyes. "Ever use one of these?"

She nodded. "Once."

"Cap someone?" I asked, my voice neutral.

She shrugged. "I dunno. It was . . . chaotic. Probably not, to be honest. I wasn't really . . ." she trailed off, unsure how to finish her statement.

I knew what she meant, though. "In gun battles, the majority of shots fired miss. An untrained kid, scared, in a gangland shootout? I doubt you came within a dozen feet." I overrode the objection I saw bubbling up. "You didn't want to hurt anyone, you were just going along with what was in front of you. Doing what you had to do."

She nodded. "I'd hoped to never be in that position again."

"Don't blame you, sweetheart." I dropped my palm on her knee and squeezed. "You don't want it, I sure as hell won't think less of you. But if you want to keep this with you for protection, it's yours."

"You think I should?"

I shrugged. "I'm not gonna lie to you, shit could

very well get worse before it gets better. This has been way too damn easy so far. I'm just offering it to you. Choice is yours."

She stared at the heavy black .40. After a moment's thought, she gingerly nudged it back toward me with an index finger. "I think I'll let you do the shooting, if that's okay. If it comes down to it, I'll do what I have to, but if I don't have to shoot anyone . . . I'd rather not."

I slid the pistol back into my pocket. "Fair enough. I'll do my damnedest to make sure you don't have to use it, how about that?"

She smiled at me. "I would appreciate that."

At that moment, my ever-wandering gaze latched onto a pair of men across the street, seventy-five yards away. The way they were eyeing me, the brisk, crispness of the way they walked, and the way both of their right hands remained shoved into the pockets of identical black windbreakers . . .

"Layla," I snapped, raising my voice just enough to be heard. "Incoming."

"I see 'em."

"I'll handle it, but be ready," I said. I nudged Colbie with my knee. "Go over and sit by the others. Follow Layla's lead."

She didn't hesitate but also didn't obviously hurry. She stood up, strolled over to where Layla and the others were, and found a seat on the arm of the bench, immediately engaging in conversation.

The two men were close. Their eyes flicked from me to Temple and back, and then scanned the rest of the park. One of them said something to the other, gesturing with a free hand, and the two men separated.

The last thing I wanted was a public shootout, especially with so many innocent people around—aside from the eighteen women in my care, there were other pedestrians on the sidewalks, cars passing back and forth, bicyclists. All I had aside from the pistols was the three-inch folding blade I'd taken from Anton on the plane, which was better than nothing but not much against two armed assailants.

I was sitting on the bench closest to the street, so I remained where I was for the moment. I cast a quick glance behind me at the park, doing a headcount and a scan of the layout: the park was a rectangular lot between two rows of buildings, with a walkway bisecting the rectangle from the sidewalk to the center of the park, where there was a brick-paved courtyard, three rows of benches arranged in a semi circle around the center, facing in. A giant oak tree served as the centerpiece of the park, with a few smaller saplings around the perimeter of the park. The sides and rear of the park were formed by brick walls, the back and sides of buildings, with only the street side facing open. Most of the women were sitting on the benches closest to the oak tree.

As the two men approached the park, crossing

the street, I stood up and slid my hands in my pockets. I had the folding knife in my hand, thumb ready to flick the blade open. The men had separated far enough apart that their tactic was obvious: one was going for me, the other for Temple. I decided to trust Layla to handle the one headed her way, and focused my attention on my immediate opponent.

He was a similar height to me but slimmer by about thirty pounds, and probably a decade younger, although the coldness in his expression made me think he was no novice to these kinds of situations. I stood my ground and let him approach. He got within six feet and then stopped, withdrawing his hand from the windbreaker pocket. He had a nine, finger on the trigger.

"Hands," he barked, in a thick accent. "No funniness or you die."

I kept my expression neutral as I raised my hands slowly. Of course, I had the little folding knife in my right fist, and it was just long enough that it didn't quite fit in my fist. His eyes went to my hand, and he jerked his chin at the hint of black peeking out from the bottom of my fist.

"What is?"

I lowered my hands and opened my right palm to show the knife. "Here."

He held his gun low, at his hip, aimed at me, and shuffled toward me, arm outstretched. Dumbass. Had he told me to drop it, kick it to him, or toss it,

I'd have been fucked, but he looked young enough and naïve enough to maybe fall for this little trick. And yes, he did. He inched toward me, reaching for the closed knife in my hand, trusting the threat of the gun to be enough of a deterrent.

Dumbass.

I waited until he made his move, stretched his hand out to snatch at the knife. There was a split second when his attention was on my hand, on the knife, rather than on me, and that was when I struck. I lashed out with my left fist, batting his gun hand away and darting forward into him. My left hand fastened onto his wrist, and I crushed down with all the force I had, hard enough that I felt bones grinding, and he cried out. The instant I made my move, I flicked open the knife blade that thankfully had a nice smooth action and decent spring to the blade, so one little push of my thumb sent the blade snapping into place. My hand was already low, at belly level, which made a throat shot tricky. I crashed into him, keeping a crushing grip on his gun hand wrist, and jamming the knife between us, angling down, down. I felt the rough scratch of denim and the bulge of his zipper; I angled a little lower and then drove the blade into the meat of his inner thigh, high up. He grunted in pain and I twisted the knife, dragged it back toward me through muscle, and then I withdrew the blade, my knuckles dripping and hot and wet with blood. I slammed the blade into his throat just beneath his Adam's apple, and his groan and scream of pain turned to a nasty wet whistle. I backed away, dropped him, stripping him of his pistol as he fell, blood spurting in thick bright red gushes from his severed femoral artery.

I heard a shout and turned my attention to Layla and Temple. The other thug had Temple held in front of him against his chest, arm across her chest, but he didn't have his gun to her temple. He had orders to bring her in alive, obviously, since she wasn't worth anything dead. Which made his posture as a hostage taker an empty bluff.

I made sure he got a good look at his buddy, bleeding out. "Let her go, dickhead."

"*Nemaye . . . vpadit' nizh,*" he said, jerking his chin at me.

"I don't know what you're saying, bud, but for your sake, I hope it was 'I'm a pussy, I give up.'"

Colbie snickered. "Actually, he told you to drop the knife."

"No shit. Some things translate themselves." I met her gaze. "Tell him to let her go, or I'll kill him slower than I did his friend."

Colbie rattled something off in Russian, and the dumbshit was foolish enough to pivot away from me to face Colbie, leaving most of his torso open. I chucked the knife at him, and as soon as the knife left my hand I drew the .45 from behind my back. Life ain't like the movies, though, and folding knives aren't weighted for throwing, so unless you're an expert, that shit ain't sticking blade first into anything, and even experts would say that was nearly impossible. And in my case, I wasn't an expert knife thrower. So the knife hit the asshole right in the center of his chest with the handle. Didn't do jackshit to hurt him, but it did provide exactly what I needed: a distraction. He jerked his attention back to me, and the moment Temple felt his focus shift, she tore herself out of his grip and hit the ground. Smart girl. Now the playing field was even. By the time the stupid fucker realized what was happening, I was already inside his reach and had my pistol barrel shoved up under his chin. He blinked stupidly for a second, and then raised his hands.

"Shit," I groaned as I took his weapon. "This complicates things."

"What does?" Colbie asked.

I grabbed the guy by the hair and shoved him into the ground at the base of the oak tree. "This cockmuncher," I said, gesturing at him with the barrel of the pistol. "He surrendered, so I can't just shoot him, now."

"Oh," Colbie said. "I suppose that wouldn't be very nice, would it?"

"No. It'd be downright unfriendly, I'd say."

People watched, staring at the dude bleeding out, wondering what was going on. I had to make this whole scene less conspicuous right the hell now or we'd have to find somewhere else to sit, and I was kinda starting to like this park.

"Hey hooker, grab his ankles," I said to Layla.

"Don't call me a hooker, dickhead," she retorted.

Layla tucked her pistol into the waistband of her jeans at the small of her back with practiced ease and grabbed the now-dead dude by the ankles. I grabbed him by the armpits, and we carried him to the back corner of the park and dumped him. Not much I could do about the giant pool of blood on the sidewalk where he'd bled out, but at least there wasn't a body lying out in plain view. He wasn't exactly hidden where he was; mind you, just . . . less obvious.

A quartet of men in business suits drifted past the park just then, and my heart slammed in my chest as one of them glanced our way, but he didn't seem to see anything amiss, and they all kept walking. This park was some distance from the busiest roads and didn't have much traffic, pedestrian or vehicular—thank god, too, because that hadn't exactly been the most unobtrusive of situations.

Layla sat back down on the bench with Kyrie and Lola, who were comforting Temple. Layla had her pistol out and was positioned to keep an eye and a gun barrel on our hostage, who seemed content to sit and not be dead, for the moment, at least.

I picked up my knife off the ground, folded the blade back in, and pocketed it, then resumed my seat on the bench. After a moment, Colbie returned to sit beside me.

"You make that look so easy," she said.

"Which part?"

She gestured at the spreading pool of ruby-red blood. "That. Killing people. I'm not even sure what you did, or why he bled out so fast."

I grabbed her hand, placed her fingers on the inside of my thigh, high up, so her knuckles were inches from my crotch. "There's an artery here, the femoral artery." Colbie's breath caught, and her fingers splayed out on my thigh, digging in, as if fighting the urge to move higher yet; I released her, but her hand remained on my thigh. "The femoral is one of the biggest arteries in the human body, transporting over three hundred fifty millimeters of blood per minute. If that motherfucker gets severed, you will bleed out in less than five minutes."

She tightened her grip on my thigh, and I felt myself going hard behind my zipper even though she was inches away from my cock, and we were discussing a man's death. "So . . . if you'd severed his femoral artery and he was going to die of blood loss anyway, why did you stab him in the throat?"

I rested my palm on her knee, and then gently, slowly, hesitantly slid it up her thigh in minute increments, under the hem of her skirt; she let me, and my heart started doing a ridiculous pussy virgin teenager *thumpity-thumpity-thump* just from a fairly innocent palm to her leg.

"So he wouldn't scream and draw attention to us."

"Oh."

"Do I scare you?"

She nodded. "Yes, you do. It shouldn't be so easy to end a life."

I sighed. "I agree. But that's where my life has taken me. I don't do it lightly, and I don't do it easily. I'm not a serial killer or a sociopath, Colbie. But if someone threatens me or those I've sworn to protect, I will not hesitate, and I will not feel guilt. These jackholes are all stone-cold killers, and I'm doing the world a favor by getting rid of them."

"Do you have any regrets?"

"In terms of what? In general, or people I've killed?"

She shrugged. "Both, I guess."

I thought for a moment. "Hmm. In general . . . maybe not making more of the time I had with Raquel. I wish I'd been more open about how I felt, shown her what she meant to me. I was young and stupid and an emotional caveman, thought being manly and macho meant never being . . . like . . . sweet or tender or whatever. I really cared for her, but I was just a . . . a churlish dick all the time. Surly and closed off, kept my emotions shut down."

Colbie looked at me, surprised. "Wow, I wasn't expecting that answer."

I tilted my head and shrugged. "Just the truth.

She deserved more from me than she got, and then she died, and I'll never be able to give her that."

She hesitated a long moment, and then her palm skated down the inside of my thigh to my knee and back up, closer to my groin, this time. "So if you were ever in a real relationship again . . .?"

I knew what she was getting at, what she was asking me. "I'd do things a lot differently. I got no problem being real about what I'm feeling. Maybe it's being older, realizing life is too damn short to act tough when you don't gotta be tough."

"So you can be sweet and tender, is that what you're saying?" she asked, with a wink and a twinkle in her stormy gray eyes.

I smirked. Slid my palm a little higher, and now my hand was fully under her skirt, up to mid-thigh, and her skin was silky soft and luscious and warm. "I can be a lot of things that might surprise you, babe."

"Like what?"

"If I told you, it wouldn't be much of a surprise, now would it?"

She snorted. "Cop out."

"Hey, I've surprised you quite a bit since we first met, haven't I?"

She conceded the point with a tilted nod of her head, her mahogany locks swaying. "I guess you're right."

"I can't give away *all* my surprises right off the bat, can I?"

"Fine, fine," she said with a laugh. "So, change of subject. Tell me about the virgin."

I tilted my head back and blew out a sigh. "You're sure you want to hear about this?"

She nodded. "Yes, I do. I'm curious."

"And you'll tell me something about yourself in return?"

She nodded again. "I will. Something revealing and personal of a sexual nature."

I held out my hand, and she took it in hers, and we shook.

"All right, then. Here it goes. I was thirty-two at the time. Working for the FBI in the forensics department. I was a field operative, one who went to the crime scene and figured out what happened based on the evidence. Kinda like Dexter, except I wasn't a secret serial killer. No attachments. I'd just finished a particularly gruesome triple homicide case, and I went to a bar to have a few drinks and see if I could find some company for the night. Like I said, the case I'd just helped close had been pretty nasty, and I'd put in a good eighty hours of work the previous week, so I was . . . not really looking for someone chatty, you know? I just wanted to have some fun and spend the weekend catching up on sleep." I realized, at that moment, that after shaking hands in agreement, neither of us had let go, so we were holding hands, my right in her left, with my other hand under her skirt on her bare thigh, and her other hand on my leg—lots of touching, none of it overtly sexual. Very weird for me. "So . . . two, three drinks in, I still hadn't scoped anyone. All the girls in the bar were either clearly with someone or in a group. I've discovered it's always more trouble than it's worth to try and separate one particular chick out of a group. I was losing hope and getting ready to just toss it in and go home. And then I saw her. Young, maybe twenty-one, twenty-two, really young. A lot younger than I usually go for, but for sure legal. Pretty, sweet looking, and all alone. She was wearing this dress, not sure what you'd call it, kind of a sundress or something. Cute, flowers on it, mid-thigh length, with a belt and a cardigan over it. I don't know why I remember what she was wearing, or why it should be significant, but it just . . . was. Her outfit wasn't meant for anyone but her, meant to be comfortable and pretty. She was alone, like I said, sitting at the bar, nursing a glass of white wine. Long shiny blond hair. Cute—really cute, really pretty . . . and obviously lonely. Now, that shit is *not* my type. If I'm at the bar trying to score a hook-up, I go for the obvious types, the easy pickings. The kinda girl you'd clearly expect to be able to pick up at a bar for quick and easy one-night company, okay? Just the facts."

"And this girl was way outside that type."

I nodded. "Way, *way* outside it. Probably wasn't even looking for company on the stool next to her, let alone what I had in mind. I'm still not sure what came over me. I was in a shitty mood, I was exhausted, I was frustrated, and I was horny. I'd been too busy that week for anything but work, so all I really wanted, to be blunt, was to get my rocks off and then sleep for twelve hours. So why did I sit down next to a sad, lonely, cute girl? I don't do *cute*. Cute is a death sentence. Cute is . . . just no. But there I was. I bought her a glass of wine, and I struck up a conversation and ended up closing the bar with her. Just talking. We didn't even drink that much, or at least I didn't. She did, though. So by the time the bar closed, she was blackout drunk and couldn't even tell me her own name, much less where she lived. So, I—"

Colbie eyed me sidelong, eyes narrowed. "Puck. You didn't."

I stared at her, not bothering to disguise my anger. "*Fuck* no! Jesus, Colbie."

She raised both hands in a gesture of apology. "Hey, we don't know each other very well."

"If you can't see by now that I'm not the type of guy to rape a blackout drunk chick, then either you're a terrible judge of character, or I come across as a lot more of a skeezy shit-ball than I thought."

"Or maybe I was feeling you out, seeing how you'd react to the insinuation." She shrugged and smirked at me. "The vehemence of your response goes a lot farther in telling me about what kind of guy you are than anything else you might say."

I blew out a calming breath. "I'm glad I passed

your test, in that case."

She reached out and trailed a finger through my beard. "So. Lonely drunk girl . . . what'd you do?"

"Took her back to my place. I couldn't just leave her there."

"You could have gotten her address from her purse."

I cocked my head to the side. "I suppose. But everything life has taught me says to never ever dig in a woman's purse. Especially one I don't know."

"You said you'd been talking to her most of the night."

"Doesn't mean I knew her well enough to go hunting in her purse." I waved my hand. "Point is, I put her in my bed, made sure she wasn't gonna choke on her own vomit, and then set some Gatorade and Tylenol on the bedside table."

"What did you guys talk about?"

I waved a hand. "Just . . . random bullshit. Politics, movies, music, surface shit. Nothing deep, nothing about ourselves." I paused. "The only reason I brought her to my place was because it seemed safest. Even if I had gotten her address, she was so clobbered she would have needed monitoring, and she'd mentioned that she lived alone. I slept on the couch and got up a few times to check on her, make sure she hadn't upchucked in her sleep."

"So then in the morning . . ."

I hesitated. "In the morning . . . she woke up at

like eleven, and I made coffee, and we had a super awkward conversation. The first thing I told her was that, in case the fact that she'd woken up completely clothed wasn't enough of an indication, she'd passed out in the cab, and I'd tossed her in bed and that was that. I wasn't sure what kind of girl she was, if she'd assume we'd banged or be worried about it . . . I just wasn't sure. Like I said, we hadn't discussed ourselves, like at all. She seemed embarrassed, but also upset, still."

"Not seeing where this is going, to be honest."

"Eventually, I flat out asked her what was wrong." I let silence hang for a moment, thinking back. "She didn't answer for a long time. When she did, it was to tell me that she'd planned on getting drunk, going home, and killing herself."

"Holy shit. Why?"

"That's verbatim what I said, actually. She told me she was twenty-one, a virgin, and had terminal cancer."

"Oh my god," Colbie breathed.

I nodded. "Now you see where it's going."

She sighed. "I think so, yeah."

"She reached up and pulled her wig off, because I guess she could tell that I was feeling a little skeptical, maybe. She didn't look sick, you know? When she took the wig off, she was completely bald."

"Jeez. What did you do?"

"What does anyone do in that situation?" I

laughed. "I completely blanked. Froze. Like . . . what was I supposed to say? Ask how long she has left? Seems cold, to me."

Colbie nodded. "I can see the difficulty."

"At that point, I experienced what still remains the longest, most tense, most awkward silence of my life. I'm not an emotionally comforting sort of guy, you know? I'm still not, and I was even less so, then. I was still pretty hurt and pissed off and fucked up over Raquel, wasn't really in a place where I knew how to comfort a pissed off dying girl."

"So what happened?"

"She asked if I'd take her home, so I did, and that was that, I thought." I glanced at Colbie. "This is where it gets interesting. Two months pass, I pretty much forget about her. Then the door buzzer thing goes off at like three in the morning, Tuesday night, Wednesday morning, whatever you want to call it. I answer the door in a pair of underwear, because what the fuck? Nobody I knew even knew where I lived. It was her, the girl. I never got her name, and she never offered. By the time morning came around and she was admitting to being terminal and a virgin, it seemed kind of late to be like, 'oh hey, by the way, what's your name?' You know? So I never got her name. Then she shows up at my door at three in the morning. She's crying. No wig, a lot thinner, looked sick this time."

"God, Puck."

I nod. "So, I bring her inside, and she sits on my couch, and says she has a favor to ask." I pause, and then pitch my voice high. "'You can't say no, because I'm dying, and you're not allowed to deny a dying person their last request.' That's what she said to me, verbatim."

"Dear god."

"Yeah, pretty much. So I'm like, 'all right, what's your request?' She tells me she doesn't want to die a virgin. She'd been waiting for the right guy, the right time, and then she got sick, and it would be cruel at that point to get involved with someone emotionally. Apparently there was a guy, but she'd pretended she wasn't in love with him so he wouldn't get all invested with a dead girl walking. That was her phrase—dead girl walking."

"This sounds like a novel."

"Felt like one," I said. "So I tell her I assumed she wanted me to . . . be the one. And she just nodded. My head was spinning. Like, what the fuck? What was I supposed to do? Again, I was at a complete loss. She said . . . she didn't know my name, and I didn't know hers, and she wanted it to stay like that. She didn't want me to pretend feelings, don't make it weird. But she also didn't want to just . . . get it over with, right? She wanted to enjoy it, but keep it impersonal to a degree."

"Goddamn, Puck."

"So, I agreed. Like she said, I couldn't be like,

no, I'm not doing that. I mean, it felt fucked up, you know? But, at the same time, if you look at it from another perspective, it didn't have to be that much different than any other random hook-up. I just had to put aside the fact of her terminal illness and just pretend she was . . . just some nameless chick I'd picked up at the bar."

"And that's what you did?"

I nodded. "I did."

Colbie was silent for a while. "So?"

I eyed her. "So . . . what?"

She snorted. "You can't stop now. What happened?"

I blinked. "Um, well . . . I slept with her."

"And?"

"And what?" I paused. "What is it you want to hear? A play by play?"

"Was it good? Was it hot?"

"It was . . . yeah. It was good. It was hot. I told her the only way I could make sure she had a good experience was if we had sex more than once. I'd never been with a virgin, but I knew enough to know the first time was never very good. And I didn't want her first time to be her only time, and have it be . . . anything less than memorable, I guess. So we started out kissing. Good place to start, right? The girl could kiss, too. I mean, damn. She had that shit down. I let her just sort of . . . dictate things, to start with. Figure out whether she really wanted to carry through with it, you know?" I hesitated, feeling oddly protective of the details. "She was . . . eager. After that first time, she was . . . insatiable. She stayed with me for two days. I called off work, said I had a family crisis to deal with. A boldface lie, but whatever. I made sure she had the time of her life. We never exchanged names, and we never talked about our pasts. Basically, we spent the better part of 48 hours eating, fucking, and sleeping."

"Wow."

I shrugged. "I . . . I wasn't ever quite able to completely forget . . . the circumstances, but I like to think she was able to do that for those two days."

"How'd it end?"

"I woke up, the morning of the third day, and she was in my bathroom, sick. She asked me to call her cab, so I did. She kissed me, told me thank you for giving her a priceless gift, and then left."

Colbie was silent for a while and then sighed. "And you never saw her again?"

I shook my head. "Nope. Well, not in person. I was reading the local newspaper one morning about a month later, and I was trying to fold the fucking thing so I could read the comics, and the obituary section fell out. I saw her face." I paused, tugging on my beard. "I threw the paper down before I could read anything about her. Threw the paper away and went to work."

I could tell this threw Colbie. "Why? You didn't want to know? Not even her name?"

"I wanted to know more than anything. But her request was that she remain anonymous to me."

"Why do you think that was?"

"I don't know. It's something I think about, sometimes." I shrugged. "My best guess is that she wanted me to remember the time we spent together for what it was, rather than associating it her with her life. She didn't want to become some mythic, tragic figure for me."

"Is that how you see her?"

I shook my head. "Honestly, no. It worked. I know absolutely nothing about her. All I know, all I remember, is two days of what was, if I'm honest, really great sex. When I start to feel nostalgic or start to put some kind of tragic angle on my feelings toward her, I think about those two days spent naked, making her feel things she'd never felt before. I think about the sex, and I make it about that. Because I like to think that's what she wanted. And also because otherwise, I might go a little crazy over the whole thing."

Colbie eyed me thoughtfully, and I waited for her to ask the questions I could see percolating behind her eyes. "So was it the best sex you've ever had?"

I shook my head. "Nope."

"No?"

I shook my head again. "If I said yes, I'd be romanticizing it. It wasn't the best ever. It's up there, but not the best."

"So who was the best?"

I laughed. "You don't mind asking the hard shit, do you?"

She laughed with me. "Hell no. That's how you get to the good stuff. And if someone isn't willing to answer the hard questions, they're not worth my time."

I tilted my head. "How do you figure?"

"Life is too short for bullshit, Puck. I OD'd, I told you that. I realized then that, as cliché as it sounds, life is what you make of it. After that, I became aggressive about going after what I wanted, and ever since, I refuse to waste time on people who aren't worth my attention. If you can't be real with me, if you can't be upfront with me, if you can't handle me asking the hard shit, then what's the point?"

I accede the point with a grunted *huh* sound. "Fair enough. Well, then, I guess the answer would be . . . this chick named Maya. I met her on vacation and we spent a week together in a tiki hut, in bed. I think I had more sex in that week than any other entire month. She was . . . fucking wild, man. Totally batshit crazy, like legit, she was a goddamn lunatic, but she was a fuckin' wildcat in the sack." I squeezed Colbie's thigh. "Your turn."

"Okay, I guess it's only fair. So, something revealing and personal of a sexual nature." She twisted a strand of my beard around her finger and tugged on it; I debated telling her that the way she tugged on my beard was a crazy-ass turn on, but decided to leave that tidbit for later. "Okay, I've got it. So it's no secret that smack junkies will do just about anything for a hit, right? I'm sure you're familiar with the stereotype, right? Well, I made a rule for myself that I'd never use sex as a tool, no matter how desperate I got. And I never did. Even when I was in the depths of withdrawal desperation, I refused to trade sex for a hit. I was terrified of getting trapped in prostitution, because that was something I saw all too frequently. There was a group of us, homeless people, junkies, alkies—the dregs, the losers, the . . . the castoffs and the lost, you know? We lived in this little community under an overpass. It was hell, but it was better than an alley, or somewhere alone. I wouldn't call any of those people friends, really, but we looked out for each other, to a degree. A lot of the women, they'd get desperate, and they'd turn a trick to get money for the next hit, and then they'd need another hit, and the only way they could get money for another hit was turning another trick. It turned into a trap, and I guess I always held out hope, deep down, that I'd figure out some way out. Part of me didn't want to believe that was really my life, or something like that. But I just . . . I refused. I'd been a virgin when my uncle raped me, and I think that helped make it easy to never let that become a way out. The only experience I had was rape, and it felt like even if I willingly let some guy fuck me in exchange for money or drugs, it'd still feel like rape, still be that same thing Uncle Craig had done."

"Makes sense."

"I did a lot of other gnarly shit to get drug money, though. Lots of stealing, scams, and begging. It was an ugly time."

"That's personal and revealing," I said, "but not sexual . . . about sex, but not sexual."

"What I consider my first time, my first voluntary time, was after I got clean. He was a lot like me, recovering addict, homeless, trying to pick himself up and restart his life. Older than me by a few years, really sweet guy. Perfect kind of guy for my first time after everything I'd been through. It was hard to find privacy in a shelter, but we managed it, and it was . . . nice, but underwhelming."

"After what'd you experienced, I'd imagine it'd be hard to . . . want that, I guess."

She nodded. "You'd be right. I wanted to be normal. I didn't want what Craig had done to define me anymore, or to hold me back. And Paul . . . he made it easy for me to get past my hang-ups. I thought maybe he and I would have something, you know? Like we could lean on each other as we worked on staying clean and figuring out how to start life over."

"I sense a 'but' coming."

She nodded. "But then he vanished. I threw myself into focusing on the SATs and scholarships and college applications. And then, a few days before I left for Harvard, I ran into him. He was using again. I could see it, feel it, smell it. He was strung out and desperate for another hit. I don't think he even recognized me. And that was sort of the final mental turning point for me, seeing Paul like that. High, crazy, desperate, dirty, so fucked up he didn't even recognize me. I realized then that I'd never, ever, fucking *ever* go back to that."

"And you haven't."

She shook her head. "I barely even drink. The idea of losing myself to anything scares me. Even being drunk feels like something I could get hooked on and then somehow I'd be back out on the street. I know it's silly or stupid, but even if I let myself drink regularly, I have this fear that I'll become an alcoholic. Having known plenty of those, I know how ugly it can be, how completely you can lose yourself to it, and I just . . . I refuse."

I withdrew my hand from her leg and put it around her shoulders, drew her closer against me. "Not silly, babe. Not at all. My old man was an alcoholic, and that shit will rule you and it will ruin you, if you let it. I've lived a life hard, I don't mind admitting. But I'm very much aware of the fact that Pops was a drunk, and I won't let myself go there either. I'm careful about it. I take regular hiatuses from drinking, just to prove to myself, I guess, that I'm in control, that I don't need booze to have a good time."

"I'm glad you understand." Colbie rested her

head on my shoulder, and even though this conversation hadn't gone how I'd meant it to, I felt like this was better, somehow.

I wanted the trade of revealing sexual stories to be hot, to fan the sparks between us into something more. I meant it to make things between us sizzle even more, give me an edge. That backfired, it became some kind of intensely personal, emotionally packed moment of revelation. I just told her shit I'd never told anyone, shit I'd never admitted even to myself.

"So, who was your best?" I asked, in the interest of trying to regain the sparks.

"Alex Caldwell. The TA of my first Russian class. His mom was Russian, like had moved to the States while she was pregnant with Alex. She ended up marrying some American dude when Alex was two, which was how he had an American last name, but he'd grown up speaking Russian and English, since his stepdad learned Russian so he could talk to Alex's mom better."

I smirked at her. "Okay. And . . .?"

Colbie rolled her eyes at me. "There's nothing lascivious about the story. We dated for six months, and he was great in bed. Alex was the one who showed me what sex could really be, I guess you could say. He was my TA, but we made a rule that we'd never talk about the class, and he'd grade my papers like anyone else's, and I'd never get any kind of special treatment. And then the class ended, and that stopped being something we had to worry about."

"Why'd you break up with him?"

"Oh, he graduated, got a job in Los Angeles, and that was that. I was sad about it for a few months, but I'd never really been in love with him, and I knew he hadn't been in love with me either. We had good sex together; we got along, had fun, but when he landed the job there was no question of how it was going to go. It wasn't, like, *painful*, you know? It wasn't some big drama, do I stay for Colbie, or do I move for the really great job I just got? Nah, it was just one of those things that happens in life, and we both knew it."

"What made the sex so good?"

She lifted a shoulder. "He paid attention to me, figured out what I liked. And it didn't hurt that he had—" she broke off, blushing a little.

"A big cock?"

Colbie nodded. "It was very nice, yes."

"Very nice," I echoed. "Did he make you go crazy in bed? Did he make you come so hard you fainted?"

She rolled her eyes at me. "No, Puck."

"You say that like I'm asking stupid questions."

"You are."

I leaned in and bit her earlobe, lowered my voice to a whisper. "See, I don't think I am. Best sex ever should make you absolutely crazy."

"Like you and Maya?" she asked.

I nodded. "We'd finish, and I'd just laugh, because it was so fucking crazy. Every single time I was like, *whoa, holy shit.*"

Colbie frowned at me. "So if I've never fainted from an orgasm, if I've never gone *whoa, holy shit,* then I'm not doing it right?"

I shook my head. "Not what I'm saying. But you should experience that at least once."

"And you can show that to me, can you?" she asked, skepticism rife in her voice. "Crazy, make-me-faint sex?"

"Absolutely."

"And what if I have sex with you on the promise of earth-shattering, life-changing sex, and you don't deliver?"

I smirked at her. "Colbie, babe . . . it feels like you doubt me."

She stared up at me, and her expression was difficult to read. "You're promising an awful lot, Puck. Dozens of orgasms, orgasms so intense I faint, sex so good I go crazy. You're building this up a whole hell of a lot, and I'm skeptical of anything that sounds too good to be true." She wrapped an index finger in the end of my beard and tugged on it again. "Call me cynical, but I'm wary of someone promising me the things you're claiming you can do."

"You raise a valid point."

She quirked an eyebrow at me. "But?"

I shrugged and shook my head. "But nothing. It's a valid point. You're absolutely right to be cynical and skeptical."

She laughed. "You're not helping your case, Puck."

I touched her knee, traced up the inside of her thigh a few inches, and she shivered, tensed. "I barely touch you, and you shiver. You *like* the way I touch you, and you want more." I murmured this to her. "You want to know what my fingers will feel like touching your pussy. You want to feel my face between your thighs. The way you tense and catch your breath when all I'm doing is whispering to you and touching your leg . . . when I get my mouth on you, you'll lose your fucking mind, Colbie. You know you will. You already can't breathe, and all I'm doing is talking about it. You can imagine it, can't you?"

She was frozen in place, not breathing; her thighs clamped down around my hand, arresting my upward progress under her skirt. "Yes, Puck."

"Yes, what, Colbie?"

"I can imagine it."

"And you want it, don't you?"

"Hell yeah."

I teased the outer shell of her ear with my tongue. "What else do you want?"

"You."

"Me, how?"

"Naked."

"And?"

She shook her head. "And . . . everything."

I laughed, a low rumble. "You want me naked

. . . on top of you?" I brushed my lips against her ear. "You want me to tie you up so can't escape and eat you out until you're begging me to fuck you? You want me tied up, wearing a cock ring, so you can ride me and fuck me and not let me come until you're ready? You want to feel my cock sliding down your throat? You want to feel me come all over your tits?"

"That'd be a start," she answered, a little breathless.

I laughed again, genuinely surprised by her response. "A start, she says."

"Yeah, a start. You got more?"

Her thighs loosened, and I slid my touch a little higher. "I got plenty more," I murmured. "Enough to keep you coming for days."

"Promises, promises." My phone rang, a short shrill chirp, surprising me. She nudged me. "You better answer."

"Oh. Right." I lifted the headset to my ear and answered it. "Ivar."

"The first vehicle is two minutes from your location." A brief pause. "I would get my hand out of that woman's skirt and be ready for action, if I were you."

I jerked my hand away from Colbie and stood up, searching. "You've got eyes on us."

"I would not survive very long if I went blindly into situations." His laugh was disconcerting. "I have been observing you attempting to woo that woman for some time."

"It ain't an attempt if I succeed, now is it?"

"I suppose not. Now, if you please, attend to the job at hand."

"I'm attending, bro, I'm attending."

"Then you are aware of the four men approaching on foot from the east?"

I pivoted, scanning, and found the men he was talking about—on foot on the sidewalk across the street, less than a hundred yards away, each with a pistol out, eyes fixed on me. "Now I am."

"Do you wish to dispose of them, or should I?"

"Let's split the fun," I suggested. "You silenced?"

"Of course."

I put the phone on speaker and set it down, went to one knee, pistol in both hands. "First to take down two wins."

"Stakes?"

"Bottle of Pappy Van Winkle."

Ivar chuckled. "Very well. Begin on three. One . . . two . . . three."

The moment he said three, I squeezed the trigger, felt the pistol jerk and my ears rang with the report, and I watched the rear-most man jerk backward, his head flying back on his shoulders. At the same moment, the one in front collapsed abruptly, a hole blossoming his forehead. I was already pulling aim on the next man forward, but he already had a hole between his eyes, and the third a split second later. In my defense, I'd already fired twice, and my bullets hit them each a fraction of a second after Ivar's.

"Goddammit," I growled. I picked up the phone and clicked off speaker. "Anselm wasn't kidding about you."

"What did he say?"

"That you made him seem like a cute little puppy or something."

Ivar laughed. "He was being modest. It would be an unnerving thing indeed to be on Anslem's bad side."

"No shit." I stood up, chuckling. "Three to one. Guess I owe you a bottle of Pappy."

"I will take you up on that. I have a taste for American whiskey."

"Ever have Pappy?"

"*Nein*, I have not. Surprisingly difficult to get in Europe."

"Hell, that shit is hard to get in America."

"The truck is arriving. Load the first group onto it, the larger group of women. The driver will greet you by name. If he does not, shoot him."

"Roger that," I said.

"I will be with the second truck, arriving in five minutes."

"See you in five, in that case," I said, as the truck squealed to a halt at the curb.

"*Jawohl*."

The truck was an ex-military, two-ton, huge military transport truck, painted black. I jogged over, pistol still in hand, halting a couple feet away as the driver threw open the door and hopped down.

"Puck Lawson," the driver said, extending his hand toward me.

"That's me," I answered, shaking his hand.

"Lars." He eyed the group of women sitting in the park, huddled in separate groups, looking scared and worried. "Let's load them, *ja*?"

I waved them over, and slowly, gradually, hesitantly, they approached me in twos and threes. I glanced at Colbie, gestured for her to join me. I addressed the gathering group. "How many of you speak English?"

Only three women raised their hands.

"Can you communicate with any of the others?" I asked.

One of them nodded, pointing at another cluster of four women. "They speak Portuguese," she said, in a thick Spanish accent, "and I know a little."

"Okay, here's the deal. This guy is a friend. He's going to take all of you somewhere safe."

"Where?" the one who'd spoken up asked.

I shrugged. "Dunno."

"Then how do we know is he a friend?" she pressed.

"Because he works for someone I trust."

"What is happen to us?" she asked.

"They're going to help you in any way they can," I said. "If possible, they'll help you go back home, or if that's not possible, they'll help make you as safe and comfortable as possible."

Colbie repeated it in Chinese and Russian, but there were still two groups who didn't seem to understand any of it, a trio of women who looked to my admittedly inexpert eyes to be from India, and another two from the Middle East somewhere. The two groups watched as the other women voluntarily climbed into the back of the truck, which seemed to communicate well enough that whatever was happening, it wasn't something bad.

There were sirens off in the distance, which weren't necessarily about us, but considering the number of dead bodies in the immediate vicinity, I felt it safe to assume they were headed toward our location.

The women were all aboard the truck, and the driver lowered the flaps, fastened them, and climbed into the cab. The diesel engine groaned and rattled, and the truck pulled away, and then it was just the five women and me.

An older model Range Rover halted at the curb where the truck had been, and a man exited from the driver's side. He was not what I was expecting—I'd been expecting a younger guy, based on his voice. This man was past forty, had blond-brown hair parted to one side, wore a drab, ill-fitting brown suit without a tie, thick round glasses, and had an unkempt goatee. He was the kind of man absolutely no one would give a second glance to or thought about. Which, I supposed, watching him approach me, would serve his purposes well.

He clapped me on the shoulder, and we shook hands. "I am Ivar. You are Puck." He glanced at the women. "The rest of the introductions shall have to wait. I do not have an interest in dealing with the local authorities."

"Me neither."

He glanced past me at the man we'd taken hostage, sitting with his back against the tree, knees drawn up, looking green around the gills. "Who is he?"

I shrugged. "He surrendered. I couldn't just—"

Ivar reached into his suit coat, withdrew a compact 9mm, fired once, and replaced it, the whole thing done as casually as anyone else might swat a fly. "Loose ends kill you." He gestured at the Rover. "Shall we?"

I blinked at the now-dead guy, a neat round hole directly between his eyebrows, and nodded. "Let's get this shitshow on the road."

6

NO FOOLIN'

I'D SEEN SOME CRAZY STUFF IN MY LIFE. AS A homeless person, especially in New York, you saw some crazy ass shit go down. People wearing all sorts of goofy nonsense, fights, murders—I saw a group of guys trying to steal a grand piano; I saw a guy in full clown costume running from three policeman, cackling; I saw drunk people fucking in alleys on a regular basis; I watched a guy get caught cheating and then get chased mostly naked down the street by both women. Point was, I'd seen death, and I'd known violence.

What Puck was capable of . . . was different. He was frighteningly good at it, made it look easy, effortless. Yet he was articulate, and surprisingly open with me, and seemed in touch with his emotions. He was an enigma. Like, if I'd met him on the street or at the bar, I probably wouldn't have thought about him twice. I meant, he just wasn't my type. I wasn't sure I had a type, but if I did, Puck wasn't it. The guys I'd dated mostly fit into a mold: a few inches taller than me, clean-cut, well dressed, well educated. And I hadn't dated any one of them for more than a couple months, because they were all fucking boring. Nice, easy to talk to, decent in bed—and boring.

Or at least, if I compared them to Puck, that was how they seemed now. I meant, he was anything but boring. He was a natural storyteller, and he was educated, obviously, but he cursed like a sailor, and the clothes he wore were . . . um, interesting. That shirt? I used to panhandle outside a bar that hosted a lot of heavy metal bands, and I got to know a few of the regular patrons, most of whom wore shirts like Puck's, which was the only reason I knew what all that angry red lettering was supposed to say. And his build? He was the exact opposite of the guys I usually dated. They were tall, sleek, elegant, and Puck was . . . not. Decidedly not. He called those kinds of men pussies, I surmised. They never took me anywhere that could have even possibly led to physical violence, but if we'd ended up in some kind of situation, looking back . . . I'd have been the one to jump into a fight before most of those guys. I could walk down the darkest, scariest street anywhere in the world, and if Puck was with me, I'd feel perfectly safe.

With those guys, conversation never went anywhere deep. We talked about movies, or books, or
social issues, or mutual friends, or business, and
we never really got to anything deep or personal. I
mean, we talked about important political issues, but
it never got personal. I never told any of them about
my parents or what Craig did, and I sure as hell never discussed my heroin addiction. I had the feeling
none of them would understand, and I knew several
of them would have cut all association with me had
they known.

Puck was just . . . different. I didn't know.

And the more I talked to him, the more I found
out about him, the more interested I was. He talked
a good game, that was for damn sure. Dirty talk had
never really been a thing for me. One guy tried, and I
just laughed, because it sounded so stupid and corny,
like he tried to sound like a porno. When Puck talked
dirty . . . it was fucking hot. Why, I wasn't sure, but it
was. The timbre of his voice, the way it rumbled in my
ear . . . the heat of him, the way my skin tingled when
he touched me . . . I don't know. And that beard, god.
The whole time we were on the park bench talking, I
wanted to bury my fingers in that beard and pull him
closer, jerk him in for a kiss. And he would've liked
that, I could tell. When I touched his beard, when I
tugged on it, his nostrils flared and he sucked in a
breath, and I could just tell he'd like it if I used his
beard to make him do what I wanted.

The other thing about Puck that had me hot and bothered was the forcefulness of his personality, how intense and dominant he was. He'd let me have my way when it suited him, but he'd be in control. And . . . I liked that. Most of the guys I'd dated or slept with weren't like that. I was always in control. I was a pushy, in-control sort of girl. I was in charge of myself. I didn't allow anyone to push me around or manipulate me. But deep down, I wanted to give in, a little. It'd have to be the right circumstances, which was why I'd never let anyone see that part of me. But with Puck, I saw it.

He'd take care of me. I'd be safe letting him push me around a little, letting him have control.

What that would look like, where it would go, I didn't know—and that was what scared me.

He sat in the front passenger seat, talking to Ivar. I tuned into the conversation, but it was mostly about guns, which I'm not super interested in. I was behind Ivar, and Layla was beside me with Temple on the other side of her; Lola and Kyrie were stretched out in the trunk.

Layla nudged me, keeping her voice low. "So, you and Puck?"

"So me and Puck, what?"

"You like him?"

I snorted a laugh. "A little soon to tell."

"Oh, bullshit. You like him." She teased my kneecap with her fingertips. "He had his fingers under your skirt."

I blushed. "He's . . . different."

"That's one word for him." She indicated the road behind us with a nod of her head. "All this, what are you thinking?"

I lifted a shoulder. "It's scary. But Puck seems to be able to handle whatever comes at us."

"I don't trust many people, but I trust him."

I eyed her, hesitating. "You trust him in terms of all the shooting, and I get why, watching him do what he does. But on a personal level?"

Layla gave my question thought, which I appreciated. "Honestly, I don't know. If you can handle his personality, I think there's a lot more to Puck than most people would give him credit for. I don't think he's ever been serious about anyone, but I don't know for sure. We don't get into a lot of deep personal discussions. Either we're working, or it's poker night with the guys at the compound, and we're drinking and bullshitting. Not exactly share-circle moments, you know?"

As close as Puck and Layla seemed to be, it didn't sound like he'd told her anything about his past, which made everything he'd told me seem pretty important. I had the feeling he didn't talk about his past any more than I did. Which meant our conversations . . . *meant* something. But what?

Hell if I knew.

I wasn't sure what to say to Layla, though,

because it was obvious he hadn't told her what he'd told me.

Layla's expression brightened, and she poked me in the ribs. "He shared with you, didn't he?"

I shrugged uncomfortably. "We talked."

"He did!" She muffled a squeal. "He totally shared with you."

I eyed her. "Why are you getting so worked up about this?"

She grabbed my arm and shook it. "Because Puck doesn't share. I've killed people with the man, and he hasn't told me dick about himself. All of the guys are like that—they only share with someone they feel is different, someone that means something. We're all family, but we tend to keep our own counsel when it comes to heavy personal shit."

"So what are you saying?"

She let go of me and folded her hands on her lap. "Nothing."

"Layla."

She shrugged. "I'm not saying anything. I'm just pointing out a pattern. Make of it what you will." She was suddenly subdued.

I noticed Puck was watching us in the rearview mirror.

"Stop interrogating the woman, Layla," Puck growled.

"I'm not interrogating," Layla said. "We're just talking."

Puck just snorted. "You were pumping her for information."

"Girl talk."

"Gossip."

"Idle backseat chitchat."

"Puck, it's fine." I met his eyes in the mirror. "For real."

Ivar cut in from the driver's seat. "There is trouble."

"Company?" Puck asked, leaning forward to check the side view mirror.

"*Ja*. We are still some ways from the airfield yet, and I would like to dispose of them before we get there."

Puck checked the magazine of his pistol, then set another one in the cup holder, handle facing up. "Let 'em get closer. I can handle them."

"Better yet," Layla said, "if Temple switches places with me, we can both handle them."

"How many people does this Cain guy have on call to send after us?" I asked.

"A lot," Layla, Puck, and Ivar all answered in unison.

"Oh."

"He has a lot of resources," Puck said, clarifying. "He can put the word out that he needs someone killed or captured, and anyone from the criminal element in the area will respond in droves, because Cain can and will pay out big. Plus, he has operational cells all over the world."

"He sounds like a problem," I said.

Puck snorted. "That's an understatement."

Layla had traded places with Temple and ejected the magazine of her pistol, then replaced it. "Only got a few rounds left in here, and no spare."

Without taking his eyes off the road, Ivar reached out with his right hand and opened the glove box, withdrew another pistol, and handed it back to Layla.

Puck eyed Ivar. "Yo, you got any heavy iron in this ride?"

Ivar smirked. "Reach under your seat."

Puck bent over, reached under his seat, and straightened up, holding a compact black machine gun. "Hell yeah, now this is what I'm talking about!"

"And what you do call that?" I asked.

My time in a gang had only exposed me to handguns, and even then, it never really mattered what type or brand, since they all shot the same to me, and I hated touching them regardless of what they were.

Puck checked the magazine, pulled back a slide, and extended a shoulder butt thing. "This, hot stuff, is a Heckler & Koch MP5K. A fully automatic ultra compact submachine gun."

I just blinked. "Oh."

Puck laughed, opening the window, Layla following suit. "Just means little boom stick shoot many bullets very fast."

I rolled my eyes at him. "Jackass."

Ivar cut in. "Traffic around us is minimal. Time to make the move. Ladies, the shooting will be very loud in the auto. You should all lie down on the floor, for maximum safety, and cover your ears as well." He glanced over his shoulder, then at Puck and then Layla. "Ready? *Eins . . . zwei . . . drei*."

On *drei*, Ivar swerved to the left and jammed the brakes hard, and we were thrown forward, tires skidding. A black four-door sedan shot forward on our right side, and Ivar floored the gas pedal, pinning us back against the seats as we rocketed forward once more. We were parallel with the sedan, and Puck had the ultra-auto-submachine gun aimed out the window. He squeezed the trigger, and three loud concussions blasted the air, making my ears ring from the deafening reports, and then Layla's gun barked. Temple was on the floor between the seats, and Lola and Kyrie were flat on the floor of the trunk. There wasn't anywhere for me to go, so I leaned forward a little, at least I felt like I took some kind of precaution rather than just sitting there all nonchalant while bullets flew. The other car had their windows opened too, and a figure leaned out the window, with a gun similar to the one Puck had.

As seemed normal, Puck's shots hit first, shattering the driver's window and painting the interior red, and then a split second later, one of Layla's shots hit the guy with the gun, and he vanished in a spray of crimson. The sedan continued forward for a few seconds, and then the dead driver slumped to one side, and the steering wheel twisted, and the sedan veered away, turned sharply at speed, and then bucked over into a roll.

"Left side," Layla said. "Another one."

"Colbie, roll down your window and get out of the way," Puck ordered. "Layla, get 'em."

I depressed the button to lower the window and then pressed myself as far back against the seat as I could. Layla, rather than trying to switch spots, a laborious and time-consuming process, just draped herself across both Temple and me, bracing one hand on the bottom of the window opening, extending her pistol with the other hand. I heard a deafening concussion, and then another, and then another, making my ears ring. A slightly more distant *BANGBANGBANG,* and I felt the door panel jerk as bullets hit, and then again, and again, and then I felt something hot sting my calf. I scrunched down as far as I could, and kept my eyes shut, waiting for something horrible to happen. Layla was pressed against me, her frizzy, curly, crazy black hair tickling my nose, her shoulder against my chest, and I felt her body jerk every time she shot her pistol.

I heard a window shatter, and Puck cursed. "SHOOT THE FUCKING DRIVER, GODDAMMIT!" Puck shouted.

"I'M FUCKING TRYING!" Layla bellowed back, her voice muffled in my ears.

"TRY HARDER!"

Layla actually stopped what she was doing to level an icy fuck-you glare at Puck. "Think you can do a better job of shooting *at* a moving vehicle *from* a moving vehicle while lying across two people?"

Bullets plinked into the side of our car, and smashed another window.

"*Shiesse ihn—JETZT!*" Ivar barked.

That didn't need any translating. Layla turned back to the window, hesitated, took aim . . . and fired once. The silence from the absence of gunfire was deafening. I opened my eyes just in time to see the sedan go into a flat spin and then into a bouncing, glass-shattering roll.

Layla shifted awkwardly off Temple and me, returning to her seat behind Puck. "Well that was fun," she said, without a trace of irony.

"You two bicker like children," Ivar pointed out.

"That's because she's basically like a really ugly, really annoying little sister," Puck said.

"I'm sexy and you know it, bitch," Layla snarked back.

Puck twisted and stuck his tongue out at her. "I'm not a bitch; you're a bitch."

"Pussy."

"Dick."

"Twat."

"Ass-face."

Ivar sighed. "Enough, enough. You are making

my head ache."

I watched the whole exchange with bemusement. If any man ever called me any of those names, even in jest, I'd probably have—as my gang friends used to say—popped a cap in his ass. Of course, as a white girl from the suburbs, they never let me talk like that; it was kind of a joke among us. Puck and Layla seemed to have that kind of a relationship, though, where the vilest of insults were used as a way of expressing friendship. I thought for Puck, at least, it served as a reminder that she was one of the guys, so to speak.

The rest of the hour's drive to the airfield was uneventful, if noisy, since several windows had been shot out. The airfield was . . . well, more of a field than anything I'd recognize as a place designated for airplanes to take off and land. There were a pair of those long half-barrel shaped hangars side by side, and then another pair facing them, on the opposite side of what I supposed was the runway—essentially just a wide, neatly-mown swath of grass. A twin-engine prop plane waited, and the moment the Range Rover appeared, the airplane's propellers spun into life, flashing in the sun.

I half expected a helicopter to appear, or a fighter jet, or more cars, guns blazing . . . but we loaded onto the waiting aircraft and took off without incident, Ivar waiting until everyone was loaded before following us into the airplane and closing the door after us, taking the co-pilot seat.

I took a seat in the last row of chairs, and Puck settled into the seat beside me. I don't know if he saw or felt me tense as the props roared to full speed and the aircraft bumped into motion, but he seemed to know without having to be told that I was nervous.

He threaded his fingers into mine. "Not a fan of flying, huh?"

I shook my head. "Nope." I let out a frightened breath and squeezed his hand as we picked up speed. "Especially on a plane this small. It's always the little planes you hear about crashing."

"It's gonna be fine, babe."

"Is that it?" I asked, once we were airborne.

"Is what it?"

"Cain, the bad guys, the shooting."

Puck winced. "Probably not, if you want the truth. We're not going directly back to the States from here, certainly not in a puddle-jumper like this."

"Then where are we going?"

"Prague, in the Czech Republic."

"I think they're calling it Czechia, now, actually. And I am familiar with European geography, thanks."

"Oooh, gettin' snippy, are we?" he asked, but the smirk and the twinkle told me he was teasing.

"If you haven't already picked up on the fact that I'm just a *tad* sarcastic," I drawled, "then you *really* haven't been paying attention."

He grinned at me. "Oh, I've noticed, believe you me."

"You have, huh?" I couldn't help how flirty that came out, and at this point, it seemed kind of silly to keep resisting . . . except that it was so much fun to fuck with him.

He gave a sassy little smirk and bobble of his head. "I don't mean to brag, but I'm kind of smart. I'm trained to notice these things."

I laughed. "Things like the fact that I'm a serious bitch with a serious attitude?"

"Tiny, minor little details like that, yeah."

"So you don't deny that I'm bitch?"

He shrugged. "Why should I? Serious bitches with serious attitude make my cock hard. I'm weird that way."

I shook my head, snorting in disbelief. "You're unbelievable."

He touched my chin and turned my face to his. "I'm teasing, Colbie." He quirked an eyebrow. "Mostly. I do like your attitude. But you're not a bitch; you just don't take any shit. And that really does make me horny."

"What doesn't?"

"We've covered this already, remember? Nuns, centipedes, and the IRS." He let go of my hand so he could explore closer to the hem of my skirt. We were alone in the row; everyone else sitting in front of us, so there wasn't anyone to see where his hand went this time. "Some things make me hornier than others, though." His voice was pitched low enough that only I could hear him.

"Oh yeah? Like what?"

His hand snuck under the hem of my skirt, and I held stock still, barely breathing. "Like the fact that you're totally cool under pressure. No hysterics, no howling, no freezing, you just do what's gotta be done and don't whine or bitch or argue."

"That makes you horny?"

"What it says about you does. The fact that you're tough."

I laughed. "Oh I'm tough, all right. Most guys find it intimidating. I don't take bullshit, I take charge, and I get shit done. I started as a PA at the firm where I work, and now I'm in charge of several of the biggest accounts we have in China and Russia. I got there by being tough, by never taking anything sitting down. And the guys I work with make no secret of the fact that they think I'm an ice queen bitch."

"Then they're pussies."

"I agree. The hypocrisy is astounding, though. They call me ice queen and bitch and butch and all sorts of names because I refuse to put up with misogynistic horseshit, and because I'm focused and determined and all business at work. Yet if I show so much as a hint of cleavage or wear a skirt that's anything less than business length, they'll go out of their way to hit on me and act like I must obviously be hankering to ride all of their dicks."

"On the basis of a little cleavage and leg?"

I nodded. "Pretty much."

"Sounds like you work with a bunch of pieces of shit."

I shrugged. "Not gonna hear too much argument out of me about that. Some of them are okay, like the four or five guys I play poker with. But they've accepted me sort of like you have Layla, as one of the guys. If I show up for poker night, it's in jeans and a T-shirt, with a baseball cap on."

"I'd think you'd dress to kill, just for distraction value," Puck noted.

I laughed. "I've done that, actually. Wore a killer push-up bra and a low-cut dress, teased my hair out to look all just-fucked, did a lot of leaning over."

"Bet you cleaned up that night."

"Hell yeah, I did. Didn't even have to count cards, and it was still a slaughter. They were so busy staring at my tits and daydreaming that most of the guys in the game forgot how to hold a poker face." I grinned, remembering. "I made twenty grand that night."

"Damn, babe." He eyed me. "If I got to see you like that, I wouldn't mind losing all my money to you."

"Something tells me you'd stare the whole night yet still win."

He chuckled. "Got that right. Although I did lose two grand in one hand to a chick once, because of something like that."

"And all she did was show some cleavage?" I teased.

"Takes more than cleavage to distract me, sweetheart. No, she went full-on intentional nip slip. I watched her do it. She kept wiggling her shoulder all weird, and the strap of her dress kept drooping lower and lower, and I knew exactly what she was up to, but it still worked. Eventually the strap fell completely, and her tit fell out right as I was about to win on a ballsy fucking bluff. She called my shit, swept the table, and pulled her strap back up. Walked away with eight grand, and my eternal irritation. I don't like being played, especially when I can see the play coming and yet still fall for it."

"I'm gonna say that's mostly on you, although that is a dirty trick to play."

I realized then that he'd used the distraction of the conversation to work his hand most of the way up my skirt. His fingers were passing mid-thigh, and I was suddenly hyperaware of his touch, of how close his fingertips were to my core.

I reached up and tugged on his beard. "What's your plan with that hand, Puck?"

He smirked at me. "You aware of what you do to me when you tug on my beard like that?"

I smirked back. "Let me guess . . . it makes you horny."

He flicked his gaze away from mine and down

to his crotch. "I don't know, why don't you tell me?"

My gaze followed his, and I could clearly see the ridge of his erect cock outlined against the material of his pants, thick and angled slightly to one side. God*damn*, what a cock. I swallowed hard, and forced my eyes to his.

"Jesus, Puck."

He winked. "Tug on my beard like that, you'll end up tugging on something else."

My breath caught, because now that I'd seen the outline, I wanted to see the rest. Hell, I *wanted* to end up tugging on his something else. I wasn't about to let him know that, though.

I let go of his beard and tried to shift away from his touch.

He didn't quite let that happen, though. He leaned into me, and his beard tickled my ear. "Keep pretending you don't want it, Colbie. I'm enjoying our little game."

"I'm not pretending," I whispered.

His fingers had crept higher yet, and now my heart was pitter-pattering in my chest, and my thighs were tingling, and I couldn't quite make myself close my legs to keep him away. His teeth latched onto my earlobe, and his tongue flicked, and his breath was hot, and I had to catch my lip between my teeth to keep from letting out the moan bubbling up in my throat.

"Puck . . ." I whispered.

Higher, higher. A fingertip nudged and brushed against the gusset of my underwear.

"What, Colbie?" he whispered back.

"Don't."

He hooked his finger inside the gusset, tugged it aside, and I had to swallow a gasp.

His whisper was hot against my ear. "Don't what?"

"Stop . . ." The word was more of a moan than a word.

"Is that a 'please stop' or a 'please don't stop'?" He brushed his fingertip against my slit. "I'm not quite clear."

That little grazing touch, the nudge of his finger against my swollen nether lips . . . god, it was too much. And not enough. But I still refused to give in to the begging I knew he was trying to get out of me.

I clenched my hands into fists and ground my molars together. Forced my eyes to stay open and locked on Puck's. I was torn between wanting to knock his hand away to prove that I could, and wanting to scootch lower in the seat and widen my thighs so he could touch me more. So, I remained frozen, not moving an inch, barely breathing, neither helping nor hindering.

He was amused, his brown eyes twinkling, searching mine, a ghost of grin on his lips. "You're a stubborn one, Colbie."

I didn't answer.

Couldn't.

He'd worked his fingertip between the lips, and my heart was hammering, and I was aching, and I felt wetness flooding me. I knew he had to feel that, feel how wet I was. Especially when he wiggled that finger deeper, deeper, until he was knuckle deep inside me. Oh . . . oh shit. Shit. That felt good, so good, too good. And then he slid that finger out, and I think I may have let out a little sound, something like a cross between a mewl of pleasure and a growl of irritation. One finger, just one stupid, talented finger, and he had me clutching my knees with all my strength in an effort to keep from writhing, had me biting down on my lip so hard it hurt.

Thankfully, the cabin of the aircraft was pretty noisy, which worked to drown out the sounds I was making, sounds I couldn't help at that point. He was doing something to me, some sort of witchery. Sex magic, or something. Just a single digit, one stupid fucking finger, but I was going nuts, squirming, biting my tongue—literally. Sliding it in, then out, slowly, achingly slowly, then back in, curling, rubbing deep inside me, then flicking upward, his finger now wet with my essence, to smear over the hard button of my clit.

No hurry. Just a slow exploration of my sex with one thick, talented finger. I let my head fall back against the headrest, eyelids fluttering, chest heaving, thighs quivering. It wasn't enough. Dammit,

dammit, dammit—it wasn't enough. I needed more. I was close, so close, I was teetering on the edge, shuddering on the brink, and he was so unhurried, just sliding that finger in and out, occasionally brushing my clit, and fucking hell, he had to know, he *had* to know he was driving me crazy, that I wouldn't be able to come until he gave me more, gave me the pressure and friction against my clit. He knew. The bastard, he knew.

"Puck," I whispered. "*Dammit*, Puck."

He didn't quite laugh, but I could hear the aroused, pleased mirth in his voice, saw it in his eyes when I turned my head to stare him down. "What, Colbie?" He plunged his finger into me, and I bit down on my lip to suppress a gasp. "You want something, all you gotta do is say so."

"No."

He did laugh that time. "Stubborn girl."

Make me, I wanted to say. *Make me beg. Take control from me.* But I couldn't say it. The whole point was I wanted him to take it without having to be told.

God, that sounded stupid and manipulative even to myself, but I wasn't backing down on it. Wouldn't. So I bit my lip and forced my breathing to slow down, and kept the moans locked down inside me, and forced myself to stay still, and refused to ask him to make me come.

"You have no idea," was what I whispered back to him.

He made a sound that was halfway between a *hmm* of interest and a laugh of amusement. "Good thing I love a challenge, huh?"

"Yeah," I murmured, "good thing."

He leaned close again, his lips nuzzling my ear. "I can feel how close you are, Colbie. You want it, don't you?" He gave me a tiny but potent nudge to the clit, enough to make me flinch as a bolt of zinging pleasure shot through me. "You're crazy sensitive. A few little circles, and you'll be coming all over my hand. But you're so stubborn. You won't give in, will you?"

I shook my head. "Uh-uh."

"Because you're a strong, stubborn, independent woman."

"Damn right."

"Problem is, Colbie honey, you've never met a man like me."

He accompanied that statement with another brushing touch of his finger against my throbbing clit; my inhalation of surprise became an involuntary whimper. My teeth ground together as I bit down on the sound.

"I have absolutely no problem admitting that much, at least, is true," I muttered.

He slid his finger back in, and this time, he did it swiftly, a sudden insertion, fast enough that the movement gave off a wet squelching noise. I cringed, and my thighs clenched together.

He did it again, and whispered in my ear. "Does

that embarrass you?" Again, another squelch. "That embarrasses you, doesn't it?

I nodded. "Yes."

"It shouldn't. It's fucking hot, Colbie." He nipped my ear and slid his finger a few more times then added a second finger, and I had to bite down with my molars so hard they ached. "That's the sound of you being hot and bothered, sweetheart. You're all wet for me. It means you dig this, what I'm doing to you. It means you're fighting yourself. It means your hot, wet, tight little pussy wants more. You don't have to admit to shit, babe. I know. I can feel it, I can smell it. I know *exactly* what you want, Colbie."

I was fighting it so hard. I did want it. I wanted more. I wanted to come. I wanted him to keep touching me. I wanted to hike my skirt up and rip my underwear off and ride him. Fuck, I wanted him to just give me that one goddamn finger against my clit, right now, just enough to let me come. I was trembling with need. He felt it, he knew it. Yet instead of letting me come, he slid those two fingers into me, drew them out, almost but not quite brushing my clit, and then back in.

My underwear was in the way. The gusset was stretched to the side, preventing him from having a full range of movement. If he had his fingers inside me, the gusset would slide back into place higher up, and he'd have to fight them on the way out to have access to my clit. I wanted them *off*. Goddammit.

I'd be damned if I'd admit it and double damned if I was to going to give him the satisfaction of watching me shimmy out of them. That's what I wanted, but the battle was engaged now, and I refused to lose. Even though winning meant I was only piling sexual frustration upon myself. And on him.

The whole thing was stupid. I should have just wiggle out of the stupid underwear and asked him to give me the orgasm and then, when we had more privacy, I'd let him fuck me, and I'd go my way and that would be that. End of story.

That was how this would normally go. And for some reason, I wanted this to be different. So I held out.

He slid his fingers out, and the underwear fought him, and he cursed under his breath. "These stupid underwear are in the way."

"Are they?" I breathed. "I hadn't noticed."

He laughed. "Oh yes you have. You want them off as much as I do, you're just too stubborn to admit it."

"You're wrong."

He didn't bother responding to my blatant lie. Instead, he hooked his finger inside the gusset again, but this time, instead of sliding that finger into me, he curled it around the gusset and tugged down. Oh. Oh no. I froze, stopped breathing. He wiggled and tugged, and I felt the waist band roll down over my hips. He worked that finger back and forth, front to back along the length of the gusset, pulling downward. Slowly, inexorably, the underwear slid down. The waistband caught on my butt, yet all he had to do was give a firm tug and they'd skipped free, and then a few more tugs, a few inches, and they were loose, and he drew them down my thighs, letting them fall around my feet. Lifting one of my feet and then the other, he had my underwear dangling from his index finger.

Shit. I stared at him, glanced at my erstwhile undergarment, and then back at him. They weren't plain cotton granny panties. What I hadn't mentioned, when we talked about what kind of underwear I preferred to wear, was that my idea of fit and comfort usually tended toward a full coverage bra and a thong. I just found thongs most comfortable. I didn't like briefs—*hated* might be a more accurate term, really—and even when I did wear something with more coverage than a thong, it was still on the skimpier side. The only exception was if I was hanging around the house. When Puck talked about his mental image of me watching cartoons in nothing but a pair of little boy superhero briefs, he wasn't far wrong—the only detail he had wrong was that for Saturday morning cartoons, I wore my favorite pair of stretchy cotton boy short underwear.

But at work, I rocked a thong. But not to feel sexy or any of that nonsense, just because I found them comfy.

Which meant the underwear Puck had dangling from a finger was a tiny little scrap of blue lace—yes, I wore matching sets, sometimes. Not always, but occasionally. The day I was kidnapped just happened to be one of those instances.

"You lied, Colbie Danvers."

I quirked an eyebrow at him. "Did not."

"You said you picked underwear for fit and comfort, not style or sexiness."

I reached for the thong, but he kept it out of reach, stuffing into a hip pocket. "Give 'em back, Puck."

He snorted. "Hell no. I'm keeping that shit."

I crossed my arms over my chest. "I didn't lie. I just happen to find thongs comfortable."

He rested his palm on my thigh again, and I realized we'd be starting all over, his hand creeping gradually back under my skirt. *Skip that part*, I wanted to say. But, as per the rules of this idiotic game, I said nothing. Just held still and waited.

He didn't take as long, this time. He even went so far as to pull my leg aside. I didn't fight that as hard as I should have, but hell, I was all worked up and still trembling from how close he'd gotten me to orgasm, and I wanted that release, *needed it* at this point. Dammit, I needed it. I wanted his touch, ached for it. He touched me like I belonged to him, like he knew exactly what I wanted.

Somehow, I was lower in the seat, and my thighs were falling open. If Puck had drawn attention to that, I'd have sat upright and closed my legs, but he was a smart bastard, so he said nothing, just took advantage of it. Found my sex waiting, hot and wet and ready. Slid that finger into me, and immediately drew it out and brushed it against my clit. My eyes closed and my teeth ground together, and my chest heaved, because somehow that short reprieve as Puck removed my underwear had only served to make me wetter, more sensitive, more ready. Closer. God, so close.

He was teasing, now. He'd slide his finger in and pull it out, tease my clit, then slide it back in. Two fingers, middle finger and ring finger, and then he'd tease me once more, and yet somehow he never quite gave me the pressure I needed to get any closer to orgasm. Yet the urge, the need, the heat, it all kept building. Each time he brushed my clit, each time he slid those fingers into me, I wanted it more, needed it more desperately, and each time I got the teasing burst of sizzling pleasure from the brief touch to my clit, I'd hope and silently beg that this time he'd let me come, yet he never did. And the desperation was intense, now. Almost unbearable.

I had my fingers curled into fists, my jaw clenched. Eyes closed. I was breathing deeply, long sucking inhalations and slow shaky exhalations—resisting the urge to give in each time he touched me.

And always, his touch was slow and unhurried and gentle.

A squelch as he slid two fingers in.

I bit down on a whimper when he brushed my clit.

And this time, when I clamped my teeth around the breathy little sound, he did it again. Two fingertips stroking my clit, and my hips flexed. Again, and I felt my butt cheeks squeeze together, and my thighs tremble as I fought the urge to lift my hips, to grind into his fingers.

"How long are you gonna fight it, Colbie?" His whisper was close, so quiet I had to strain to hear him.

"I . . ." My train of thought was derailed when he grazed my clit a third time; the pressure, the pleasure, and the searing need were all tangled and wild and throbbing—one more touch like that, maybe two, and I'd be gone. "I . . . *oh*—"

One fingertip, pressing firm against the bud of my clit, pressing, just touching, and I was shaking all over, barely able to breathe, fighting it, needing it, wanting it, refusing to give in. He wanted this; he had to take it from me. He had to know I never gave up, that he'd earned it.

And god, holy shit, he was close.

Because I was right *there*. And he fucking knew it. Yet he didn't take it.

Instead, he plunged his finger into me so deep his palm bumped against my clit, and I was rocked forward as a blinding clenching burst bit through me.

Grind that palm . . . right there, right there. That was what ran through my head, but never passed my lips.

Yet my hips were flexing on their own. A slight, subtle movement, but I knew he felt it.

Out again, and that was it—one more even accidental nudge and I'd be toppling over the edge, coming harder than I ever had in my life.

Yet he didn't give it to me. He fucking knew *exactly* how close I was—how the hell he knew, I had no idea, but he knew. Frustration boiled through me, tangled with raw need and rippling desperation.

"Puck—god*dammit.*"

He had the audacity to laugh. "You want it, Colbie. You're there, beautiful. I can feel it. Your thighs are shaking. You can't breathe. Your hips are moving." He slid his finger back in, agonizingly slowly. I gasped as I felt his finger press in. "Two words."

"Two words?" My eyes flew open and met his.

In and out, in and out, slow, consistent—finger-fucking me. Hot, erotic, pleasurable, but not what I needed. He was silent, watching me as his fingers glided smoothly through my wetness.

"Two words, Puck?" I prompted.

I couldn't help it any more. My hips were grinding with his movements, seeking what I so desperately wanted. I was crazed with it. I had to come. *Had* to. He'd been working me to the edge and back for I couldn't remember how long. Forever, it felt like. Too long. If I didn't come soon, I'd explode with frustration.

"Please, Puck," he murmured.

"Fuck you," I snarled, under my breath.

"Got that backward, hot stuff. Pretty sure I'm the one fucking you." He increased his speed, but never quite let any part of his hand touch my clit. "Say those two words, and you'll be coming all over my hand so hard you'll see stars."

"No."

"Fair enough." He withdrew his touch completely.

"What are you doing?" I asked, hating the edge of panic in my voice.

"My wrist is cramping," he said, a smirk on his lips.

"Goddammit, Puck."

He trailed his touch back in, closer, closer, and my thighs splayed apart, a wanton gesture. "What's wrong, Colbie?"

"You're an asshole."

He nodded. "Yes, I am." He teased my slit, tracing up and down, tickling, nudging in and out ever so slightly. "I think that was one of the first things I told you."

"Fuck."

I was normally not much for swearing all that much, but when I was worked up and horny and frustrated? Filter went away. And right then, I'd never been so worked up, never been so frustrated. Never been so horny.

I just wanted to come. I just wanted to feel his fingers on my clit, just wanted to hit that high and shake and feel his fingers and daydream about what he could do if we were alone and naked.

God, I needed it.

"Fuck it," I breathed. "Fine. You win."

I twisted my head, reached up and grabbed his beard, pulled his ear to my mouth. "Please, Puck." I gasped the words as quietly as I could, finally relinquishing this tiny victory to him. "*Please* . . . let me come."

I felt his grin spread across his face. His unoccupied hand lifted, and he pinched my chin between finger and thumb, and I felt his breath on my lips, and his finger slid into me, gathering moisture. His lips brushed mine, and I stopped breathing entirely.

He kissed me, and his fingertip struck against my clit at the same moment his tongue slid into my mouth. I moaned helplessly, caught up in tidal wave, toppled and twisting and crazy. Climax crashed through me with a blast of searing ecstasy, and he kissed me through it all, kissed me like I'd never been kissed by anyone, swallowing my moans and my gasps and my mewling shrieks. I came and I came and I came, and he held on to me, his hand around the back of my neck, crushing me closer to him as our lips fused. I reached up and scraped my palm over his scalp, cupping the back of his head, and I kept a grip on his beard with my other hand, and I gave in to the movement of my hips, flexing and grinding against his fingers as they whirled around my clit in a perfect union of speed and pressure and friction, touching me just right, exactly right, touching me so perfectly I couldn't have told him how to do it any better. I burst apart, felt something explode inside me. I was wrenched into spasms of gasping intensity, wave after wave.

When the climax finally subsided, I was left quivering, helpless. I collapsed against him, burying my face in the side of his neck, gasping for breath I couldn't quite catch. "Jesus, Puck."

He pulled his hand away from my sex, and I watched, mesmerized and horrified and turned on all at once as he licked his middle and ring fingers clean, sucking at the glistening essence from my pussy coating his fingers. "Two fingers, Colbie. Fully clothed, on a plane, surrounded by people."

I blushed hard, remembering for the first time that we were in fact in a small airplane cabin with five other people. "Ohmygod."

He laughed. "Relax, babe. Look around. Nobody is watching." And then he winked at me. "Now think what I could do if I had . . . say . . . an hour and you were naked."

I glanced up, looked around, and he was right. Layla and Kyrie were lost in conversation together, as were Lola and Temple, and Ivar was in the co-pilot seat scrolling on his phone. None of them even glanced back this way. Then the last part of what he said registered, and became an image, a daydream—me, stripped naked, lying on my back on a bed, Puck's face between my thighs, his tongue lapping at me, his big strong hands fondling my breasts . . . his huge hard cock driving into me . . .

"Dammit." I breathed the curse, squeezing my eyes shut, trying to pretend I wasn't still quaking from the orgasm, trying to pretend I didn't want Puck more than I'd ever wanted anyone or anything.

"You want this, Colbie." Puck's voice was in my ear, speaking the truth I was too stubborn to voice myself. "You can pretend you don't all you want, but you ain't foolin' me, sweetheart."

"I'm not trying to fool *you*," I muttered, the words spilling out unbidden.

He just palmed my cheek, smirking at me with that stupid, sexy, knowing smile of his. "I know that too."

Of course he did. Obviously, I wasn't fooling either of us.

7

TEASING

Holy motherfucking shit—COLBIE DANVERS having an orgasm was hands down the most erotic thing I'd ever witnessed. My cock was throbbing, and I was pretty sure I was leaking pre-come in my underwear. I hadn't even seen her tits, much less gotten a glimpse of the pussy my fingers had just been in, but I was already half in love with the woman's body.

Maybe that wasn't a smart thing to joke about, though.

Only, I wasn't really joking, was I?

I'd give up another finger to get thirty minutes alone with Colbie, and I'd be content with my bargain even if all I got to do was *look*. If I got to touch—and kiss and lick and fuck—I would die a happy man.

I knew she was still freaking out, which I understood. She'd clawed her way out of hell, and when you do that on your own like she had, giving up even the tiniest amount of control was like surrendering your soul. I got it, I really did. I respected the hell out of her, and that was the damn truth. What she'd come out of, what she'd fought her way through, that shit took guts, it took balls—which I mean in the euphemistic sense, obviously—and it took furious determination and fierce strength, along with an unwavering sense of independence. I respected that shit down to my fucking toes, inside and out. But I also knew—or rather I strongly suspected—that there was another part of her deep down that wanted to be able to let go, just for a minute. She couldn't, she didn't know how, she flat out refused. Which I also understood. She'd fought me down to the last possible second; she'd made me earn every inch I took from her. She wasn't just going to fall onto my dick, and she wasn't going to be dropping to her knees any time soon just because she felt sexual desire for me. If she wanted easy no-strings sex, she could get it any time she wanted, and I thought she knew that. I wasn't under the impression that she was that kind of girl, but you never knew. It didn't matter. The point was, she and I both knew she could get sex whenever she wanted it. This dance of ours wasn't about sex. It was about control, it was about trust—it was about sex, too, yes, but not sex of the wham-bam-thank-you-ma'am variety. It was about . . . something more. What, I wasn't sure.

Maybe it was about me earning her trust enough that she'd eventually give me control. I wasn't a dominant, not in the traditional sense. Not even close. I didn't care how shit went down, most of the time. I had no problem letting a chick tell me how she wanted it, and I had no problem going with that. I'd go along for the ride, because most of the time, we both got our pleasure and that's what it was really all about. For Colbie, it was about more than body parts, about more than who touched whom where. It was about more than orgasms. She could give those to herself, if that was what it was about. Was it about deeper meaning? Emotions? I wasn't sure. I just knew I had to play this right, or it would vanish in a heartbeat— *she* would vanish. She'd shut me out, shut me down, and tell me to go to hell. So even though I knew she wanted me, knew she wanted this with me, I also knew she wouldn't give it up easily.

I glanced at her; she was still breathing hard, her beautiful chest rising and falling swiftly as she sucked in deep breaths and let them out. Her eyes were closed, but I knew she was awake. She was twisted in the seat slightly, facing me, her reddish brown hair draped over her face and obscured her lovely features. Her skirt was still slightly rucked, showing me a bit of her legs. And god, those legs. Long, smooth, elegant.

As I watched her, Colbie's eyes flicked open and

met mine. "In the name of honesty and fairness, I have to admit that you were right about one thing, at least."

I quirked an eyebrow up. "And what's that, honey?"

She dropped her voice to a whisper so soft I had to strain to hear, even when I leaned close enough to feel her breath. "I've never come that hard in my life."

The smile that curved my lips then was pleased and satisfied. "Colbie, sweetheart . . . that was just a little teaser."

She furrowed her brow. "I'm still feeling aftershocks."

"When you have multiples, they build on each other. Each one is stronger than the last. Give me the opportunity, and I swear, no lie, no exaggeration, I'll have you begging me to let you *stop* coming." I grinned broadly. "And *that's* when I'll take you."

"Oh really?"

I nodded, letting her see how serious I was. "You'll be dizzy and shaky and hypersensitive from coming so many times you've lost count, and I'll put you on your hands and knees, and I'll wrap my fist in that fucking gorgeous hair of yours, and I'll drive my cock into your tight wet little pussy and I'll spank your ass as I fuck you into oblivion."

"Holy shit," she breathed. "Where do you come up with this stuff?"

"That's what I've been fantasizing about since I

met you."

"You're serious about that." She stared at me hard. "You really intend to do all that?"

"Why would I joke about it?" I grabbed her hand and placed it on the aching ridge of my erection. "Does that feel like I'm joking?"

She jerked her hand away as if burned. "Jesus, Puck. Are you gonna be all right? You feel a little . . . stiff." She managed to say this straight-faced, somehow.

I winked at her. "I'm kinda achy. Wanna help me out? Relieve the pressure a little?"

She rolled her eyes. "Yeah, I'll just go down on you right here and now."

"I wouldn't argue."

She snickered. "No shit. You'd love that, wouldn't you?"

"Actually, as much as it does ache, I'd rather wait until I can get you alone."

She tilted her head to one side. "Really?"

"Sure." I shifted, adjusting myself as she watched, trying to relieve some of the pressure. "If and when you go down on me, I'll want you naked. I'll want you to take your time."

"So you're not an exhibitionist?"

I shook my head. "Not really, no. I like to be daring, yes, but the thrill is in the danger of getting caught, not in actually getting caught." I jerked my chin at the rest of the cabin. "There's no way we'd pull that off without someone noticing."

"I could give you handy." She smirked, and I knew she was just fishing for what I'd say.

"And put the come where? It's not gonna be a little bit, sweetheart." I adjusted myself again, more for her benefit this time. "When I come, it's gonna be a flood."

"I see." She couldn't seem to keep her gaze from wandering back to my groin, to the visible outline of my still-erect cock.

"And babe, if I were you, I wouldn't make suggestions you don't have any intention on following through."

She met my gaze boldly. "What, you think I wouldn't?"

I huffed a laugh. "No, Colbie, I don't think you would."

Her eyes blazed.

Oh.

Oh hell.

I forgot—she doesn't like being challenged.

"Switch spots with me," she said. She lifted up and slid onto my lap, and I shifted to the window seat. "Now. Take off your underwear and give them to me."

I quirked an eyebrow at her. "You're serious." I glanced forward—Temple and Lola had their heads resting on each other, dozing; Kyrie and Layla were across from them, deep in conversation; Ivar was still busy on his phone.

She quirked an eyebrow back at me. "Do I look like I'm joking?"

Why not go with it? Could be fun. So I unlaced my combat boots enough to slip my feet out, shucked off my pants and underwear, and then tugged my pants back on, and handed her my black boxer briefs. I left my pants unbuttoned and unzipped, then glanced at Colbie. Her eyes were wide, her expression one of shock and desire. Her lower lip was caught between her teeth, and her gaze was locked on my cock. Hard as goddamn marble, pre-come beading and smeared on the tip. Obviously I was better endowed than she'd anticipated, judging by her expression.

"Jesus, Puck," she breathed.

"I love the way you say that," I murmured.

Her eyes flicked to mine, and then roamed the cabin before returning to me. She hesitated, taking a deep breath, and then shifted closer to me. Reached for me, nudging the flaps of my zipper aside to fully reveal my erection in all its glory. Took everything I had to play it cool, to tamp down my disbelief—I really hadn't expected her to actually do this. I wouldn't have pegged her as the type to give me a public hand job in a million years. Yet it seemed as if that was exactly what was happening.

OH.

Oh yeah. Yep. Her delicate little hand slipped around my cock, and I had to bite my tongue quite literally to keep from making a sound. Her fingers were so small, so thin, so delicate—she couldn't get her hand all the way around me. Part of that was me, I suppose I should admit, as I was not a small man in any sense of the word except in terms of height, and even then, my cock was longer than my overall height would lead most to assume, and thicker than they'd guess. I've never measured, because who does that, for real? So no, I don't know how many inches. I could guess, but why? Plenty, and more than enough.

Her touch slid down slowly, and I watched, rapt, as she glided her fist back up, rubbing her thumb over the tip, through the smeared clear sticky fluid. My teeth ground together—her touch was . . . perfect. Soft. Warm. Gentle, yet firm. Confident. She knew exactly what she was doing, and she was enjoying it. Not as much as I was, that was for fucking sure. God, her hand felt incredible. My heart crashed in my chest, my stomach sucked inward involuntarily. My balls ached.

We were both acting as if nothing was going on, her gaze roving the cabin now and again, like mine was. She plunged her fist down again, and my eyes fluttered closed momentarily. Up then. God, each stroke was heaven, her warm smooth touch making me crazy. I wanted to move, needed to push, to thrust, to flex. But I didn't. I held stone still, only my eyes and chest moved. Let her do this, her way, in her time.

She was as unhurried as I'd been, touching her. No rush, just a slow, teasing exploration. Up and down. She paused at the bottom, squeezed a few times, then moved her hand up, rubbed the tip again, maybe played a few short shallow strokes. I swallowed hard, teeth grinding, lungs expanding as I took deep, steadying breaths.

Casually, she leaned a little closer, her eyes flicking up to mine, assessing me, watching my reaction as she cupped her other hand over my balls. Oh god, oh fuck, that was almost my undoing. I blew out a harsh breath through my nose, focusing on keeping still, on not making any sounds. Her beautiful mouth curved in a pleased smile, seeing my efforts to contain my reaction.

Her lips brushed my ear. "You have a gorgeous cock, Puck."

"Thanks."

"Having trouble holding back already?" she asked, gliding her touch a bit more swiftly, then, teasing me, drawing me closer to the edge.

"Nope. I'm fine." I wasn't, and we both knew it. "Just fucking fine."

She laughed quietly, her gaze moving away from mine and down to my cock. "I hope your poker face is better during actual poker."

More slow, teasing strokes, her palm cupping and kneading my balls. Faster then, just a little. Enough that my hips started flexing, and a soft grunt escaped me.

"Wouldn't take much now, would it?" she

whispered in my ear, her breath warm, her words making it harder to hold back. "A few quick jerks, and you'd make a mess, I bet."

"Think so? Try me." I was bluffing. It was all false bravado; she was more right than she knew.

She laughed again. "Oh, you'd like that, wouldn't you?" Colbie paused with her hand around the head of my dick, caressing the tip, squeezing. "That's not how this is going to go, Puck."

"No?"

She shook her head, hair tossing. "You like to tease and play games? Well, so do I."

I growled. "Of course."

"You think you could tease me and edge me and force me to beg for the orgasm and not have some kind of payback?"She let go of me, letting my cock rest against my belly. "Silly Puck."

I let out a breath slowly, seeking control. "I'm well aware I earned this."

"All you have to do is ask, Puck. Beg, like you made me beg."

I grinned at her. "Joke's on you, babe, 'cause I have absolutely no problem with that."

She smirked back at me. "Oh no?"

I shook my head. "Nope." This part was no bluff, at least. "Please, Colbie."

"Please what, Puck?"

"Touch me again." I flexed my hips. "Make me come. Please, Colbie."

She made a face, one which seemed to say *hmm, I COULD, but* . . .

"Make you come, huh? Just like that? Finish jerking you off?"

"Yes, please."

She flicked open a button of her blouse, letting the blue silk of her bra spill out a bit, along with a tantalizing expanse of creamy cleavage. "What if I decide to toy with you a bit more?" She undid the next button, and she was bared for me, a sapphire blue full-coverage bra enclosing a pair of plump, firm, luscious tits threatening to overflow the confines of the cups. "It was a little too easy to make you beg. It didn't seem . . . genuine enough. It wasn't desperate enough."

She twisted toward me, eyeing the cabin to make sure no one was watching us.

"Shit, Colbie."

"Yes?" she asked, sounding all innocent. "Is there something you'd like to ask me?" She breathed, tracing the edge of the cups, tugging at them a little.

I got a hint of darker skin, the outside rim of her areola. My cock throbbed even harder at the prospect of seeing those gorgeous tits bared. "Fuck," I growled. "You're good, babe."

She smirked, teasing with the cups again, pulling one down just enough to give me a tantalizing glimpse of more of her breast before letting go. Then the other. And she still wasn't touching me. Letting me cool off, backing away from the edge—only, the torturous teasing she was doing was pushing me right back toward the edge, even though she wasn't touching me.

"You want to see these? Is that it?" She tugged down one side, and I got a peek of nipple.

"Fuck yes, I do."

She smirked again, a cruel little grin. "You know, this bra is a front clasp." She grasped the edges and lifted to open the bra, pulling the edges apart a little, enough to tease, to give me a glimpse of the insides of her breasts, and then closed it again. "Super easy to open and close."

I groaned at the tragic loss when she closed it, and then groaned again when she began buttoning the shirt back up. "You're evil."

She laughed, a pleased, erotic huff of enjoyment. "I like front claps bras. My boobs are small enough that they're still supported." She unbuttoned again, holding the clasp of the bra. "And then at the end of the day, a front clasp bra is just so easy to take off. One little pop . . . and it's off." She undid the clasp, but kept the tension and didn't quite open enough for me to really see anything.

"What is it you want to hear me say, Colbie?" I whispered. "My dick is aching so hard it hurts."

She held the edges of her bra with one hand, and reached for me with the other. "Oh no, poor Puck. It hurts?"

"Throbs."

"So bad?" She hesitated a quarter inch away from me.

"I'm dyin', babe." I thrust, vainly, trying to get closer to her hand.

"You need me to finish you off, is that it?"

"Might just die of frustration if you don't."

"I wouldn't want that," she said, circling her fingers around my cock. "The only problem is, now my bra is undone. I can't finish you properly with one hand, but if I let go, my boobs will fall out."

"That would be epic," I breathed. I met her eyes, let her see my sincerity. "Please, Colbie?"

"Hmm. I don't know."

I groaned as softly as I could. "Shit, shit, shit." I thumped my head against the seat. "I *need* to see your tits."

"Just see them?"

"Hell no. I need to bury my face in them. I need to paint my come all over them." I heaved a deep breath as she squeezed my cock, a teasing pressure. "But for now, I'll settle for the privilege of seeing them."

Her smile was genuinely flattered. "Privilege?"

"Fuck yes, Colbie. It would be an honor and privilege—and probably the hottest thing I've ever seen."

"Promise not to tease me anymore?" she asked.

"Hell no." I lifted my chin. "What will I promise is to tease you just enough. I promise I'll always follow through. I promised you an orgasm you wouldn't believe, and I made good, didn't I? You *like* the teasing, Colbie. You love the game as much as I do."

She stroked me, and we both watched as her hand traveled from root to tip, slowly. "Damn you for being right."

8

SEX, GUNS, AND GANGSTA RAP

MY HEART WAS HAMMERING SO HARD I WAS worried I was having some sort of attack or episode.

I absolutely could not believe I was doing this. At all. Much less with a man I had just met, let alone in this situation, on a small passenger plane full of his friends and coworkers. Any one of them could turn around at any moment and catch us, and then what would they think of me? I was not like that. I didn't do that. The last guy I had sex with, I didn't so much as kiss him until we'd been on three dates—not because I believed in the three date rule per se, but because I generally didn't like to go there with a guy until I was comfortable with him, and it usually took a while for me to be comfortable with anyone. Yet

Puck, somehow, made me feel totally at ease, comfortable, daring even. He didn't dare me or challenge me to do this, he just didn't believe I would, and for some stupid reason it triggered something in me that wanted to prove him wrong.

And also, I wanted to do this. I *wanted* to feel him, to touch him. I also wanted to get him back. I wanted to prove to him that I could play the game too, that I could push his buttons and read his reactions and make him beg. It was equally portioned between the two reasons, honestly. The way he'd made me feel, the intensity of the orgasm, had only made me hornier than ever, made me want him more. And then, after I'd recovered from the climax, I'd looked over and he'd been sporting a monster erection. And he also seemed to genuinely not expect or anticipate anything in return despite how hard he was. And god, he looked *huge*. And then, when he took off his pants right there beside me, I got my first look at his dick, and I actually stopped breathing for a second. The damn thing was even more perfect and enormous than I'd imagined. Seven or eight inches long at least—so fucking *thick,* though. My fist didn't fit around it, it was so thick. One glimpse, and I had to touch him. I wanted that smooth firm flesh in my hand.

I wanted to feel him lose control. I needed to know, for myself, and I needed him to know that I made him crazy, that I made him beg. Drove him to the edge and pushed him over, but not before toying with him.

And holy shit was it satisfying. Watching him squirm, watching him grind those teeth together and fight the urge to go caveman on me . . . watching him try to stay still and quiet, and lose the battle. So fucking hot. I was all wet again, and now I didn't have any underwear on, so the wetness was seeping out of me, dripping down; he could probably smell me, I was so wet.

And now I had him on the edge again. Teased, and teased, and tortured. Pushed him close to orgasm, backed him away. Gotten him to reveal desperation, the need to feel me touch him again, the need to see me. He was sitting there, chest heaving, jaw clenching, stomach tensed. I had his huge gorgeous cock in my hand, and all I'd need to do was stroke him a few times and he'd come all over the place. I had his underwear on my lap, ready to use them for easy clean up. I wasn't about to tell him this, but I was actually—foolishly, stupidly, probably—considering using my mouth a little. I wouldn't swallow it all, not this time. But I might let him feel that. Give him that much, just because he'd made me come so hard I had legitimately gotten dizzy from it.

I'd surprise him with it; that was what I'd do.

His eyes were flicking from my hand on his cock, squeezing and shallowly caressing it near the base, and my hand on my bra, holding it closed—then up to my eyes, roaming my features, and back down.

"No touching me," I said.

He slipped his hands under his butt. "Okay."

I glanced one more time around the small cabin, noticing Layla and Kyrie had finally dozed off, Kyrie leaning against the window with Layla's head on her shoulder, and Ivar was using both hands to type on his phone, absorbed, ignoring everything, the big bulky headset on his ears blocking out any sounds we made. As private as we'd get, under the circumstances.

I released my hold on the clasp of my bra, and my boobs bounced free, swaying gently. I reached up and brushed the straps off my shoulders so the garment hung open, baring my breasts completely. His cock throbbed, jumped in my hands, and he shifted, clearly fighting the urge to touch me. I liked seeing that need in his features, how badly he wanted to touch me.

I focused on his dick. Wrapped my right hand around his shaft above my left, and stroked downward. His eyes were fixed on my tits as I stroked him, so I gave a little shimmy, setting them to swaying, and he made a soft grunt in the back of his throat, his hips flexing, pushing his thick, firm, warm cock through my fists. God, it was hot, watching him edge closer to release, and the public setting made it hotter yet.

I felt a gush of wetness seep through my sex, and I clenched my thighs together. He was so close. Hips thrusting, cock pulsing in my hands.

Then I did something crazy, something I've never done before, never even considered: I tugged the hem of my skirt up, baring my pussy to Puck's gaze, and as he watched, I slipped two fingers inside myself, gathering my essence . . . then I smeared it onto the tip of Puck's cock, mixing it with his own leaking pre-come. He growled low in his throat, his eyes raking over my bared, glistening core.

"Holy motherfucking shit," he murmured. "Your pussy is fucking perfect."

I grinned, couldn't help but touch myself again, smeared more of my wetness onto his dick. Plunged my fist down his length, coating his shaft with sticky wet essence, his and mine mixed. Stroked faster, using both hands now. Skirt up, shirt undone, bra opened—tits bared, pussy bared . . . his thick hard cock in my hand. People mere feet away. One loud noise and they'd all look back here.

"Fuck," Puck growled.

"Not yet," I whispered.

"Trying," he said through gritted teeth.

"You're holding back?" I asked, plunging my hands around him, twisting my fists around his plump pink glans then stroking down to his base.

"Yeah." His eyes fluttered closed then snapped open, staring in turn at my hands, my tits, my slit.

"Don't come yet."

"Why not?"

"Because I told you not to. I want you to wait."

"I can't much longer." He tensed all over, hands fisted under his thighs, jaw clenched, breathing hard.

"A little longer. It'll be worth it." I kept stroking smooth, even motions from tip to root and back up.

I made him wait, slowing down enough that he started thrusting helplessly, needing the release.

"Puck," I whispered, and his eyes flitted up to mine.

"Yeah?"

"Say 'please, Colbie.'"

His mouth twisted in a grin. "Please, Colbie?"

"How many more orgasms are you gonna give me if I let you take me somewhere private?"

"As many as you can handle, plus one or two more."

"And I'm gonna pass out from it?" I slowed nearly to a stop, backing him slightly away from the edge.

"Most likely, yeah." He was thrusting, needing touch, movement, friction.

"Say my name again, Puck."

He laughed, a huffing grunt. "Colbie."

I couldn't hide the pleased smile as I leaned toward him. "Keep saying my name."

He blinked at me, disbelieving, as I bent over him. "Colbie . . . Jesus—*Colbie*."

"Mmm." It was all I could manage, because I had him in my mouth.

I tasted him and me. Flesh. Salt. Musk. Sex. Heat, man. My jaw was stretched, and I felt him on my tongue, sliding past my teeth sheathed behind my lips. He let out a long groaning breath, which I realized belatedly was my name, he was groaning my name like a prayer, drawn out, as I wrapped my lips around him and gave him the heat and warmth and wetness of my mouth.

I couldn't take much and didn't try. I stroked him underneath my mouth, moving my hands quickly now, because I knew I couldn't make him wait any longer. And I didn't want him to.

He sucked a breath in, a sharp inhalation, and then his teeth clicked together. "Colbie, babe—holy shit. I can't—I'm gonna—fuck, fuck, *fuck*—"

I backed away slowly, let him pop free of my mouth, my saliva connecting my lips to his cock in a string, or maybe it was saliva and his pre-come mixed together. He tensed, hips locked in a forward thrust, head pressed back against the seat.

"Now, Puck," I whispered.

I gathered his underwear and cupped it under the broad head of his cock, shielding the tip with the stretchy black cotton. Stroked him in long fast jerks, my hand a blur around his root. I felt his breath catch, felt his cock throb and pulse. Shifted my hand up around the top of him and kept going, hard and fast. He growled, a sound from the bottom of his throat, from his chest, muffled as he buried his face in my hair.

"Ohhhh . . . god, *Colbie* . . ." he breathed.

And then he came. I watched his come jet out of him, soaking into the underwear, kept stroking him as fast as I could. He murmured something unintelligible, thrusting into my hand, and come shot out of him again and again.

I couldn't stop myself. I bent over him again, guided him into my mouth and flicked my tongue over his cock as he spurted one last little drip. I tasted his seed, thick and salty and tangy and musky, and I licked again and swallowed the little bit that leaked out of him and glided my fist around him as he gasped. I backed away, and kept going with just one hand, slow deliberate strokes to milk every last little bit of his come out of him, white droplets beading at his tip and sliding down the underside of his cock. I licked them away and kept stroking until he hissed.

"Colbie, holy shit—Colbie."

"Yes, Puck?"

"Can't take any more." He was still hard, but wouldn't be for much longer.

"Oh no?" I bent over him one more time, grinning at him. "Then . . . *this* would just be too much, huh?"

I took him in my mouth and sucked as hard as I could, working him with my tongue, using both hands to jerk him faster than ever. He moaned, hips flexing so hard he left the seat entirely.

"Ohh fuck fuck fuck, Colbie, Jesus, Jesus . . ." he groaned.

I was laughing as I sat up. "Now we're even." I tucked him back into his pants, zipped him up, and buttoned the fly closed.

I folded his underwear up so the come was as contained as it would get and stuffed the wad into one of his cargo pockets, which I then buttoned closed.

"Holy hell, woman," he murmured. "That was . . . *damn*."

I felt pleased with myself, because Puck was totally limp, head lolling back on the seat, eyes closed, breathing hard. I happened to glance forward, and I saw that Layla was awake, mid-stretch, twisting in place. She saw me, shirt open, boobs hanging out as I wiped my lips with the back of my hand. I blushed so hard my cheeks went hot and forced myself to remain calm as I fastened my bra. Layla made the international sign for blowjob, moving her fist toward her mouth and sticking her tongue into her opposite cheek so it appeared as if a dick was poking the inside of her mouth.

Which only made me curse under my breath. "Shit. *Shit!*"

Layla just grinned and gave me two thumbs up.

"Shit, what?" Puck asked, his eyes still closed.

"Layla saw."

"Saw what?" He lazily opened one eye and shot her a look.

"Me, with my shirt open, wiping my lips." I was mortified, shaking. "She knew what I'd just been doing, obviously."

Puck's eye closed again. "She won't judge, trust me."

"I'm still embarrassed."

"Don't be." He took my hand in his, met my gaze. "Hang around this crew long enough, you'll probably get an eyeful of her doing the same thing. She gives her man so many BJs it's absurd." He squeezed my hand. "She'll probably congratulate you later."

"She just gave me a big grin and two thumbs up," I admitted.

"See? She's happy for us."

"Happy for *us*?" I asked, my voice sharper than I'd have liked.

"Yeah, for us." He tangled his fingers in mine. "You can't say there's anything normal about this thing you and I have going. I know I've never done anything like this before, and I don't think you have either. And then there's the fact that however you and I may both feel about this whole thing, it's sure as fuck *more* than either of us know what do with."

"I can't deny any of that, but—"

He spoke over me. "So yeah, *us*, wherever that takes us, whatever it looks like." His gaze shot to mine, and his voice was just as sharp as mine had been a few seconds earlier. "And no, I'm not just saying that because you gave me a hand job so epic I'm having trouble feeling my toes."

"There was some mouth in there, too," I couldn't

help pointing out.

"Whatever word or phrase you want to use, then. Blowjob with hands, hand job with a little mouth, whatever—it was fucking incredible. Hands down, without a doubt, unequivocally, the hottest goddamn thing I've ever experienced."

"Including everything with what's her name . . . Maya?"

Puck snorted. "No contest. Not even close."

"Not even close? She was the best ever, I thought you said."

"Best ever up until now. What you just did blows that whole week out of the water. No joke."

"Don't bullshit me."

"I'm not!" He sat up straighter. "You really think at this point I'm the type to blow smoke up your ass just to make you feel a little better?"

"So what could I have done better?"

"You're not insecure, are you?"

"No, but I'm not sure I believe you."

"So if I tell you it was perfect, you wouldn't believe me."

"I'm not saying that."

He frowned. "Then what are you saying?"

"I don't know!" I threw up my hands. "I've never done this kind of thing before. On a plane, in public? With a guy I've known a matter of hours? I don't usually make out with a guy on the first date. I'm not a prude, but I don't trust easily, and I have to have some level of trust before I feel comfortable enough with a guy to let him touch me, to be naked around him. Not because I'm insecure about how I look—I eat healthy and workout and I like how I look. It's more just . . . I don't know. But there's something about you that I just . . . *trust*. So I don't know why I did any of that with you. Why I let you touch me, why I touched you, why I'm even thinking about having sex with you, much less feeling like I need it more than I've ever needed sex in my life."

"I'm not a stranger to casual sex, you know that about me at this point. But this is different for me, too. When I'm working, I'm normally laser-focused. This is a job for me, and also more than a job. Getting Layla and the girls back safe to their men, who happen to be not just my co-workers but my friends, my brothers in arms . . . it's more than a job—it's personal. So for me to get distracted? That's *never* happened. Not since that shit with the madam. I learned my lesson. After that, I avoid temptation while working no matter what. Work is work, a job is a job, and I do *not* allow myself to be distracted. But you . . . you're not a distraction. You're . . . fuck, I don't know, Colbie. I don't fucking know. I can't *not* do this with you—shit, that sounded stupid. I just mean . . . I could no more stay away from you than I could just stop breathing." He palmed my cheek, and his hand was big and rough and warm and comforting. "Hear me when I say this: I need this more than I've ever needed anything or anyone, too. I absolutely *have* to feel you, naked and pressed up against me. I have to be inside you. It's imperative. I don't care what it takes to make that happen, I'll fucking do it."

I heard the sincerity in his voice, and I believed him.

And that scared the bejeezus out of me.

We landed at a tiny airport that Ivar informed us was several kilometers outside Prague—this one at least had an actual paved runway. A new Mercedes-Benz passenger van was waiting, with several men standing around it, each armed with a submachine gun, a larger version of the one Puck had used in the Range Rover, with an actual barrel and stock.

"They are friends of mine," Ivar reassured Puck, as we descended. "This airport is secure."

"Secure from Cain?" Puck asked, sounding skeptical.

"Even from him, *ja.*" Ivar pointed at the control tower, and I could see several figures dressed in black on the roof. "Snipers. Two of them, one with eyes on us, one with eyes on the approach. Another with an RPG, in case of breach."

Puck seemed impressed. "Red carpet, huh?"

Ivar shrugged. "Precautions." He gestured at the waiting van. "*Bitte.*"

"What's the plan, Ivar?" Puck asked.

"My associate operates in Prague. The plan is simple. We drive to her flat, she removes and deactivates the tracer in Miss Kennedy, and then I deliver you to Mr. Roth."

"I like simple plans," Puck said.

Puck climbed in, and I followed and somehow ended up sandwiched between Puck and Layla, the other women behind us, Ivar in the front seat, and two of the armed guards in the very back. Once we were in motion, Layla leaned close to me and whispered in my ear.

"So . . . you and Puck, huh?" she asked, for a third time.

I felt my cheeks redden. "Layla, what you saw—"

"Colbie, if you apologize or say some stupid shit like 'I don't do that sort of thing, normally'"—her voice took on a whiny, simpering tone—"I swear to fuck, I'll punch you, and take away any and all cool points you've earned with me up till now."

I eyed her. "But—"

She put her finger over my lips. "No buts." Her voice was pitched low enough that only I could hear her. "Puck is a cool guy. Not my type physically, but that doesn't mean I don't recognize the fact that he's sexy. He's a badass, and I'd bet any money he'll rock your motherfuckin' world."

I snickered, a sound awfully close to a giggle. "He already did."

"So don't you dare try to *explain* that shit or make it seem like you have something to hide." She bumped me with her shoulder. "Sister, when you decide you like a man, you get to choose what you do about it, and you don't owe fucking anybody any explanations. So what if you just met him? If you trust him, you decide you want him, then you jump on that dick and ride him like a goddamn rodeo champion. That's your right as woman, as a person, and as a responsible adult. And when you're done, you're done. That's it."

"What if . . ." I wasn't quite sure if I could even formulate the question out loud.

"What if you don't wanna be done?" Layla filled in, her voice more normally pitched, and I nodded. "Then go with it. I was scared shitless when I realized Nick and I were a thing. But if what you got feels like it's worth it, then you hold on and you don't let go. When it stops being worth it, then you know it's over. For Nick and me, it won't ever not be worth it, so I keep holding on."

"You make it sound simple."

"Simple, yes. Easy, no." She laughed. "Nick is an asshole. But he's *my* asshole, and I love him, and his qualities far outweigh the fact that he can be a dick, that he's a little controlling, a lot bossy, and super protective."

"Controlling, bossy, and protective don't seem like bad things."

"When you're a badass boss chick, it is. You seem a lot like me—independent to a fault, with a hair-trigger temper if anyone tries to make you do something you don't want to do, or tries to keep you from doing what you want to do."

I giggled, and yes, this time it was a stupid girly giggle. "You got that right."

She nodded sagely. "When your man is used to giving orders and being obeyed but you're the kind of chick who thinks it's funny to defy orders just for the hell of it . . . things get tricky. And when that same man is bound and determined to make sure you never so much as chip a goddamn nail, much less see any real action, and you've developed a bit of an addiction to the thrill of danger and feeling like a badass boss chick . . . it gets even trickier."

"He didn't like you wanting to be part of the team?"

"The stupid caveman tried to order me to stay home."

"What happened?"

"I ran off. Shook the tail he'd put on me, hunted his dumb ass down." She grinned, remembering. "He has an office on the West Coast, doesn't go there a lot. But the op he was on required him to be in LA and I knew it, so I let myself into his office. Stripped down to my birthday suit and waited till I knew he was about to walk in, and made sure he caught me diddling myself."

I snorted. "Wow. And that worked, did it?"

She blew a raspberry. "Fuck no, it didn't work. Backfired completely. I thought I'd tease him until he agreed to let me go on the op with him."

"But—?"

"But he turned the tables on me. Zip-tied me to his office chair and teased me with his cock until I was begging him to let me have it. I've got a weakness—I see his dick, I want his dick. He was all hard and kept putting it in me and touching my lips with it, and I was all hot and wet and shit, and he wouldn't fucking give it to me. So I ended up agreeing to stay put."

I couldn't help laughing. "He must have a magical dick."

"You have *no* idea." She said this deadpan, no hint of irony or sarcasm.

"So you don't go on ops?"

She shot me a look. "Of *course* I do. What kind of pussy do you take me for? I had no intention of actually staying home, I just wanted his dick and was willing to say anything to get it into my mouth."

"Oh." I wasn't sure what else to say, because this girl clearly had zero filter, which was equal parts funny and disconcerting.

"Circumstances became such that he didn't have a choice but to let me go with him, and I ended up proving that I was game—not that he should have needed more proof at that point anyway. I'd fought my out of a previous situation, but that is a whole other story. Point is, I proved I could handle myself in a shootout and could follow orders when it really counted. And now I'm an active member of Alpha One Security's core taskforce." She leaned forward and glanced at Puck. "Ain't that right?"

He held out his fist, and they tapped knuckles in front of me. "Hoo-rah, motherfucker." He winked at me. "This bitch is stone-cold."

I laughed. "No kidding. I've seen her in action." I shook my head. "I think you're all a little nuts. You crazy assholes seem like you actually *enjoy* this shit."

Puck shrugged. "Eh, I guess we do."

"Some people like sex, drugs, and rock 'n roll," Layla said, "well, I prefer sex, guns, and gangsta rap."

I laughed and shook my head, then turned to look out the window. I'd always wanted to see Prague, and so far I hadn't seen a single thing, having been caught up in the conversation with Layla. I needed to let her advice and my own thoughts and feelings on the subject percolate a little, so I watched the scenery. We'd entered the city proper already, which meant we were on a narrow two-lane one-way road, with the buildings close by on either side, squat four- or five-story buildings with lots of windows and shops on the street level—the unmistakable look of old-world Europe. We took a twisting, looping series of turns, often doubling back or circling the same block more than once, and I realized the driver—a taciturn older man with salt-and-pepper hair underneath a flat cabbie cap—was making sure no one was following us. Eventually he must have been satisfied we weren't being tailed, because he made an abrupt left turn and drove straight for half a dozen blocks, then circled another block twice before finally pulling into a parking spot in front of an apartment building. It was four stories, flat gray, squat and square and imposing, and pretty much identical to all the other buildings I'd seen so far.

Ivar exited the van, opened the sliding side door, and gestured at Temple. "You. Come inside." He glanced at the men in the back. "*Blieb hier. Wenn es irgendwelche Probleme gibt, gehen Sie.*"

The men both nodded. "*Jawhohl.*"

Temple reluctantly, nervously, climbed out, glancing back at us, and Ivar sighed in irritation. "You wish a friend for courage, *ja*?" Temple nodded, and Lola slid out after her, and the two women held hands. Ivar rolled his eyes. "It will take ten minutes, and you will not even feel it, probably. Like a finger prick, at most. Then done. Chin up, *ja*?"

Temple nodded again, and took a deep breath, and then lifted her chin high, following Ivar into the apartment building. Puck was standing outside the van, leaning against the frame of the door, and he had the little submachine gun in his hands, although I wasn't sure where he'd stashed it up until now—certainly not in his pants; I nearly laughed out loud at my own lewd joke.

He must have caught my stifled laugh, because he glanced back at me. "What's funny?"

I indicated his gun. "I was just wondering where you'd stashed that, and thought, certainly not in your pants." He blinked at me blankly, not following the joke. "Because I did a rather—ahem—*thorough* search of that region, if you'll recall."

Layla couldn't stifle a laugh, and a grin spread across Puck's features.

"Yeah, no gun hiding in these pants," he said.

I rolled my eyes at him. "You ruined the funny."

"You wanna check again? Make sure I'm not hiding any more . . . firepower?" He winked at me. "Could be worth double checking."

I laughed. "Hmm . . . yeah, I'm good. Pretty sure I wouldn't find anything this soon anyway."

"Ohh, shots fired," Layla howled.

Puck just made a droll face. "Sure about that, darlin'? You might find yourself shocked how fast I can reload."

I felt my face heat up, knowing both Kyrie and Layla were listening, and probably the driver and both guards, though who knew if they spoke English. None of Ivar's men seemed to be paying attention, one standing near the hood, and the other near the rear end, their big fuck-off machine guns in plain view. Clearly, Ivar wasn't worried about attention.

"Oh fuck off," I said, because I didn't have a better

comeback. Mainly because I was pretty sure he'd be ready and raring to go, and I couldn't deny that I'd sure as hell like to find out.

"Can't take the heat, don't dish it out, babe."

"I can take the heat, asshole."

He smirked, and I wanted to smack the smirk off his face as much as I wanted to kiss it off. "That's not all you can take, sweet thing," he said, with a suggestive wiggle of his eyebrows.

I choked on my own shock, then growled, and slapped him across the cheek, hard enough to count, but not hard enough to really hurt. "You're a bastard, Puck Lawson."

He let me hit him, and when I went to smack his arm he caught my wrist and yanked me out of my seat and against his chest. "And don't you forget it," he said. But then, more softly, meant just for me, with a thumb grazing over my cheek: "I'm just teasing, Colbie. I didn't mean anything by it."

I gave him a lazy smile. "I can take a joke, Puck."

He laughed. "Well good, because I've got jokes."

"Yeah, just not funny ones."

"Ooh, now that's what you call shots fired," he said, brushing his lips against mine.

Ivar appeared with Temple and Lola in tow. He shot Puck a frown. "Can it not wait? We are on a timeline, you know."

Puck lifted me into the van. "Hey, I'm ready when you are, bro."

"Just do not be so distracted you miss important things."

"Not a problem."

Ivar nodded. "Now we go to another airport, and this time to a larger aircraft for the journey to the States."

We were loaded in the van again and winding through Prague. Temple was touching a spot on the back of her head, right at the hairline at the base of her skull; she twisted in the seat and lifted her hair up to show us a small square bandage.

"Get the chip out?" Puck asked.

Temple nodded, held up a corked glass tube; inside the tube was a tiny cylinder not much bigger than a grain of rice. "I felt that bump, too, but I thought it was just a pimple or something." She shook the tube, making the device rattle inside. "I can't believe those assholes put a chip in me! If Duke and the boys hadn't already killed most of them, I'd want them dead."

"Yeah, well, we're working on that," Puck said. "The real culprit is Cain. Those jackasses were just the hired goons."

"Is that thing deactivated or whatever?" Layla asked.

Temple nodded. "Dr. Emilia wiped it, somehow."

"Are you sure you shouldn't toss it, just in case?" Layla said.

"The circuitry was cooked with an electromagnetic pulse." Ivar put in. "Fried, dead. No chance of it being reactivated."

"So now we're finally going home?" This was Kyrie.

"That is the plan, yes," Ivar said.

"Well, if the tracker is fried, then we should be able to get away without a problem, right?" I asked.

Ivar nodded. "I never make any assumptions. Anything is possible." He waved a hand in a vague gesture. "They would have traced us here to Prague. If they assume you are trying to return home to the States, there are only so many places where airplanes large enough for a transatlantic flight to take off from. We are not out of the woods yet, as they say."

I didn't see much more of Prague except nearly identical roads and buildings. But then, you couldn't really experience a city properly unless you had at least three days to get out, get lost, and immerse yourself. Thirty minutes in and out didn't really count as visiting, so I'd still have to leave Prague on my list of places to visit. The airfield we were going to was another two-and-a-half-hour drive outside of Prague, which left a lot of time to think.

But, me being me, that's exactly what I wouldn't do. If I started thinking, I'd start overthinking, and then I'd upset myself, and then all the emotional reactions I've been suppressing would start springing out and, as Ivar had said, we weren't out of the woods yet, and I couldn't afford to give in to thinking or reacting until I was somewhere truly safe.

No thinking.

So I turned to Puck for distraction.

"Do you have a favorite place?" I asked. "Like, a retreat or a secret getaway?"

He wasn't fazed by the abruptness of the question. He thought for a moment, and then shot me a wink and a grin. "The back seat of that airplane."

I huffed. "For real, Puck."

He patted my leg. "Teasin', babe. My cabin has always been my favorite getaway. Although now that Cain's people know about it, I'm probably gonna sell it." He tapped his kneecap with the muzzle of the submachine gun he still had strapped around his chest. "No point to a secret hideaway if Cain's aware of it."

"That sucks, huh?"

He sighed. "Yeah, it kinda does. It's been in my family for going on two hundred years. That was where I went when I needed to get away from everything, you know? Plus, it's really all I have to remember my family by. I mean, I didn't have much to begin with, but now I ain't got shit."

I frowned at him. "You have no family? None?"

He shook his head. "Nah. Mom's dead, Dad's dead, never had brothers or sisters, or aunts or uncles. I think Pops had a brother and a sister at one point, but if they're still alive, I don't even know their names. His folks were gone before I was born, and Mom's folks both passed a while back, and I never met 'em anyway, on account of the fact that when Mom married Pops, her folks disowned her. Said Pops was a no account gambler, a drifter, and a piece of shit. They weren't wrong about him, but that didn't mean they should've disowned her."

"And your mom was an only child too?" I asked.

He shrugged again. "Dunno, and there ain't no point to finding out. What good is blood family if they're total strangers? I'm almost fuckin' forty, and I've gotten along fine without 'em so far, so there ain't no point in digging up them bones." His southern drawl was strong, for some reason; he didn't like this topic, I supposed. He glanced at me. "What about you?"

"Favorite place? Or family?"

"Yes."

"Well, you know about my family—same as you, I don't have any." I shrugged. "Only time it really makes a difference is around the holidays. That time of the year gets lonely."

"Word," Puck said. "If I'm not on an op, then I'm flat out wasted during the holidays. I have a tradition, I rent a penthouse in Vegas, order up a shitload of booze, and I stay my ass in that penthouse getting shitfaced until the holidays are over."

"And you probably also hire company, I'm guessing?" I asked, lifting an eyebrow at him.

He nodded. "Been known to a time or two, yes. Like you said, it gets lonely."

"But is hired company really any kind of comfort?"

He bobbed his head to one side. "You'd be surprised. Most of those girls don't have much family themselves, so spending the holidays getting paid to hang out with someone? Not a bad gig."

"But you're not paying them to just hang out, though," I pointed out.

He leveled a reproving glare at me. "There you go with the assumptions again, sweetheart." He ejected the magazine from the weapon, thumbed out one of the bullets, and toyed with it rather than look at me. "When I rent out that penthouse, the singular goal is not to remember those two weeks, from before Christmas to after the New Year. So if I book an escort for those two weeks, it's usually for the purpose of having someone around to make sure I don't choke on my own fuckin' puke, or do something monumentally stupid. Sometimes we do the obvious, yeah, but usually, we'd just hang out, talk, drink, and watch movies. Someone to just *be* there, more than anything. And, like I said, most of those girls are shy on meaningful family their own selves, so they're grateful to not be sitting around alone. Instead, they have me, which I realize may not be a super amazing value add for them, but it's a damn sight better than bein' lonely on Christmas fuckin' day."

I blinked, feeling my throat close as I imagined the picture he'd painted: him, in a glitzy Vegas penthouse, drunk, his only company an equally lonely prostitute or escort. Drinking to forget the time, so he would be less aware of the loneliness.

Layla, sitting on my left side, whereas Puck was on my right, reached around me and slugged Puck on the shoulder. "You're a dumbass, Puck Lawson."

He frowned and rubbed his arm where she'd punched him. "Probably, but why?"

"You waste all that time and all that money on hookers and booze and a penthouse when you could just crash with us? And what about Thresh? He doesn't have family either. Nor does Duke, for that matter. Why do you stupid, emotionally handicapped dumbass fucking men insist on being so goddamn macho about everything?"

"We get together during the holidays a few times," Puck said. "They usually show up at my penthouse for a few days."

"That's not what I mean. You guys are family. To each other, and to me and Nick." She sounded like she was choked up. "I don't have family, Nick doesn't have family, and who the hell knows about Lear and Anselm. None of us have family. So why the hell don't we act like fucking family when it counts?"

"Because we're all stupid stubborn macho men," Puck answered. "Emotionally handicapped and socially stunted."

Lola piped up, then. "Yeah, well, you can bet your ass *that* shit is gonna change for Thresh, now that I'm in the picture."

"Same for Duke," Temple put in.

I twisted to glance back at Kyrie, but she didn't say anything, although she looked like she was deep in thought.

Layla raised her voice. "Hey, Ivar."

"*Ja*?" he answered.

"You got a secure line to the boys?"

"*Jawohl*," he clipped out, and dug a phone out of his hip pocket, touched a speed dial entry, and handed it back to her.

Layla listened to it ring. "Hey, baby, it's me." She snorted. "Yes, me, Layla. Who else you got answering the phone saying 'hey baby?' Yeah, you bet your ass nobody, or I'll cut your fuckin' balls off. No, listen, you're gonna yell at me for wasting secure phone time on this, but it's important. We are, as of this moment, hosting a company-wide two-week holiday retreat for all the guys and their girlfriends, from Christmas to New Year's. I don't care where, or what it looks like, or how much you spend on it, but that shit is non-negotiable. Did you know about Puck's Vegas penthouse bullshit? . . . Yes, I'm serious, Nick. No, this can't wait. You say those guys are like your family, well I'm calling your bluff. We start acting like family. Not just protecting each other when shit goes down but investing in them outside of work."

She listened a few moments, seeming mollified. "Exactly, that's what I'm talking about . . . right . . . Okay. Yeah, I love you, too—Yeah, we're on our way to the airport for the trip stateside."

Kyrie reached forward. "Can I see that?" Layla handed it back to Kyrie. "Hey Harris, it's Kyrie. Yeah, can I talk to him? . . . Hi, babe. So you heard what Harris was talking about. Yeah, so you're going to coordinate with Harris on that, okay? Buy an island near us or something, or build a set of guest quarters for them, whatever you want, as long as there's private accommodations for all of them down with us for the holidays. You can figure out the details, that's what you're best at. Yep, so far so good. I've seen some things I'd rather have not seen, but no worse than Greece. Okay, love you. Bye."

I couldn't help but laugh. "You people are crazy."

Kyrie handed the phone forward. "Why? What's funny?"

I gestured at her and then Layla. "You two. You tell your husband to '*buy an island* or something.' For real?"

She shrugged, grinning. "He's Valentine Roth— he could buy an island from the profits of a single quarter from *one* company, and we own a dozen that I know of. So telling him to buy an island is like saying 'baby, I want a Ferrari, go buy me one.'"

I laughed even harder. "You do realize that the vast majority of humans on this planet can't just go buy a fucking bicycle whenever they want, much less a Ferrari, don't you?"

She made an *oh well* face. "True, and yes I'm aware. My point is more that for my husband, buying an island versus buying a Ferrari is pretty much the same thing. Affects him the same amount, which is to say not at all." She hesitated, and then continued. "He also donates more to charity as an individual than anyone else I've heard of, Zuckerberg and Gates included. He's just quiet about it, doesn't publicize it—doesn't *allow* it to be publicized, if you want to be accurate."

I held up my hands palms out. "Hey, I didn't mean it to sound like an accusation or something. I just thought it was funny."

She waved me off. "People get weird about it, when they find out I'm married to Valentine. I don't even think about the money for the most part. I mean, yeah, I live in a ridiculous house in the Caribbean, and we have a few people around as staff, and there are armed guards and patrol boats and things, but . . . you get used to it. I'm a stay-at-home mommy, and I do it all myself. We have a nanny for when we want to get out by ourselves, but . . . I'm the mommy. *I* raise my daughter myself. The money is more Roth's than mine, although he'd get pissy if he heard me say that. I don't really care about the money, is the point. It's really nice to have, and I'm grateful and thankful, but being rich doesn't solve all the problems people tend to think it does."

"People are weird about things they don't un-derstand," I said, "and most people don't understand what it's like to have access to unlimited amounts of money any more than they can understand what it's like to be flat broke, or homeless."

"You were homeless?" she asked.

I nodded. "From when I was sixteen till I was twenty."

"You got yourself out of it, clearly," Kyrie said.

"Sure did," I said. "Got a real job and everything, and I do okay at it, too. But having been homeless, having begged for handouts, I appreciate every damn cent I earn, because there was a time when having even two dollar bills to rub together meant not going hungry another night."

It was so weird to talk about this stuff so open-ly; I *never* talked about my homeless years, and yet these women just seemed to *get it*. They didn't look at me weird, or pity me, or whatever. They accepted me for who I was. I wasn't ready to share as much as I had with Puck, but I could see myself sitting down with a bottle of wine and spilling with these women. Even more oddly . . . I *wanted* that. I didn't tend to form close friendships. I was friendly with some of the people at work, but they were coworkers; I never truly trusted them, never spent meaningful time with them outside work. For one thing, the women seemed like they were from a different planet. Like, they were

what I might have become had Mom and Dad and
Danielle lived—normal, a little spoiled, a little vapid,
nice, stable, boring. Yeah, maybe we shared interests
in terms of enjoying shopping for nice clothes and
getting manicures once or twice a month, and talking
about how guys were assholes, but you could do that
over lunch or in the bathroom. That wasn't friendship stuff, that was acquaintance stuff. These wom-
en, though—Layla, Temple, Kyrie, and Lola—they
seemed to understand me. They'd understand the
damage I had from the various traumatic experiences
of my life, and getting kidnapped off the street in the
middle of the day wasn't the worst. If I'd actually gone
on to be sold into sexual slavery that might have been
a different story. But so far, it wasn't so bad. Scary,
nerve-wracking, gross, and I'd probably have night-
mares about this stuff at some point, but it wasn't a
life-altering traumatic experience.

Which was fucked up, when you thought about
it. But there it was.

I had no idea what was going to happen when
this was finally all over . . . maybe I'd end up back in
New York, taking the occasional trip to Moscow or
Beijing or St. Petersburg or Shanghai, playing poker
with the guys on Friday nights, eating dinner alone,
watching cartoons alone . . . but I didn't want that
anymore. Seeing the bond Layla and Kyrie had, the
easy camaraderie of Lola and Temple . . . it made me
jealous. Made me want to be part of their group.

Layla was eyeing me, watching me. "You look like you're thinking deep thoughts over there, missy."

I shrugged. "Just wondering what's going to happen when this is finally all over."

She didn't respond immediately, still searching me. "Well, if you think you're going to just vamoose back to Manhattan or wherever you live and pretend none of this ever happened, you better have another think."

"Why?" I asked.

She just frowned at me like I was stupid, or missing something glaringly obvious. "I told you, bitch, you're part of the posse, now. You don't get to crawl back into your little hole and ignore us." She jammed her elbow into my ribs. "You're stuck with us now, ho."

I eyed her carefully. "You know, if anybody else called me bitch or ho, we'd be throwing down, earrings off and everything."

Layla laughed, unfazed. "Anybody else, I'd tell 'em to bring it, but something tells me you're as tough as I am. I'll give you a little primer on being my friend: if I *don't* call you insulting names, I don't like you. And if I'm polite to you, I flat-out hate your ass. So the worse names I call you, the more I like you. Just ask Kyrie."

I glanced at Kyrie, who gave a shrug and a nod. "Layla has turned vulgarity and insult-driven affection into an art form. She only knows how to show affection in two ways: fucking and insults, and since we're all straight as far as I'm aware, she's only left with insults. She tosses out words like 'bitch' and 'ho' and 'hooker' like she drops F-bombs and references to sucking dick."

I figured since everyone pretty much already knew Puck and I had gotten down to a little business on the plane, I might as well sally forth with more honesty. "But what if—"

Layla cut in over me. "Doesn't matter. You've known Puck since this morning. Granted, we've packed a lot into today, and when you're tossed into high-stress situations like this, bonds form pretty quickly. Shit, Harris and I would probably still be dicking around with our feelings for each other had Vitaly not kidnapped me. That situation forced us to hit the afterburner on our feelings, and we never looked back." She gestured with her chin at Puck and me. "That may be the case for you two, and maybe not. Nobody's got a stake in that except you guys. All *I'm* saying is, I like you, and I really hope you decide to stick around regardless of what does or doesn't happen with you and Puck."

"Who's Vitaly?" I asked.

She waved the question away. "Someone who is now dead. He was kind of like Cain—a rich asshole criminal with a vengeful streak a mile wide."

"And he kidnapped you?"

She nodded. "Hauled my jiggly ass all the way down to Brazil. But that's a story for another day." She poked me. "Stop avoiding the subject."

I sighed. "I'm not, I just don't know what to say. I don't know what's going to happen. I don't make friends easily, or at all, really, but . . . I like you guys. I could see us being a posse."

"Hey, I'm down to be in the badass boss chick posse," Lola said.

"Me too," Temple added.

"I'm in, obviously," Kyrie said.

"Can I be in the posse?" Puck asked.

Layla reached over and patted him on the shoulder. "Sorry, Puck, girls only."

"Besides, you already have your big guns and big muscles club with Thresh and Duke," Temple said.

"Guns and muscles aren't the only big things about them," Lola stage-whispered.

Which caused a lot of howling in the van, from me included. I caught the tail end of a look between Ivar and Puck, the kind of look guys exchange when women do the whole laughing and shrieking thing guys don't understand, the look that says *why are they screaming, and how do we make them shut up?* Everyone else caught the look, which only made the rest of us laugh all the harder.

"I apologize for breaking up the levity," Ivar interrupted, "but we are arriving at the airfield. I do not have security here like I did on our arrival, so if Cain has people here, it will be down to us to deal with them."

"What he means is look sharp, ladies," Puck said. "It's go time."

Ivar nodded. "*Ja*, as he said."

This was a larger airport, albeit a rural one. There was a gate manned by two armed, uniformed guards; Ivar, sitting in the front passenger seat, showed them some kind of ID or pass, and they waved us through. My heart was in my throat, hammering and crashing wildly as we made our way across the tarmac, zipping behind the tails of airliners angled up to jetways. We left the main terminal area and continued to the area for private aircraft, a wide square, lined with hangars, the fronts open to reveal cavernous interiors occupied by aircraft ranging from single engine prop planes to massive private jets.

One such airplane waited off to one side, a set of moveable steps positioned at the doorway. It was truly mammoth, very nearly the size of the hangar itself.

Backlit by the setting sun, this jet was sleek and sexy and glossy black, with a crimson RTI stenciled in aggressive letters on the tail fin. The van halted near the steps, and Puck, Ivar, and the two guards—who'd sat silently and unnoticed this whole time—clambered out and positioned themselves to cover all directions. Ivar waved us out, and Layla went first, followed by Temple, Lola, Kyrie, and then me.

Kyrie grinned as we approached the staircase. "Oooh, Valentine sent the nice jet. Good boy."

I eyed the aircraft, which looked like it cost the

equivalent of a third world country's GDP. "This is your husband's jet?"

She nodded. "He designed this one, actually. He recently started a hyper-luxury transport manufacturing company, so making fancy jets and boats and stuff is his new hobby."

"He designed this?"

"He helped. He's not an engineer or anything, just a really smart businessman with good taste and better judgement. This is the prototype of an aircraft his new company is going to be selling. They have military grade jet engines, which means this thing goes insanely fast, and it also has things like antimissile defenses, and it's designed to be low-radar reactive or something. For the richest of the rich who want to fly incognito, he says."

I was mind boggled. "And how much is this going to cost?"

Kyrie blew a raspberry. "Shit, girl, I have no idea. Close to triple-digit millions, easily. This isn't the kind of thing your average A-lister, like Temple's mom, for example, would buy. This is the kind of thing the king of Saudi Arabia would own, or those Koch assholes. That kind of rich."

We boarded and found seats near each other, both of us on the aisle. As we sat down, the flight attendant offered us warm hand towels followed by a selection of beverages and small snacks.

I glanced out the window and saw Puck shake

hands with Ivar, taking a moment to clap each other on the arms and murmur macho bromance bullshit to each other, and then Puck jogged up the steps and into the plane while Ivar waited on the tarmac, watching.

Puck grabbed the window seat beside me, and as he settled himself, I turned back to Kylie. "You say transport like there's something besides jets and boats."

She nodded. "Yachts, jets, armored limos made out of stretched Bentleys and Rolls Royces and Maybachs, mobile command centers pulled by semi-trucks—those are super cool, actually. You can choose whether you want it to be a mobile office command center thing, or a home. Think those monster RVs rich old folks retire with, but it's got a full-size tractor-trailer. The trucks are those new Volvos that are fully electric and can go faster than most race cars. They're really awesome, actually."

She tapped a bubblegum-pink fingernail on the armrest. "What else has he come up with? Helicopters, of course. And when I say yacht, by the way, I'm talking something the size of a battleship, literally. So big it comes with its own smaller speedboat the size of a normal yacht, with a helicopter-landing pad and like twenty staterooms. And usually, the helicopter and powerboat are included. Oh, he's also working on a submarine."

I blinked at her. "A what?"

"You heard me." She grinned. "A submarine. But instead of being all tiny and cramped and full of ICBMs, it's a luxury retreat. Huge staterooms, a movie theater, a swimming pool, cameras installed outside and giant screens on the inside walls so it feels like you're seeing what's out there. I've been on the proto-type actually, and I think I'm going to have him keep one for us. It's really incredible. You can be down near the bottom of the ocean where only whales and stuff go, and it's totally silent, and you can see jellyfish and weird sea creatures and . . . it's just *so* cool."

"And there's more than, like, two people who can afford these things?" I asked.

She nodded. "You'd be surprised. There are quite a few people out there who are quietly wealthy. Never in the news or anything, but they're out there, and they have stupid amounts of money. And in the current social and political atmosphere, Valentine is wagering on a lot of them wanting to have a hyper-luxury home that can go wherever they want, away from all the craziness."

"I guess I can see that. If you can afford your own submarine, why would you live on land?"

"Exactly! Especially when it has a retractable sundeck on top of the conning tower and a glassed-in viewing bubble at the front end."

"That sounds amazing."

She nodded. "It is. I'm super proud of him." She gestured around the interior of the jet. "I mean, this is pretty incredible, isn't it?"

I wasn't sure "incredible" covered it. The outside of the jet was completely opaque, without windows at all, yet when you got inside, you discovered that the entire interior, from floor to ceiling, stretching all the way up and around, was one giant screen displaying what was outside in an unbroken, 4K display. The picture was so clear I felt like I could reach out and touch the wing, or smell the jet fumes. The seats were . . . god, how did I describe them? Like the most comfortable bed you'd ever been in, the kind of bed that had a memory foam topper and a fluffy down comforter, and you were enveloped in a cloud? The seats were like that too; they just . . . *hugged* you in softness. Creamy tan leather, with thick, plush crimson carpeting underfoot. This was the kind of jet on which you popped Dom Perignon and ate caviar and checked the time on a diamond-encrusted Rolex, and had a Rolls Royce waiting for you on the other end of the flight.

I felt distinctly out of place.

I didn't usually let my past dictate my present; I didn't hold my past against me. But when surrounded by such finery and luxury, I had a hard time forgetting that I was once the girl who dug through dumpsters for returnable cans so I could afford a single hit of smack.

Puck had been sitting quietly with his eyes closed but he let out a sigh, tracing the stitching in the leather. "I never quite get used to this kind of thing," he said.

"You must have been reading my mind," I murmured to him. "I was thinking the same thing."

He took my hand. "I always feel like I'm gonna get the seat dirty, you know? Like, even if I'm all showered and wearing nice clothes, I still don't feel like I belong. In my head, deep down, I'm still that kid from Arkansas who grew up in pool halls and poker tournaments, hanging out with strippers and cashing in stolen chips so I could I buy candy. My dad let me run wild, you know? When we weren't on the road playing poker, I was out in the woods, fending for myself, usually barefoot in a pair of shorts. Literally, I grew up half-naked most of the time, and the rest of the time I was surrounded by hookers, strippers, cardsharps, and bikers. Shit like this"—he gestured around us—"it makes me nervous. I'll never fit in, is how I feel."

I couldn't and didn't try to resist the need to rest my head on his shoulder. "Exactly how I feel. I'm sitting here thinking, I was the girl who would dumpster-dive for returnables so I could buy smack, or sit outside subway turnstiles begging for change so I could buy a burger. I'm always going to be that girl, no matter how far away I try to get from her, no matter where I live or what I do to escape her."

"That's not us anymore, though," Puck said. "May have been who we were, but it's not who we are now.

We belong wherever we decide we want to go."

I clung to his arm. "It's hard to forget, though."

"That's the damn truth."

Silence. I wasn't even aware of having taken off, but the screens displayed a darkening sky full of stars above with intermittent shreds of grayish-white clouds, city lights glowing in golden webs below.

"What happens next, Puck?" I whispered.

He squeezed my thigh. "I take you to the nearest hotel and fuck your brains out."

"Puck," I sighed. "I'm being serious."

He lifted an eyebrow at me. "So am I." He held the expression for a moment, and then winked at me, cracking into a grin. "But for real though, I don't know what's next."

KISS WITH A CAPITAL K

IT FELT LIKE IT WAS OVER. HAD THAT FEELING, YOU know? Relief mixed with exhaustion, plus a helping of *was I totally sure it was over?*

The plane landed at some private airfield owned by Roth—in upstate New York, if I had to guess, and we were met by Harris's A1S Strike Team Beta. That was to say, a dozen hard-eyed kids fresh off combat deployment, decked out in black paramilitary BDUs and body armor, each wielding an MP5SD and a personal sidearm. I knew for a fact there was at least one sniper out there, somewhere, and probably someone with a SAW—Harris didn't fuck around. The B-team was arrayed in a box formation, rifles at the ready.

Harris, Duke, Thresh, and Roth all stood together in a cluster inside the box, each looked more pissed off than the last. A line of shiny black Mercedes-Maybach G650s stood idling nose to tail, five of them, which represented something like $2.75 million—chump change for Roth, a not so small fortune for the rest of us, even though we five core A1S got paid stupid amounts of money for what we did—corporate exec money, low seven digits a year. I could afford *one* G650, but it would set me back a nice chunk. Five? I mean, no. But Roth, as I overheard Kyrie say, could buy entire islands from a cell phone. This wasn't him rolling out the red carpet, this was just Roth providing his idea of decent transportation.

LOL, as the kids said these days.

I could tell Colbie was unnerved and impressed though. I meant, it was an impressive sight. The B-team kids were chosen as much for looks, physique, and intimidation value as their combat record and résumé, meaning, they were all six-feet plus and built like gods, with ridiculously chiseled features and chins you could use as anvils. Harris used the B-team when he wanted to send a visual message—*do NOT fuck with me*. They weren't eye-candy, though, they were all seasoned warriors who could and would pull the trigger. But in this case, it was meant to communicate that he took this seriously.

Although, I knew the real work of sorting out the situation was done by the two notably absent members of A1S, Anselm and Lear. With any luck, Lear would track Cain down, and Anselm would put a

.50cal slug through his fucking skull, and that would be that.

The women, led by Layla, exited the plane in a jog, and reunited with their men in a welter of joyful shrieks and happy crying and wet kissing.

Colbie and I were the last ones to descend the steps, and she leaned close and nudged me. "Hey," she whispered, "who are all the men?"

"The guys in formation with the machine guns are the B-team, and I don't know any of their names. Harris has probably assigned them stupid codenames like Honcho and Ripper and Comanche and shit. Don't know, don't care. They're here to make sure nothing goes FUBAR at the last second. The dudes in the center are my boys. I'm sure you've heard the names by now." We were face to face with the crew, so I turned it into introductions, pointing at each in turn. "Duke Silver, the ginger pretty boy; Thresh is the one who looks like the love child of Dolph Lundgren and Arnold Schwarzenegger; Harris, the boss; and last but not least, Valentine Roth, genius billionaire playboy philanthropist—wait, that's Tony Stark. Roth is just a billionaire philanthropist, seeing as he gave up his playboy ways to marry Kyrie and, last I checked, he's not a certified genius."

Roth actually laughed. "Has anyone ever told you your mouth is going to get you in trouble?"

"All the time," I said, "but that's what makes me so much fun."

Roth grabbed me by the shoulder and squeezed hard. "I have to say, listening to Harris and trusting you and Ivar to bring my wife home was the hardest thing I've ever done. If it had been up to me, I'd have sent in a mercenary army."

I nodded and clapped his arm. "You couldn't have gotten anything together fast enough to make a difference. I was the best bet, and Ivar . . . well, he was indispensible. We literally wouldn't be here without him." I frowned. "Speaking of Ivar, I owe him a bottle of Pappy van Winkle."

Colbie stood quietly by and seemed a little awe-struck, to be honest. And I got it. Duke was blindingly pretty on top of being a burly brute of a man, and Thresh was bigger than fucking Godzilla and almost as good looking as Duke, and Harris wasn't far behind either of them in terms of build or looks, and Valentine Roth was almost as famous for being hot as he was rich and mysterious, and I said that as a totally straight male who loved tits and ass and pussy with an almost rabid intensity. So yeah, to the uninitiated, I could see how all those big, ripped, good-looking dudes in one place might be a little hard to handle at first.

"I think if you guys did a shirtless calendar, all the ovaries in the country might combust at once," Colbie said.

Which got a lot of laughter, from the other women especially.

"Hey, dickbag, who's the hot new girl?" Duke asked.

I realized I'd only done half the introductions. "Oh, right. Guys, this is Colbie Danvers. She was one of the women abducted by Cain's shitheads."

"And here she is," Harris said, "all cuddled up next to you."

Colbie was tucked against my side, my arm around her protectively, but then when Harris cracked his joke, she straightened away from me.

"That a problem, boss?" I said, tugging her back against me.

He just shook his head and laughed. "No, it's just funny."

Colbie didn't fight me as I pulled her back into a casual side-hug, but was tense and stiff. "Why is it funny?" she asked.

Harris—flanked by Thresh and Duke—gestured with his thumbs to either side. "I'm just noticing a pattern. Thresh goes down to Florida, and this whole fucking snafu breaks open. Bam, next thing you know, I'm rescuing him from the fucking Everglades with a sexy doctor hanging off him. Then Duke goes AWOL, and he turns up with a hot-ass celebrity. And now Puck vanishes only to reappear with you. Are you a doctor or a celebrity or some shit too?"

She laughed. "No, none of the above."

"By none of the above, she means she's a Harvard Business grad and fluent in three languages," I said.

Thresh made a rumbling sound, which was his cave-troll version of laughter. "Harvard educated, multilingual, and drop-dead gorgeous. I think you'll fit right in, Colbie Danvers." He reached out and shook her hand. "Welcome to the Alpha One family."

Judging by the way she ducked her head and grinned, she was probably blushing, which I noticed she did a lot and easily, despite her tough girl persona. It was cute. "Thanks, I guess."

"Don't give her too much shit about the welcome to the club business," Layla said. "She's still not sure about Puck."

"Hell, I've known the man going on ten years, and I'm still not sure about Puck," Harris said.

"None of you fuckers are being helpful," I snapped. "Lay off."

Colbie patted my chest. "Relax, Puck. I told you, I can take a joke."

Duke snickered. "Ohh shit, we've got a live one." He pointed at Colbie. "Better clean out your porn stash, Puck, you're gonna want to hang on to this chick."

"I don't think they make dumpsters big enough for Puck's porn collection," Thresh said.

"Ha fucking ha, dickheads." I tried to pass it off as another joke. "Very funny."

"You have a storage unit full of it, Puck," Duke said. "Who's being funny?"

Colbie to the rescue, apparently. "Well, at least I'll

have somewhere to store my own collection, then."

Neither Duke nor Thresh knew how to respond.

"We were . . . um, totally kidding," Thresh said, going for last second diplomacy.

"That's weird of you. I wasn't." Colbie remained straight-faced.

"You have a porn collection? I wouldn't have guessed." Layla peered at Colbie from underneath Harris's arm. "We'll have to watch porn and drink some cab sav together sometime."

Colbie shrugged. "Hey, I'm full of surprises."

"No shit," I murmured. Then louder, to the group: "Can we get the fuck out of here already? I'm hungry and I haven't slept in more than two days."

"Mount up, folks," Harris said, his voice cracking through the quiet. "We're headed to a place Roth has about an hour from here. We'll have a quick debrief and then everyone can get some R&R."

The B-team boys spread out, reforming the box in a spaced-out perimeter around the four vehicles. I noticed three blacked-out Suburbans waiting in the shadows, and as we loaded into the pimped-out G-Wagens—one couple per vehicle—the B-team jogged to the Suburbans and piled in, four to a truck. Each G-Wagen had its own uniformed and probably armed RTI driver—Roth Transportation Industries.

Once Colbie and I were buckled into the back-seat of our Mercedes, I glanced over at her, and she was drifting off. I was fading myself, and hard. My eyes were burning, and my head was full of cotton. When I said I'd been awake for more than two days that was a conservative estimate. I couldn't remember the last time I'd slept, and things had been the opposite of boring in the meantime.

The last thing I remembered was holding Colbie's hand and leaving the airfield, the caravan of vehicles winding through a quiet, hilly, rural area, a few stands of trees here and there, white fences enclosing rolling pastures, and not a single vehicle anywhere to be seen. And then warm, peacefulness as I drifted off.

I woke up about an hour later as we ascended a hill, and a sprawling three-story estate mansion appeared in the distance. We passed through a gate, which I noticed was heavily fortified, monitored, and manned by four A1S boys—a fifteen-foot-high stone block wall extended away from the gate in both directions, cordoning off what had to be a good twenty acres of rolling grass hills, leading to the mansion itself. The house was eye-wateringly huge, yet tasteful and beautiful. It looked like something you'd see in a period-piece movie about seventeenth century French nobility, all intricate columns and gabled dormers, manicured lawns and topiary shrubbery lining the fine gravel circular driveway.

"What the hell is this place?" I asked out loud, meaning it rhetorically.

"It belongs to Mr. Roth, I believe, sir," the driver said.

"Of course it does. How many houses does the bastard have?" I wondered.

"I'm sure I wouldn't know, sir."

"I wasn't asking you, kid. Just wondering out loud."

I stared as the line of vehicles halted in the circle drive, the center of which was an elaborate marble fountain carved to look astonishingly like a Greek goddess version of Kyrie. Roth was out of his car and striding toward the door, greeting a tuxedo-clad older guy.

"Yo, Roth!" I called out, as we approached him.

He paused, glancing back at me. "Yes, Puck?"

"Is that a real-deal butler?"

Roth allowed a ghost of smile to touch his lips. "Yes, as a matter of fact. Although I think Nigel would prefer the term majordomo."

"And his name is Nigel, too. That's fucking awesome." I eyed the house. "Does this place come with a bat cave, too?"

Roth let out a dignified little breath that I realized was his classy, elegant version of a laugh. "Something like that, yes. I call it the toy box, though. You'll like it, I'm sure. I'll show it to you in the morning." He turned to Nigel. "For now, however, Nigel has arranged for the kitchen to be at the ready. Rooms have been prepared, so it's up to each of you how you wish to arrange yourselves. The phones have buttons labeled for the kitchen, so all you have to do is call down and put in a request, and your orders will be brought to you. Much like room service, but better and faster. Have a pleasant evening, and let's plan on reconvening over breakfast for the formal debriefing."

We entered through the front door and into a marble and dark wood foyer that opened into the kind of room you'd envision this place having: sweeping staircases swirling in grand arcs from the third floor all the way down to the first floor, with hallways running off into three different wings on each level. Hanging in the center of the foyer was a massive chandelier that looked like it was made of thousands of tiny pieces of antique crystal. Nigel paused at the bottom of the staircases, where a squadron of staff members waited in precise formation, each man and woman wearing formal livery. I felt like I'd walked onto the set of *Downton Abby*, and should be thrown out for ruining the take with my grubby ass.

"I don't have a full menu prepared, I'm afraid," Nigel said, sounding exactly like I'd hoped, with an arch, crisp, precise British accent. A walking cliché, which tickled me pink, to the point that I had to restrain myself from dissolving into helpless laughter, but may have just been exhaustion. "Although I'm confident we can accommodate most requests."

"I'm pretty simple," I said, my exhaustion eroding my already non-existent filter. "All I need is a bottle of Scotch and some pizza."

Nigel didn't miss a beat. "For Scotch, sir, we

have Yamazaki eighteen year, Macallan twenty-seven year, and Johnnie Walker Blue Label King George the Fifth Edition. And sundry lesser varieties as well, of course. As far as pizza goes, I did have the staff start the wood-fired pizza oven, and I believe Chef Thomas has favored a margherita of late, which I would recommend."

I blinked. "Damn, Nigel, you don't dick around, do you?"

"Certainly not, sir."

I clapped him on the shoulder, receiving a slightly disapproving frown in response. "Margherita and Yamazaki sounds perfect. Thanks, buddy." I glanced past him at the staff. "Now, which one of these fine people can show me to a bedroom?"

Nigel snapped his fingers, and a young man practically leapt out of formation, bowed at me, and gestured at the staircase. I followed him, stopping when I realized Colbie was still down at the bottom of the stairs, hesitating.

"Colbie, you coming?" I asked, holding out my hand to her.

She hid a smile and swept up the stairs after me.

I was struck again by how beautiful Colbie was—even after all we'd been through, her hair was still in perfect red-brown waves around her slim shoulders, and even though her skirt and blouse were a bit wrinkled, she moved with poise, grace, and elegance, still wearing her three-inch heels. Her face was drawn, with dark circles under her eyes, but she held herself upright and smiled at me as she wrapped her hand around my elbow with the kind of formality that would suggest we were departing for the *theah-tah* or something. It was a tiny gesture, her hand around my elbow, but it made me feel . . . proud. I dunno how to else to put it. Like, I was proud she'd chosen to walk with me, to be seen with me. I imagined how amazing it would feel to be out with her, to have people watch us walking down the street together. Of course, they'd probably ask why the hell a gorgeous, classy, elegant lady like Colbie was slumming it with a meathead biker dick like me. And that would be an excellent question. One which I wouldn't have an answer for, other than I didn't know, but thank fuck she was.

Colbie and I followed the butler junior or whatever he was up to the third floor, down a long hallway, and into a distant wing of the house. He gestured at a door near the end of the hallway. "Sir, madam."

I pushed open the door, but Colbie was hesitating again, so I stopped. "Hey man, you wanna give us a moment to talk? Thanks." I put my back to the frame of the open door as the staff kid moved a good fifty paces away and stood at attention. "Okay, so listen, babe. You want a separate room, just say so. I suppose I did kinda make some assumptions, but I hope you'll feel free to correct as needed."

She showed her poker face again, the one that gave away absolutely nothing of what she felt or thought. "So if I said I wanted my own room, and then to go home—alone—in the morning, you wouldn't be upset?"

I shoved my hands in my pockets. "I'll never bullshit you, Colbie, so here's the truth. You say that's what you want, then fine. Will I be upset? Well, yeah, no shit. I like you. A lot. I was hoping to get more time with you, and I don't just mean gettin' busy, either. I like talking to you, being around you. I'd love a chance to watch Loony Tunes in our underwear eating my special homemade pancakes. But if I've read you and this situation wrong, and you're not feeling it, and you just wanna go home, then I'll head into this room and close the door and that'll be that."

I took my hands out of my pockets and stood upright to face her, only a few inches separating us. "But Colbie, honey, there's a fine line between playing hard to get and actually running away. You want me to chase you, I'll chase you. You want me to make you give over control, I can do that. But if you don't actually want this, then you gotta be honest and say so. Don't play fucking head games. I'm not saying you are, but you've got your poker face on, and you're hesitating and acting like you're not sure if I'd want you in this room with me."

She closed her eyes slowly, left them closed for a long moment, her chest rising and falling as she took several deep breaths. "Puck, I—I don't know." She breathed in sharply. "I'm just so tired, and I don't know . . . I don't know"

I stepped closer, but didn't touch her. "What don't you know, sweetheart?"

"This. You. Me. Us. What if what we did on the plane was just . . . adrenaline and hormones and stuff? I'm not saying I regret it, because I don't, but . . . *this*"—she gestured at the open door and the lavish room beyond—"is different. A lot different, and I'm having . . . doubts. I don't *know* what I want, and I don't *know* what I feel, and I don't *know* what this is," Colbie said, her voice low and tense and miserable. "I've been kidnapped, and I've been bored and scared, and I've watched people get shot and stabbed, and I've met you and Layla and all the other women, and I'm so fucking tired I can't think straight, and I'm still scared those guys are gonna show up, and I've been keeping my emotions all bottled up because if I let it all out it won't go back in, and I know I act tough, and I am, I swear, but this has all been scary and I'm—I'm just—"

I could see her eyes watering, and it was obvious she was fighting it, hard. I gathered her close, wrapped my arms around her. "Colbie, baby, you're not deciding your entire future in this single moment. This isn't a make or break, now or never, do or die moment. You wanna come in, come in, you wanna be alone, be alone. If you wanna come in but just hang out, eat, get some rest, whatever, keep it platonic so to speak, that's fine too. There's no pressure."

She didn't respond for a moment. Then she heaved a soft, slow, shuddering sigh. "Let's just get something to eat, have a drink, and go from there." She turned her eyes to mine. "Better yet, can we just crash, right now? I'm so tired I'm not even hungry. I just want to sleep."

She pushed past me and angled directly for the bedroom, crawled onto the high four-poster bed, and closed her eyes, fully clothed, shoes on. She was asleep within seconds.

And I couldn't resist . . . I paused to rip off my boots, and then I climbed up onto the bed with her, spooned up behind her, and closed my own eyes.

I didn't think it was thirty seconds before I fell into a dead sleep.

I woke up several hours later—a glance at the minimalist digital clock on the nightstand told me it was nearly one in the morning. Colbie was absent from the bed, and I heard a shower going, the bathroom door closed.

My stomach made a growling noise, and I wasn't sure how long I'd slept, or what time it had been when we'd arrived here. I'd been in a fog; it was all a blur. We'd dozed on the flight over the Atlantic, but upright airplane sleep doesn't really count, not like a deep sleep in a real bed.

Point was, it was the middle of the night and I was wide awake and ravenous. I dialed the kitchen on the room phone, got a real person on the other end who seemed a little too eager to send up Scotch and pizza. Colbie took her time in the shower, a luxury she'd sure as hell earned. Even after the shower shut off, the door stayed closed. While she was in the bathroom, a knock on the door finally roused me out of the bed.

I answered the door to find an older woman in a shin-length black dress with a white apron, her hair done in a high, severe bun, wearing sensible sturdy black clogs, the kind chefs and servers wear. She had a food service cart, on which was an absolutely humongous thin-crust margherita pizza, steaming hot and smelling delicious. Also on the tray was a bottle of Yamazaki Scotch, two crystal tumblers, and a silver bucket of ice.

"Thanks," I said, pulling the tray into the room.

She gave the same shallow upper body bow the other guy had given me and backed away a step. "Is there anything else I can bring you, sir?" she asked, her voice containing a faint Scottish accent.

"No, thanks." I tilted my head. "You know, a lifetime of living out of hotels has me feeling like I should tip you, but I'm not sure how this whole thing works, here."

The woman frowned. "I would be insulted if you tried, sir. Mr. Roth pays us handsomely."

"Oh, well, okay then." I gestured at the Scotch. "You want a tipple?"

She let out a hint of a smile. "Oh, no, sir. I couldn't, I'm working. And really, Scotch isn't to my taste anyway." She pointed at the bottle. "That's a gift from Mr. Roth to you, as a matter of fact."

She lifted it by the neck and presented it to me, sommelier style. "It's the Yamazaki Fifty-year, two-thousand-five release."

I eyed the label in disbelief. "No fucking way."

She handed it to me. "Indeed, sir." She backed away another step, bowing again. "If that's all, I shall leave you to it. A good evening to you, Mr. Lawson."

And then she was gone, and I pulled the cart into the room, cradling the bottle of Scotch in the nook of my arm like it was a baby.

Colbie came out of the bathroom at that moment, her hair damp and brushed back over her head, wrapped up in a thick plush robe.

She eyed the way I was cradling the booze. "You must really love Scotch," she said, a laugh in her voice.

"Damn straight," I answered, "especially when Roth sends me a ridiculously expensive bottle as a thank you."

She eyed the pizza. "You read my mind. I woke up hungry."

I guided Colbie to the nearest seating option, a deep, plush, burnt velvet couch arranged in front of a marble fireplace, with matching chairs on either side. She sank into the couch with a grateful sigh, and immediately went after the pizza. I followed suit, sitting down beside her, close but not touching her, pouring us both a glass of Scotch. We devoured the entire pizza in what must have been record time, and we each finished a full glass of Scotch, and we did so without a damn word passing between us, the silence comfortable.

When we were both done eating, we wiped our hands on napkins and sank back into the couch with the glasses of Scotch, sipping, and enjoying not having to be in action or under stress.

Colbie's eyes were closed, and she squeezed them shut, then blinked them open rapidly, darting her gaze away from me, her chest rising sharply as she sucked in a breath.

Reality was catching up to her, I'd guess.

I shifted a little closer. "Wanna talk about it?" I asked.

Comforting weepy females wasn't really in my repertoire of skills, but the situation was the situation, and I had to do what I could, even if it was just sit here and pat her back awkwardly like some hapless teenaged doofus.

She shook her head, and stared into space for a minute. And then with a sigh, she leaned forward and set the glass down so she could bury her face in her hands.

She stayed in that position for a long time, and I

sat beside her, content to wait and just be there. After a couple minutes of near total silence, except for our breathing and the ticking of a clock somewhere in the room, I heard a sniffle from beneath her hands. And then her shoulders shook a little. And then a little harder, and she sniffled again.

I tentatively slid my arm over her shoulders. "Hey, listen, there's no shame in letting it out, babe. You went through a hell of a hard time, and you're allowed to let it out. Now's as good a time as any. You're safe, we're safe. For one thing, I'm here, and ain't nobody getting within twenty feet of you while I'm breathin'. And for another thing, this place belongs to the one and only Valentine Roth. Nobody is getting close to us, not here, not tonight. And you will be taken care of in the future, okay? You're on a very short list of people for whom Nicholas Harris and Valentine Roth will provide personal security service free of charge for as long as it's needed, and that's no joke. Harris and Roth are among the most powerful people on the planet, and that's no bullshit. Roth could get a goddamn Apache if he wanted one, and Harris could fly it."

I pulled her closer.

"Shit, I'm rambling," I said. "I don't know how to be the sweet comforting kinda guy, Colbie. But I'm here. And if you need a shoulder, mine are plenty big."

Colbie sniffled again, but it was laced with

laughter. "Why would anyone need an attack heli-copter, Puck?"

"You'd be surprised, babe." I laughed. "You never know when a few dozen Hellfire rockets are just what the doctor ordered."

She laughed again, and then let out a sigh, and her shoulders shook. "I just can't shake it. I keep—I keep reliving the moment they took me, over and over and over again. I thought sleeping would help, but it's . . . I'm—"

"Talk it out. It helps." I held her against me. "Tell me what happened."

She swallowed hard. "It was after work. I'd ac-tually left early because I'd gotten everything done, and it was Wednesday, and my favorite sushi bar has really good happy hour specials on Philadelphia rolls, which are my favorite, and I just wanted to get some sushi and go home and relax. I'd been kicking my ass, trying to nail down a really big order, and I'd finally gotten it, so sushi was my little celebration. I walked out of the building, hit the sidewalk, started walking toward the sushi place, just a couple blocks down." She shuddered all over. "This plain white van with some generic company name on the side pulled a stop on the curb ahead of me. The doors flew open and four big men in worker's coveralls jumped out in front of me. One grabbed my feet, one grabbed my shoulders, one put a bag over my head, and then they all tossed me into the van. I heard the doors close, felt the van start to move. My hands were yanked behind my back and tied off with something cold and hard, zipties probably. None of them even said a word. I never had a chance to even scream—it just happened so fast. Literally, I had the bag over my head and was tied up in the back of the van in under fifteen seconds."

I blew out a breath. "Shit, that's pro, man. I mean, to pull off a snatch that smooth, that fast, in broad daylight in the middle of Manhattan? They must've done it a thousand times."

"I know, I had the same thought. I knew I was being kidnapped, and since there's no one to pay ransom, it was obvious what they were going to sell me for." She trembled, sniffed, and now I heard the tears in her voice, even though she was still bent over, face in her hands, hair obscuring her features. "There wasn't anything I could do. Not a damn thing. The zipties were too tight, I couldn't see, and—I started talking, asking what they wanted, begging them to let me go, which I knew was as stupid as struggling, but I couldn't just lie there and accept it, you know? But then they stuck a needle in my arm, and I passed out. Next thing I knew, I was sitting in that old airliner, still tied up, all woozy, surrounded by a bunch of other women, some tied up, some sleeping, some awake and not tied up."

"And then the flight to Kiev."

She nodded. "I had no idea where we were going,

obviously. And there were guards on the flight, ten or twelve of them, armed with machine guns. They sat in every other row and if anyone tried to move or talk, we'd get a gun shoved in our faces. No talking, no moving." She sucked in a breath, held it, let it out slowly. "I felt like there wasn't much chance they'd actually shoot us, since we were only valuable alive as a commodity, but . . ."

She sniffed. "I was scared. I thought about trying to . . . I don't know. Do something. But I didn't—I didn't want to die." Her voice broke.

I felt her shaking again, and I realized she was still fighting the urge to cry. I pulled her closer, and she nuzzled against my chest, like she wanted to burrow into me, so I lifted her onto my lap and twisted on the couch to lay her on my chest. "Let it out, Colbie. Just let it out."

She shook her head. "I don't know how."

I ran my hand up and down her back, over her shoulders, smoothed my fingers through her silky auburn hair, sticking to comforting, non-erogenous touches. I felt the tension slowly bleed out of her, felt her melt against me. I wanted to say something to her, but I wasn't sure what. *It's okay, it's okay, it's okay*? That was bullshit. It wasn't okay, and it didn't have to be okay, which was the entire point—if it was okay, why would she be crying? Shushing her? She wasn't a baby to shush and rock and shit. What else was there to say? *I'm here?* Duh, obviously I was there; she was lying on top of me, ergo . . . I was there.

What other comfort could I offer her? Not fuckin' much. Words wouldn't fix the hurt or the fear or the trauma. All I really had to offer was my presence. So that's what I gave her, my hands roaming her back and shoulders and combing through her hair, not trying to cop some kind of feel, not pushing her, not demanding anything from her.

And, apparently, that's what broke through. She didn't shake, didn't sob or howl or wail or do any of that shit. She just . . . cried. Softly, quietly. I felt her tears wet my shirt, heard her sniffle now and again, felt her body wrack now and again, and I just kept doing what I'd been doing, gliding my hands in circles around her back, massaging her shoulders, teasing my fingers through the mass of her hair.

And then I was seized by some mushy, fuckin' stupid-ass impulse—I kissed the top of her head.

I hoped she'd let it go, just accept it and not make a big deal of it.

But Colbie wouldn't be Colbie if she weren't a ball-buster.

Her crying paused, and she twisted her head to meet my gaze; her eyes were red and damp, and curious, and . . . I wasn't sure what else. "Did you . . . did you just . . . kiss my head?"

I rolled a shoulder in a not-quite-a-shrug movement thing. "Yeah, I'm not sure what came over me."

She did a weird thing where she sniffled and

tears slipped down her cheek, but she also smiled at me and laughed. "It was sweet."

I swallowed hard. "It was weird. It's like my mouth was possessed or something."

She wriggled and somehow ended up closer to my face, and it took a shitload of focus to not make it sexual, to not let my dick do the deciding.

"I liked it," she whispered.

"Yeah?"

She nodded, her hands resting on my chest, now. "It was sweet. You should do it again."

She didn't tip her head forward or lay it on my chest, so I improvised—I kissed her forehead. Like before, it was a slow, soft, hesitant thing, entirely outside my realm of experience. But if she liked it, I was willing to go with it.

Colbie's smile spread and brightened, and she wriggled farther up my body again, and it was harder to stop myself from ripping her robe off and doing some serious ravaging. I was glad I didn't, though, because what Colbie did next blew my mind. She kissed me on the cheek. Her lips were tender and sweet as sugar and warm and wet, and the slow delicate kiss to my cheek above my beard made my heart thump and hammer and pitter patter like the bunny rabbit from that stupid Disney movie about the orphaned deer baby.

My adrenaline gland was, like, broken. Skydiving, firefights, car chases . . . my pulse stayed flat. Physical exertion got it pumping, of course, but that was different. Women, well . . . they never made me sweat, much less made my heart go pitter-fuckin'-patter.

I thought I stopped breathing when Colbie Danvers kissed my cheek.

"Wow," I breathed. "Never been kissed like that before."

She frowned. "Never? By anyone? Not even your mom?"

I managed an approximation of a casual shrug. "Nah. Ma was a hooker, and she vanished when I was like three or some shit. I don't remember her, and she sure as shit wasn't the type to kiss my face."

"And Raquel—"

"Wasn't like that."

"How about another one, then, to make up for lost time?" She slid closer and ever so gingerly touched her lips to the other cheek, and my eyes fluttered closed and my heart clanged and pounded like I was suffering from cardiac arrhythmia. My other heart—the non-physical one—did all sorts of weird shit, feeling things I didn't have words for or the emotional understanding to quantify. My dick was screaming *GET SOME, MOTHERFUCKER!* and my hands were twitching with the need to grab on and never let go, and my mouth was . . .

Stupid.

My mouth was stupid.

I kissed her cheek. A gentle touch, a brush of my

lips against her velvet skin.

And she angled her face just so, nudging her lips against the corner of my mouth. I felt her breath, felt her chest swell and contract against mine, and I felt her heart slam just as hard as mine, felt her fingers on the skin of my chest just above the neckline of my T-shirt tremble.

She didn't move away but held where she was, trembling, breathing on my lips.

Waiting.

As obvious an invitation as I was going to get, I realized.

So slowly, giving her plenty of time to tell me I was misreading things, I slid my hands into her hair and cupped the delicate curve of the back of her neck and pulled her mouth to mine, sliding my lips against hers, tracing the parted seam of her mouth; her teeth and then her tongue was gliding on mine, searching and scouring and tasting and tangling.

Oh.

Oh.

This wasn't just a kiss, it was . . . a Kiss. The kind of kiss that required the capital letter because it was something more, a kiss that transcended the mere connection of mouths, but was a door to the soul, hers and mine.

A Kiss.

Colbie pulled away first. "Wow," she breathed. "Never been kissed like that before."

I laughed at her use of my words. "Me neither, sweet thing."

"Maybe we could do it again?"

"At least once more. Maybe twice."

"At least. I mean, we don't have to limit ourselves," she whispered back, a smile on her lips.

"Limits are stupid."

My heart palpitated and my hands shook on her cheeks, and my cock was hard, curling painfully against my zipper, unable to stretch fully erect, but I didn't want to let go of her, didn't want to break the kiss because it was *everything*, and I didn't care if I breathed, didn't care if I ever came up from this kiss. I could've die then and have been content, because her mouth on mine was enough to erase everything that had gone before in my life, good or bad.

She slid downward to her back, bringing me with her. Her thighs parted to accept my weight, and I levered over her, one hand now cupped under her neck, the other braced in the cushion. Her heels hooked around my back, and her hips flexed, ground against me, and her hands groped me wherever she could reach, as hungry for my skin as I was hers. I felt her fingers plucking at my shirt, finding the hem, and then she ripped it over my head, only breaking the kiss long enough to admit the collar past my face, and then her lips were on mine again, hungry, devouring, eager.

HOLY SHIT.

This girl. This girl.

I paused for breath, but only because I was actually dizzy. She gazed up at me with her gorgeous gray eyes, heavy-lidded, lust-hazed. "God . . . *damn*, Colbie."

"You're wearing too many clothes," she whispered.

10

GIVE HIM THE CRAZY

ONCE I COMMITTED TO SOMETHING, I WAS ALL in, no holding back, no half-measures. I got aggressive, and I didn't let anything slow me down or stop me; this quality had served me well in the business world, had helped me acquire accounts other reps in my department hadn't been able to land because I didn't quit and I didn't accept no and I never gave up.

I was committed to this moment with Puck. I accepted as much as I could and I had no idea what was going to come after. I might get emotionally invested and have my heart broken, but I knew I could survive that. I'd throw myself into work and probably take a vow of celibacy, but I'd survive it and wouldn't go back to drugs.

Or maybe I'd get some insanely good orgasms out of it and that'd be that.

Ha, right. I didn't believe that as the thought crossed my mind. I mean, it wasn't like I was falling in love with the guy—I'd just met him, after all. But you could be deeply emotionally invested in someone without some kind of *TRUE LOVE*, right? And if he fucked as good as he kissed, I was totally going to get emotionally involved. Hell, I already was. He saved me. He got me. I already didn't want this night to be over, and we hadn't even started yet. I was still totally clothed, and he wasn't halfway naked yet. I got rid of his shirt, at least, and *damn*, was I glad I did.

He was a beast. He was built like The Mountain from *Game of Thrones*—a foot shorter, granted, but the same essential build: solid slabs of heavy, hard muscle. Huge power, rather than sharply-etched and finely-toned magazine-cover shred. Massive arms, a heavy hard chest, shoulders like mountain ranges, abs so hard you could crush stones on them. There was a layer of fat on them, but a slight, small one, which told me he ate because he enjoyed food, but he also ate healthily, the right foods, a lot of it, and he didn't deprive himself of the things he enjoyed. He worked out, ate right, and enjoyed life—and looked damn amazing because of it.

I ran my hands over his body, exploring his skin and muscle, enjoying his physique with my hands as much as my eyes. I didn't hide my appreciation, nor my lust.

I *wanted* him.

I was going to have him, and I was going to get every last little bit of pleasure and fun and enjoyment out of this as I could, for as long as I could. If it ran its course and ended, so be it, but I was all in until that moment came.

I slid my palms over his back, across his shoulders, around to his abs, and then reached for his fly, gliding my hand over the huge bulge at his zipper. Instead of allowing me to touch him, he grabbed my wrists and pinioned my hands over my head.

"Puck?" I questioned.

He held my wrists there against the armrest until he was satisfied that I wouldn't move. "Hush a moment, babe. I want to focus on this."

"On what?"

"I want to memorize the way you look, just like this."

My body was bare, and I gasped for breath, needing him, wanting to be touched, to be kissed—to touch and to kiss. I arched my back, pressing my breasts into the air, toward him. "Don't make me wait long, Puck, please."

He didn't answer. I was naked, completely bare to his gaze, and his eyes were wide with lust and appreciation. I didn't wax or shave, but I did trim down to a barely-there fuzz, and even that fuzz was damp with my leaking essence; I was soaked, dripping with desire.

He just stared at me, his eyes raking from my face to my tits to my pussy, and back up, over and over, as if he couldn't decide which he enjoyed looking at most.

"Puck, please. Touch me," I breathed.

He bent forward, and his mouth covered my left breast, his tongue swirling around my nipple as his lips suctioned hard, making me suck in a sharp gasp as a string of heat lanced from my nipple to my core. His fingers found my right nipple, and he was licking and sucking, switching, right and left, kissing and pinching. His chest was covered with a light smattering of coarse dark hair that brushed against my belly, scraping and tickling and teasing.

"How's this?" he asked, palming my breast, kneading, squeezing, pinching, flicking.

"So good."

"You have perfect breasts."

"They're small."

"C-cup, or I'm a monkey's uncle."

"So?

"So they're perfect." He cupped one of my tits. "Just slightly more than a handful. Absolutely perfect."

I flexed my hips to press my pussy against his waist. "Puck, please."

He laughed and slid downward, slinking off the arm of the couch, and then grabbed me by the hips and yanked me toward him so my ass was on the arm of the couch and my upper body on the cushions. My heels were over his shoulders and my pussy spread open, and I felt his warmth breath on my thighs. I stopped breathing, and my eyes fluttered closed; I forced them open so I could watch.

His bald scalp was all I could see between my thighs, and then I felt his tongue.

"Ohh. Oh . . . holy shit." I cupped his head, holding him there. "God yes."

He flicked his tongue up my slit. "You like this, huh?"

I flexed my hips as he dragged his tongue through my sex, moaning. "More."

He rumbled in laughter, and I felt two fingers pry apart my pussy lips, baring my clit, and another finger slid into my channel; his tongue lapped against me, and now my moan was almost a wail, a sound of raw, distilled ecstasy. Two slow swipes of his tongue, his finger sliding in, curling, and finding that perfect magical spot nobody else had ever found, and I rocked on the edge of orgasm.

He didn't pull me back from the edge. He felt me quaking and shuddering, heard the breathlessness in my moans, and knew how close I was. He pressed his finger against that spot inside me and massaged, and his lips closed over my clit and he sucked hard, his tongue flicking wildly, and I was consumed, fire eating through me, an orgasm wrenching met with twisting power. I arched, and I wailed, and he didn't slow down. He added a second finger inside me and ground them in and out, and he released his suction and returned to slow circles around my clit, not quite touching it directly. I ached, the orgasm shaking me still, his tongue and fingers preventing the climax from receding.

He let me teeter there, shaking in the throes of aftershocks.

And then he scraped his tongue-tip against my clit, once, twice, and I was arched and spasming, gasping, unable to moan or scream as he sent me over the edge again. A wave of climax hit me like a freight train, sending me higher than any hit of smack I'd ever put into my veins, but this time the only drug was Puck, his fingers and his tongue. I could indulge in this drug as much as I wanted and never get enough. Oh fuck, fuck—the orgasm crescendoed and I found my voice in a sudden and hoarse wailing scream, yet he had no mercy on me. His fingers squelched in and out of me hard and fast, curled to grind against my G-spot, and his tongue was wild, crazy, fast, tireless.

I couldn't stop. Didn't try, but couldn't have even if I had. Again, and again, and again, quaking, wracking, wrenching waves of fiery bliss, nonstop.

I realized, in a dizzy blast of awareness, that Puck did exactly what he'd promised: made me come harder than I'd ever come in my life, too many times to count. I'd never begun counting, and I wasn't sure if each wave was its own orgasm or one continuous rushing explosion.

I was utterly powerless.

He refused to let me down from the heights of climax, and I couldn't stop him, didn't try, didn't want to. He kept me there, fingering my channel and tonguing my clit, and now I felt his fingers that had held me open for his tongue, release me and slide up my torso to pinch my nipple, adding a whole new layer to the orgasms coruscating through me.

The orgasms built, multiplied, intensified, and I lost track of time, of how long Puck had been inducing this rapture within me, lost track, drowned in it, reveled it.

He allowed me a moment to breathe, slowing his fingers and tongue, sliding those thick strong fingers in and out slowly, gently, his tongue lapping lazily, and I shook and shuddered each time his tongue touched my clit, flinched, quaked, gasped. I felt the movement of those fingers as a tease, as a poor imitation of what I really wanted.

Yet I was incapable of speech, could only whimper and shriek as he ramped up the speed once more, building me back up to another series of jarring, juddering, explosive climaxes, and I didn't know how that was possible, how he could do that, how he knew my body and my reactions so much better than anyone else ever had, including myself.

I felt faint.

He brought me to the edge, then slowed, brought me to the edge, then slowed. I'd been at or over that edge so many times that my body wanted to live there, stay there, get there, but he'd prevented me every time, teasing me now that I was at the raw and ragged end of my limits, gasping, limp, unable to flex my hips or grind into his touch anymore, whimpering nonstop, moaning and nearly crying with the intensity of it all. Needing desperately to reach that edge one last time.

He palmed my breast, squeezing, fondling, flicking my nipple, and then he suckled my clit in a sudden rough scrape of hypersensitive erect flesh between his teeth, and his fingers pinched my nipple so hard I screamed and he added a third finger and began fucking me with them hard and rough and fast, squelching wetly, and I was nothing at all but his touch, I was only the blinding bliss he dragged out of me. He didn't stop, this time, and I knew this orgasm would be too much.

"PUCK . . ." I whispered, breathless.

At the edge . . .

Teetering, rocking, gasping . . .

And then I toppled over it, dizzy, lungs aching, my whole body spasming wildly.

Screaming so loud my throat went hoarse.

Blackness subsumed me, and I felt myself fall under, twisting into darkness.

I woke up lying on the bed, my shirt and bra removed from my wrists. I blinked my eyes open, and

Puck was standing beside me, sucking on his fingers.

"You weren't kidding, back in Kiev." I sat up, reaching for him.

He smirked at me. "Told you, some things I don't joke about."

His zipper was bulging still, but he was slightly out of reach. "Come here, Puck." I slid off the bed, hit my feet, but my legs were wobbly and weak and gave out.

Puck caught me. "I made you come so hard you can't walk," he said, letting his hands roam. "And you've been unconscious for almost a full minute."

I held on to him, let him hold me upright. "No kidding. That was more intense than all the orgasms I've had in my life combined." I bit his lower lip between my teeth, sucked it into my mouth, and then kissed him, tasting my essence on his lips, on his breath, on his tongue. I moaned at the taste of my pussy on his breath, and he moaned back as his hands cupped my ass.

"Jesus, this ass."

"Mmm-hmm?" I moaned, making it a question.

I was too busy to actually ask the question, since my mouth was otherwise occupied on his throat, his cheek, his ear.

"God yeah," he breathed. "The things I want to do to your ass, Colbie."

I found my feet, and my legs finally decided to hold me, which thank god left my hands free, since I didn't need to hold on to Puck for balance. I used this to great benefit, clutching at the broad hard curves of his body, the bulging muscles. Chest, arms, abs . . . so much muscle, so hard, so beautiful, so much to touch, and I touched it all, humming in pleasure as I slowly, unhurriedly found my way downward.

"What do you want to do my ass, Puck?" I found the button of his fly, and popped it open. "Tell me."

"Once you free that beast, babe, foreplay is over," Puck warned.

I lowered the zipper and grabbed the waist of the jeans to shove them down, using my foot to press them against the floor, and he stepped out of them. His boxer-briefs I took more time with, toying with him. Running my finger around the elastic waistband. Tugging it away so his cock sprung upward, then letting the elastic snap back into place, but he was so huge and so hard the tip peeked up over the band. I rubbed the tip with my finger, teasing him.

"That's the plan," I murmured. "Now, you never answered. I want to know your plans for my ass."

He palmed the bubble in question, squeezing and kneading and cupping and caressing. "God, everything."

"You want to fuck me there?" I breathed.

"Eventually."

"Then what else?"

"I want to scrub you clean in the shower, and then get on my knees and kiss every beautiful inch."

He lifted the globes and pulled them apart, then let them fall, bouncing. "Then I'll lick you until you beg me to put something inside you."

"Something like what?"

He traced a finger over the crack, teasing. "Like this."

I leaned forward, against him, pressing my lips to his ear. "Say please, Puck." I tugged his underwear down, and he stepped out of them, and I curled my hand around his huge erect length. "You never know what I might let you do unless you ask."

He stroked that seam again, and I nuzzled my face into the side of his neck, stroking his cock slowly. I shifted my feet apart, pressing my body against his.

"Can I put my finger in your ass, Colbie? Please?" His voice was low and rough.

I bit him on the side of the neck. "Do it." I squeezed his cock as I spoke, jerking him roughly.

"Jesus, Colbie."

"Just a little."

I held on to his scalp with one hand, his cock with the other, and kept my face buried in his neck, leaning forward to offer him access. He palmed my ass cheek, held it for a long moment, and then I felt him lift his hand to his mouth. His nose sank into my hair and he inhaled deeply, and one hand tugged my cheek aside, and the other pressed against me. I felt wet warmth, and then pressure. I moaned at the sensation, alien and somehow pleasurable.

"Never . . . oh—*oh* god . . . I've never let anyone
. . ." I breathed. "Until you. Until now."

"Never?"

"No, never." I stroked him again, slowly, gently,
and then held onto him as he wiggled his fingertip
against me. "Never trusted anyone like I do you."

He palmed my face and turned me toward him,
and he kissed me. And as his tongue tangled with
mine, his hand left my face and traveled south, between us. Found my slit, drifted in. Teased the seam
and then found my clit, slathered in my own juices.
I groaned as he filled all of my senses, his mouth on
mine, his finger wiggling deeper and deeper inside
me in that place no one had ever touched.

I batted his hand away from my pussy, lifting up
on my toes and tilting his cock toward me. "This—I
need *this*."

"Now?"

I hooked a leg around his hip, nudged the fat soft
springy head of his beautiful cock into my entrance
and worked my hips back and forth slowly until he
was inside me. And then I wrapped my arms around
his neck and held on, whimpering when his finger
penetrated me enough that I was left gasping and
shocked at the fullness, because *fuck fuck fuck fuck
FUCK* he was huge, stretching my pussy apart and
making me ache and burn, unable to move for the
throbbing, glowing, burning ache of him inside me,
so much more than I'd thought, so much bigger now

that he was inside me than he'd felt in my hand.

"*Puck* . . ." I moaned.

"Okay, sweetheart?"

I bit his earlobe hard enough that he grunted in surprise. "More."

He flexed his hips and drove fully into me, and I cried out, because I hadn't had half of his length inside me. *Now* I was full and beyond full, because he'd used the moment of surprise to slide his finger deeper.

Puck thrust in, then stopped abruptly. "Shit. I'm not wearing a condom."

"Damn it." I sagged against him. "I need this, Puck."

"Me too."

"I'm covered, and I'm clean, but . . ."

"Me too," he agreed, "but we can't take any chances."

I shook my head. "No." I ground against him, taking him deeper. "But you feel so fucking good like this."

He returned my movement, thrusting into me, making me bounce upward. "So fucking good. Too good."

And then he took two easy steps forward and tilted toward the bed, bending over, depositing me on my back, kissing me as he pulled out of me completely.

I actually whimpered at the loss of him. "Come

back, Puck."

He ripped open the drawers of the nightstand tables on both sides slamming them closed as he found nothing. Then to the bathroom, and god he was hot, his ass hard and taut. Drawers, cabinets, rifling, cursing. Then one last cabinet, and a triumphant shout.

"Thank fuck!" He stood in the doorway with a box of condoms, unopened.

My eyes latched onto his dick as he swaggered back into the bedroom from the bathroom. It was such a lovely organ, thick and hard, long, straight, glistening. Bulbous head, taut heavy balls, a shaft I couldn't wait to get my hands around, couldn't wait to feel inside me again. He ripped open the box and set it aside, tore a square packet free and tossed the rest of the string on the bedside table next to the box. I grabbed his cock and plunged my fists around him, stroking him from root to tip eagerly as he tore the packet open with his teeth.

I snatched the condom from him, held his cock in one hand and rolled the latex on with the other. When he was covered, I rolled to my back on the bed, not letting go of his shaft, pulling him with me.

He was levered over me, brown eyes on mine, palms in the pillow beside my ears, arms like pillars on either side of me. I guided him to me, not taking my eyes off his. Mine went wide as I was split open by him, my mouth locked in a breathless moue, brows drawn. I felt every glorious inch of him as he slid into me, felt the incredible, electric rippling perfection of his cock as it glided into me, and fuck, oh god, so much. I couldn't breathe for how he felt inside me. I spread my legs apart, and he pushed as deep as he could go, and I found my breath enough to gasp in rapture when his hips bumped against mine, his balls slapping against my taint as he buried fully inside me. He focused his weight on one arm and palmed my breast, purely for his own pleasure, and yet the feel of his rough callused strong hand on my tit scraping my nipple was so delicious I shuddered, and then he bent and claimed my mouth, and I rolled my hips, because I needed more, more.

"Oh fuck, Puck, please." I clutched his ass and pulled at him, tugging him closer to me.

He gave me exactly what I wanted, movement, his huge perfect dick pulling out and stretching me as it slid, and then just the plump head was left in me, and he hesitated, teasing, grinning down at me. He teased me, nudging not all the way in, backing off when I flexed to beg for his length inside me.

"Don't tease me, Puck."

"No?" He laughed. "It's so fun, though."

He apparently needed to learn that just because I was on bottom didn't mean I was helpless. I reached between us, cupped his balls in my hand, massaging them, and then slid my two middle fingers toward his taint, and with my other hand clutched his shaft. Stroked him over the condom, cradling his balls, teasing his taint. He moaned then laughed.

"Fine, fine." He bent and nipped my upper lip sharply. "No more teasing."

I released him, and he pushed into me, and I moaned as he filled me. "Oh god, Puck. Puck." I gripped his ass in both hand and held on, urging him to move faster, to give me more. "How do you feel so fucking amazing?"

It was like whatever I might have felt before with anyone else had ceased to exist in my memory. There was nothing else, no one else. Size, strength, build, looks; it wasn't because of any one of those things. It was something I didn't have any explanation for, he just felt better. *Was* better, in ever way.

"I dunno, Colbie, but you . . . Jesus, babe. You are *it*."

I matched his movements, meeting him thrust for thrust, both of us going slow, not willing to rush this. "I feel like . . . I don't know how to explain it. Like I was doing it wrong my whole life. Or like everything else, every*one* else is just . . . a pathetic imitation."

And this was missionary; I didn't even *like* missionary.

He moved in me a few more times, and I felt something rising inside me already. I slid my fingers between us, found my clit.

"Yeah, Colbie. Let me watch you touch your pussy." He leaned back on his knees, pushed my knees up, tucking my feet against his chest so I was opened and splayed apart for him. And like this, oh god . . . I could feel him deeper like this, almost like he was thicker and harder and longer, and his eyes focused on my fingers as I pressed them to my clit. He glided into me slowly and smoothly, so his thrust in was indecipherable from the withdrawal, and my fingers flew around my clit, and I felt tension ratchet up inside me, torsion focused low inside me, heat building, desperation rising, my chest heaving as my breathing went ragged, sending my tits bouncing, and I watched his gaze flit to them as they swayed and swung and bounced, to my fingers, to his cock driving in and out of me. I lifted up for a moment, to watch as his cock vanished inside me, watched in rapt fascination as my pussy swallowed his enormous length.

The orgasm stole over me, starting slow, beginning deep inside me, different entirely from the climaxes he'd given me with his fingers and mouth. Those were sharp and fast and hot; the orgasm that detonated slowly inside me now was something else, slow and expansive and deep and starting dull but gaining strength and heat and sharpness as I neared the crescendo. My hips were bucking and he was holding on to my thighs, just below the bend in my knees, keeping my legs pushed back against my torso, stretching me open, and his amazing cock was driving into me, pushing me higher and higher. I watched him move, watched his body flex, watched those beautiful massive slabs of hard muscle shift and ripple under his skin, watched his eyes roam my body, and I knew he was devouring me with his gaze, loving the way I looked naked beneath him, my tits bouncing as he fucked me, his hips slapping against my ass, and his eyes met mine, and I gave him all the vulnerability I had in my returned gaze.

"Come for me, Cole."

Cole . . . Nobody had called me that since my sister died; my eyes watered and my breath caught in my throat, choking me.

He didn't miss it, and his movement faltered. "Holy shit—Colbie—what'd I say, honey?"

I shook my head, found my voice. "Don't—don't you dare stop, Puck Lawson." My voice shook though.

I wasn't going to come, or break apart, I was going to shatter.

Puck thrust into me, holding my legs, watching me carefully, and I was too much of a mess to push anything down or block any emotions or take anything back.

I gave in to everything going on inside me, the need to cry, the need to scream with pleasure, the need to reach this precipice with Puck and throw myself over it.

My fingers went wild, and I gasped and felt it slash through me, the beginnings of the orgasm. Tears leaked, and I ignored them, letting them fall unheeded.

Puck released one of my legs, reaching down to brush my tears aside. I caught at his hand, nuzzled into his palm, one cheek and then the other, smearing my tears on his skin, and kept my gaze locked brazenly on his with all my crazy volatile emotions on full display. Gave him the full force of my craziness, to see if he wanted more.

I nuzzled into his palm again, and my heart squeezed as he moved with me, filling me beautifully in thrust after thrust, fucking deep until my breath caught from the aching thrill of him filling me.

"Ohh—oh god, Puck . . . fuck, I'm coming, I'm coming, Puck, Jesus, I'm coming so hard—"

It was exactly what I'd thought it was going to be, a shattering, all-consuming nova of ecstasy centered on our joined bodies. I cried out as I broke, sobbing as it smashed through me in a drowning wave of gutting heat and releasing pressure. I felt the walls of my pussy clamp down on Puck's cock, gripping so tight he hissed in surprise.

At the peak of my orgasm, while I was shuddering and screaming, I hooked my leg behind Puck's and pushed on his chest, flipping us over, and he rolled so I was on top. The moment his back hit the pillow, I caught my weight on his chest and draped my hair around his face and slid the tips of my tits against his mouth and sank down on him as slowly as I could.

"Ohh my holy fucking shit, Colbie, Jesus," he

ground out through gritted teeth, breathless. "Holy fuck."

His sounds of pleasure were muffled then, as I brushed my nipple through his lips, and he latched on, suckling on me until I yelped from the sharpness of his suction and teeth. I lifted up, closing my eyes to focus on the feel of his cock sliding between the lips of my pussy, and then I drove down to sink him into me, and I reveled in that sensation too, taking my time with each thrust, each stroke, whimpering and gasping and moaning because I was still coming. Puck's hands gripped my hips, and he helped me with my thrusts, lifting me up, tugging me down, and we set a perfect rhythm together. I braced one hand on the center of his chest and slid my other between our bodies and touched myself as we fucked together.

"I love how you touch yourself, Colbie," he murmured. "I love watching you touch your pussy while I fuck you."

"I think I'm the one fucking you right now," I said, bringing my knees beneath me so I could slap my ass down on him, showing him how hard I could fuck him.

He groaned, lost his words as I took him the way I wanted him, harder and harder, my ass crashing against his hips and thighs, his cock driving into me in beautifully hard thrusts, and all he could do was keep up, hold on to my hips and bury his face in my neck.

"Admit it," I whispered in his ear.

"You're fucking me," he rumbled.

"No, not that." I pressed my forehead to his, and our eyes met and my fingers flew and his cock brought me to another orgasm, and I felt him shuddering beneath me, heard him groaning, felt sweat break out on his body and mine, and I knew he was close too. "Admit that nobody has ever fucked you the way I'm fucking you right now."

"Never . . . ever . . . fucking *ever*," he breathed, gasping, grunting. "And no one ever will."

I bit his lip and then he smashed his mouth against mine in a bruising kiss, and our tongues found each other, soared and danced.

My lips whispered against his. "When you come, say my name." I spoke through gritted teeth, because my climax was endless and furious, and I could barely speak past the shuddering wracking bliss. "Call me Cole, like you did before. Pray to me when you come, Puck."

"Right now, baby, it's happening now, and I can't stop it."

"Don't stop it. I'm still coming. Come with me."

His grip on my hips was bruising, and I loved the pain of it, reminding me of his strength as he shoved me onto his cock. "Cole, oh my god, holy shit—Cole, Cole . . ."

I didn't need to touch myself to finish coming, because his cock did all the work, sliding against me just right, smashing into me, gliding against my G-spot so I broke apart all over again. I clung to him, my hands sliding over his scalp, my arms under his head, my lips stuttering over his mouth, our breathing matched in ragged gasps.

He came, he unleashed himself with a guttural roar, and I was shattering and drowning and crying because he was chanting my name, my nickname, the nickname that no one had called me in twelve years. He came and he chanted *Cole Cole Cole* a thousand times as he thrust into me, fucking me through our orgasm.

Finally, I couldn't move anymore. I collapsed on him, my cheek on his chest, my heart over his heart. I could hear our heartbeats hammering . . . *thumpthumpthumpthump* jackrabbit fast, his breath heaving, sweat slicking his skin, mingling with my own sweat, smearing together.

11

DON'T SAY IT

I'D NEVER CRASHED AFTER SEX. LIKE, I MADE HER pass out, as promised, but I'd never been brought to that point myself. Yet Colbie managed it. I came, and I felt her pussy clamp down around my cock as I came harder than I'd ever come in my life, and then Colbie collapsed on me, and her weight was like a blanket warming me, her hair tickling my nose, her scent in my nostrils, my cock stiff and throbbing and twitching inside her, her pussy clamping spastically. I couldn't move. Couldn't. Wouldn't. Moving never entered my mind. I wrapped my arms around her, felt her fingers tighten into a knot on my chest under her chin, and my eyes fluttered and I just gave in.

And when I came to an unknown amount of time later, Colbie was still on top of me, but I felt wet warmth where her cheek was.

"You're crying," I murmured.

She nodded. "My sister, Danielle . . . she was the only person who'd ever called me Cole before, and when she died, I thought that nickname had died with her. I loved it when she called me that. It was just our thing, and I . . . I don't know. I just loved it."

"Oh god, Colbie, I'm so sorry, I had no idea—"

She lifted up, straddling me, and pressed her fingers over her lips. "Don't. Not all sadness and pain is . . . bad. Yes, I miss her. Yes, there was pain when you called me that. But it also felt . . . *right* . . . to hear you call me that. I'm not going to avoid it just because it still hurts a little. I want you to call me that."

She carefully slid off me, reaching between us to hold the condom in place as I flopped out of her. Clear of me, she glanced at my cock, and at the tip of the condom, drooping heavily with my come. "You came a *lot*," she said with a smirk.

"You do that to me."

"And you came a lot on the plane, too."

"You make me crazy, Colbie. I feel like a fucking teenager around you."

"With a teenager's refractory period?" she asked, sounding eager and hopeful.

I laughed. "Pretty damn close," I said.

She leaned over me, her soft warm breasts flattened on my chest. "Go take that off and come back."

"Yes ma'am," I said, sliding off the bed. Like she

had earlier, when I hit the floor, I wobbled, my legs shaky. "See what you do to me, hot stuff? You fucked me so good I can't walk."

"Get back here and I'll do it again. Except better."

I felt my heart flipping in my chest. Legit, how could sex get any better? More to the point, why on earth would I ever leave this room? I disposed of the condom and returned to the bed, and Colbie's gaze was locked on my cock the whole time, watching it bounce and jiggle and sway as I walked toward her.

"My turn," she said, hopping off the bed.

And you bet your ass I watched that perfect heart-shaped ass of hers as she left. She closed the door and came back out a minute or so later, and she'd teased her hair out. Posing in the doorway, she leaned against it, popping a hip out, one foot crossed over the other.

I sat on the edge of the bed, staring at her. "Colbie, for real, do you have any goddamn idea how perfect you are?"

Flawless creamy skin, tight high full breasts, just wide enough hips, a perfect ass, long thick strong legs, hair that glowed reddish brown in the low lights of the room, an expressive mouth with plump kiss-able lips, eyes that shone like diamonds, storm gray and roiling with emotion she didn't bother hiding. No more poker face. She let me see exactly what she was feeling: she was nervous, letting me stare at her like this, nervous to come back and do this again with me, no longer in the heat of a moment but going in sober and knowing it wasn't just sex but something more, and she was also flush with need, desire raging in her eyes, in the way she pressed her thighs together, one crossed over the other to almost hide the blossom of her pussy.

"Take a shower with me," she murmured. "I wanna play with you in the water."

"I told you what I want to do to you in the shower."

She twisted in place and bent to present me her ass. "Why do you think I'm suggesting it?" she asked, palming her ass cheeks in a teasing bounce.

She swayed back into the bathroom, reached into the stall and turned on the shower, tested the temperature, and then stood waiting for me. I didn't keep her waiting long. Fuck no. I wanted to run in there and fall to my knees in worship, but I didn't want to seem as desperate as I was—and then I thought *fuck that*, yes, I did want her to know exactly how I felt. So I may not have run, but I moved at what I might call an aggressive pace. I pushed her backward into the shower—which was a luxurious affair, of course, a palace of marble, with benches lining two walls, multiple rainfall shower heads with plenty of pressure, all the gels and conditioners and shampoos and soaps one could want.

And yes, I fell to my knees, and I worshipped her body as the hot water soaked her, dampening her hair

and running down her body. I kissed her legs, and
her hips, and her stomach, and her breasts; I kissed
her waist and her sides and the backs of her thighs,
and I kissed the taut round bubbles of her beautiful
ass cheeks, and her spine, and the back of her neck.
I grabbed a bottle of shower gel and squirted it onto
her breasts and into my hands, and I slathered her
with it, roaming her incredible body with hands until she was white with lather, cleaning every inch of
her as thoroughly as I could, and then she twisted in
the spray to wash it away. Standing with her, I twisted
her in place to face the wall, guided her hands to the
wall, and she grinned eagerly at me over her shoulder
as I sank to my knees behind her. I took the shower
gel once more, squirted some into my palm slathered it onto her ass. Pulled apart those firm globes
to bare the sweet tight little rosebud of her asshole.
Worked the soap over it, scrubbing gently, and then
more firmly, watching her reactions as I touched her.
She was watching over her shoulder, biting her lower
lip in anticipation. I reached out blindly and found
the detachable hand-held wand, using it to rinse the
soap away. And then I touched my mouth to her skin,
kissing in circles, random patterns, edging closer and
closer. She hummed nervously as I finally touched
my tongue to her, and then, when I began to flit my
tongue in circles, she whimpered in surprise.

"Oh . . . *ohhhh*. Oh god, Puck. I *really* like that,"
she breathed.

"Oh yeah?"

"Mmm-hmm."

I stiffened my tongue and kept going, and she whimpered again.

"But—"

I glanced up at her. "But what, babe?"

She blushed, which seemed silly, but I had a feeling she wasn't used to asking for what she wanted, not in so many words, and especially not this, which she'd admitted she'd never done before. "Your finger."

I spat on my hand and applied the saliva to her, working it against the knot of muscle, and I felt her tighten at my touch. "Relax, babe."

"I'm trying."

"Don't try—just enjoy it." I teased her with my finger, touching, pressing, but not pushing in.

She moaned at my torture, flexing her hips toward me as she warmed to the feeling. "What if— what if I touched myself . . . while you touched me back there?"

"I have a better idea," I said. "Stay just like that, hands on the wall."

I pivoted and put my back to the marble floor and slid underneath her, and saw her staring down at me past the mound of her breasts.

"Oh god." She reached down and cupped the side of my head. "Yes. That. That's a much better idea."

She guided me where she wanted me, holding on to the back of my head as I moved in to taste the sweet sugar of her pussy. Because she tasted like heaven, sweet and smoky and delicious, a taste I'd never get tired of. I worked my finger slowly inside her and used my tongue to work her up to orgasm, bringing her there as fast as I could, no games, no teasing. Just my finger in the tight clamping channel of her asshole and her pussy grinding on my mouth, her hand clutching me hard against her, rocking into me, crying out, wailing loudly as she came apart. I tasted her as she came, lapped and licked and sucked away her juices as she gushed all over my face, my finger pulsing in and out of her. She was still convulsing through her orgasm when I stood up behind her and slid into her, helpless to stop myself. Her pussy clamped down around me as I fucked into her, and she moaned even harder, moving with me until I was at the edge myself, and her fingers were still moving on her clit, and I felt her clamp down and heard her cry out as a second orgasm wrenched through her.

I nearly didn't pull out in time. I felt it hit like an earthquake, and only barely yanked myself out of her tight warm slit. Colbie whirled as I pulled out and wrapped her hands around me, sliding her fists along my length until I collapsed forward against her, pressing my face into her wet tits and gasping raggedly as I exploded, my come spurting all over her sliding fists, all over her belly, all over mine.

"Holy shit, Puck," she breathed into my ear.

"Holy shit," I agreed. "You're always gorgeous,

but you're never sexier than when you're coming."

She pushed me backward, and we both glanced down at the mess I'd made. "Good thing we're in the shower, huh?" she asked, laughing. "The truth is, I feel sexy when you make me come." She grabbed the shower gel and began working it into my skin, "Feel free to make me come as much as you want, as long as you want, any way you want, whenever you want."

I let out a harsh breath at her words. "That's an awfully open-ended invitation, Colbie."

She was lathering the soap over my ass as she answered, taking extra time there, playing with me as if she enjoyed my ass as much as I enjoyed hers. "It was meant to be, Puck." She worked the soap up my back and then down my chest again, and then sank to her knees to wash my calves and then my thighs. "This— you and me, how you make me feel—I don't think I can let go of it. I can't give it up. It feels too amazing. Emotionally, physically, you just . . . you get me."

"Colbie, I—"

"You get me, Puck." She gazed at me so I could see the genuineness and vulnerability in her. "You get me, so . . . you *get* me. For as long as you want me."

I let out a breath. "Cole, honey." Her face twisted in an expression that was equal parts pain and pleasure. "What if I never stop wanting you?" It was a rhetorical question, and she knew it, didn't bother answering, but her sweet, hopeful smile told me everything I needed to know.

We washed each other's hair and rinsed once more, and finally shut off the now lukewarm water.

We dried off, wrapped ourselves in towels, and then sat on the couch, and the conversation that followed was easy and endless, helped along by more of that amazing Scotch.

I'd long since lost track of time, and the only clock was in the bedroom and the blinds were drawn, and I didn't care what time it was. Late night, or early morning. I didn't care. When we were both buzzed, I tugged Colbie to her feet, yanked the towel off her, shed my own, and we fell into bed. I pulled her against my side, her head on my shoulder, the blankets up around us. She threw her leg over mine, pulled my face down hers, and kissed me stupid.

Kissed me breathless.

A kiss that was a Kiss, another one that swept me away, sent me delving into the depths of this wild powerful thing I'd found in this wild, powerful woman.

This time, though, the kiss faded, and our eyes closed, and we fell asleep like that, nuzzled together.

I woke hours later, sunlight peeking around the blinds. Puck was asleep in front of me; his butt snuggled up against my front. I slid my arm under his to clutch his chest. He wiggled his ass against me, burrowing deeper. I was lazy, sleepy, and so comfortable I could lie there forever. I faded back to sleep that way, my face against Puck's broad back, my nose between his shoulder blades, my arm over his hip, my hand on his belly.

I woke again, in the same position. Hours later yet, judging by how drowsy and foggy I felt. Refreshed, but still lazy. Content to lie there and drift.

Puck shifted in his sleep, making a soft sound of contentedness as he burrowed back into me, seeking out and finding my hand in a partially conscious gesture. He held my hand like that, and I felt him drift back to sleep, his grip loosening until he let go.

Depositing my hand right onto his hard cock.

I smiled against his back, remembering our time in the shower last night, what I'd done to him. A lot of work, but so fucking worth it to feel him lose control, to see him so completely consumed in pleasure. Especially after the way he'd made me come, the sheer quantity and quality of mind-blowing orgasms he'd given me; I'd wanted to blow his mind as completely as he had mine.

I gripped his cock, unable to stop myself. And why should I? I shifted so I could see his erection with my hand on it. And then my eyes landed on the string of condoms he'd set on the nightstand.

Oh.

Oh *yes*.

I reached out, leaning over him to snag the

string, tore one free, tossed the rest who knew where. Ripped it open with my teeth and tossed the wrapper aside.

Rolled the condom down his hard length. He moaned, murmured, but didn't wake.

I smiled, glad he was staying asleep.

I pulled at his shoulder, and he moaned and murmured again, but rolled with me so he was behind me, spooning me, now.

Perfect.

I snugged my ass back against him, reached between my legs to find him, and guided him into me. I moaned as he filled me, and I felt him shift, heard him murmur and mumble. I rolled my hips back against him, pressing my ass against his thighs, sighing in pleasure as I felt his thickness spread me apart. I reached behind us to clutch his ass, holding on for leverage as I slowly pushed back against him, again and again.

He moaned low in his throat.

Began unconsciously moving with me.

"Cole . . ." I heard him mumble, sleepy, maybe still asleep.

I rolled my hips again and craned my head around so I could press my lips against his. "Puck," I whispered.

He made another sleepy, unintelligible sound, and his hand slid along my hip, searching, and his hips flexed to push his cock deeper into me. "Cole . . .

so good."

I believed he thought he was dreaming, and the fact that he was moaning my name even in his sleep sent thrills of deep satisfaction and happiness through me.

I sighed in pleasure, letting my hips move in a sinuous slide, holding on to his hard ass, head twisted to keep my lips pressed against his cheek. His hand clutched at my hip, gripped and released, and then squeezed again, pulling at me.

"Unnhh . . . Cole . . . Colbie." He sounded more coherent now, more awake. Still thought he was dreaming, though.

"Puck, god, Puck," I breathed.

I heard him grunt in surprise, and his subconscious thrusting faltered. "Colbie?"

I rolled my hips and clutched his ass, found his mouth and kissed him, morning breath and all. "Keep going, Puck."

"Holy shit."

"I know, right?"

He slid his hand up to my tits, fondling them, taking both in one hand and squeezing as he let himself move again. "Jesus, Cole. You really know how to wake a guy up."

I breathed a laugh and nuzzled my nose into his cheek, his beard tickling my chin. "Couldn't help it. Accidentally got a handful of your hard-on, and I wanted you, so I figured why not?"

He slid his palm down my belly and between my legs, found my clit and sent me soaring. "I wouldn't mind waking up like this more often."

"Me either." I gasped as his touch brought me from merely enjoying sex to riding the edge of climax within seconds, with a speed and intensity I'd only ever felt with Puck—would only ever feel with Puck, something told me. "Of course, I wouldn't mind waking up one morning with your cock inside me. Or your mouth on me."

His teeth latched onto my shoulder, and I felt his abs flexing against my spine as he drove into me slowly, lazily. "I think that can be arranged."

"Yeah?"

He groaned against my back, his breathing beginning to stutter, his thrusts to gain power and intensity. "How about every morning?"

I heard what he was saying, and understood what he wasn't. "I think that could be arranged," I echoed his words from a moment before.

"Yeah?"

I dug my fingernails into the iron hard muscle of his butt, clawing at him as his fingers whirled and blurred and stroked me toward a gasping, thrashing climax. It didn't take long for either of us. I fell into shattering climax within a handful of strokes, and he was right there with me, grunting into my ear, breathing my name. I moaned as I felt him come, his climax blasting through him as I dissolved into thrashing, wailing orgasm, taking him hard, taking him deep, his thrusts wild and frenzied.

He was chanting my nickname again—*Cole . . . Cole . . . Cole*—in time with his thrusts, and I had my teeth buried in the thin skin of his neck, biting as hard as I dared, groaning—growling, really—as our mutual orgasm seared through us. I felt him, not just his orgasm, not just the release or the heat as his come filled the condom, or his hands clutching me everywhere he could reach, or how deep he went as he fucked me furiously through the last wrenching shuddering waves of our climax.

Not all that. But *him*. I felt bound to him, connected to him in a way I'd never connected to anyone, no matter how good the sex. This was the best by several orders of magnitude, but also *more*, deeper, more meaningful. Not just deeper like he could fuck me so deep—which was true and delicious and incredible and I wasn't even done coming and I wanted him to fuck me again, and harder, and deeper—but because I somehow was meant to do this with him. No point in over dramatizing it or putting labels on it or sticking it into boxes, but it was just . . . meant to be. And I had absolutely no plan or desire to let go of him until it was obvious we were done, and if that day never came, so be it, and maybe I'd learn how use the L-word with him, and we'd have one of things that start with the letter 'M' and rhymes with carriage, something that's never even crossed my mind until

I met Puck . . .

Jesus.

Fucking yesterday?

Really? Felt like longer.

We were gasping, stilled, his cock still stiff inside me, his hands clutching my tits possessively. He seemed content to let me lie on him like that as I caught my breath and recovered from the orgasm, and I was content to stay like that as long as he'd let me; he was a very comfortable man.

"Where do you live, Puck?"

"Where do I live?" he repeated the question. "Um. Nowhere, really. I have an apartment I rent in Boulder, because it's within driving distance of Harris and Layla's compound, but I don't stay there much. I'm on the road a lot when I'm not working. Just riding."

"No plans to find somewhere to stick, though?" I asked, endeavoring to sound casual. "Like, no intention of putting down roots?"

Puck shifted his hips so he pulled out of me, and we both groaned as I lost him. He tied off the condom and tossed it onto the floor, and then I rolled so I was facing him, lying almost completely on top of him, my head on his chest, his beard tickling me, his hands stroking through my hair.

"Never had a reason to stay in any one place before," he said. "Don't have anything against sticking around, I've just . . . never had a reason."

"What if you had a reason?"

His touch skated down my back. "Then I'd stay."

"Where?"

"Wherever the reason was."

I allowed a long silence to grow, until I summoned courage and my voice. "How do you feel about New York?"

"How do you feel about long weekend trips on my Harley?" he countered.

"I end up working from home on Mondays quite frequently, and most of my work can be done with a cell phone and a laptop, so as long as I have signal and Wi-Fi, I can work from pretty much anywhere." I paused. "So if, say, a motorcycle trip was to last from Friday after work until late Monday evening, would that make up for having to be in the city during the week?"

He chuckled. "I have nothing against the city. I've always enjoyed Manhattan."

"Actually, I live in DUMBO, I just work in Manhattan. It's too expensive to live downtown Manhattan."

"What's dumbo?"

"It's a name, it stands for Down under the Manhattan Bridge Overpass," I answered. "It's a neighborhood in Brooklyn."

"Oh. Well, whatever." He gripped my ass with both hands, as if he couldn't help himself, and god knew I didn't mind. I loved the way he couldn't kept his hands off me, and as I thought that, I realized I'd used the L-word, and tried not to panic. "As long as you don't try to turn me into a hipster."

I snorted. "Dear god, no." I lifted up and tugged on his beard. "Don't change a single thing about yourself."

"Nothing?"

I tilted my head to one side, thinking. "Maybe fewer metal shirts?"

He chuckled. "That one's easy enough. I usually only wear them while I'm working anyway."

"What about me?"

"What do you mean, what about you?"

"Anything you would change?"

He pulled me into a kiss. "Cole, baby . . . not a goddamn thing."

I wiggled against him. "Good answer."

He palmed my ass again, and kissed me in response.

The kiss was endless, drowning. Minutes, or hours, or I didn't know how long. It stole my breath, and made my pussy drip, and I felt him harden.

I writhed, and wriggled, and shifted, and felt him slide bare into me.

"Get ready to get messy, sweet thing," Puck murmured to me.

I moaned as he moved. "I like getting messy with you." I slid off him and rolled to my hands and knees, swayed my ass at him. "Like this. That way when you pull out, you can make a mess all over my ass."

He growled. "God*damn*, Cole. I *really* like the way you think."

"And then we'll need another shower," I said, letting my voice make the obvious suggestion.

Puck just laughed again, but it was a growling, eager, pleased sound.

I laughed with him, but the laugh turned into a groan as he slid into me, and then the groan turned into a whimper as he started fucking me, and the whimper turned into a wail as he spanked me in time with his thrusts, one cheek and then the other in turn, harder and harder, until he was fucking and spanking with crazed abandon, and I was slamming back into him and I didn't need to touch myself to come. I still did, though, because I liked—*loved*—touching myself while Puck fucked me, feeling his cock slam into me as my fingers flew.

He growled again, and I felt him falter, stop, and pull out. I lowered myself so my chest was on the bed and my ass was in the air for him, and I watched over my shoulder as he jerked his cock rough and hard, and our eyes met, and I grinned in delight watching his come squirt out of him. I felt it splash onto my ass, again and again, more and more and more come in thick wet hot viscous puddles, dripping down my crack and tickling my asshole.

"God, that was hot," I breathed, when he was done.

He groaned wordlessly, holding on to my ass with both hands for balance, gasping. "Yeah, babe, it was . . . fucking intense."

"Intense fucking, you mean," I laughed.

He laughed with me, sliding off the bed and stumbling as if half-drunk to the bathroom, where he snagged a washcloth, wet it with hot water, wrung it out, and came back to me, wiping me until I was thoroughly clean.

He finally collapsed onto the bed beside me. "Jesus. Twice before breakfast. I think that's a new record, even for me."

"I'm all about new experiences," I said, grinning at him.

"And I love that about you," he said, and then blinked at me as if realizing what he'd just said. "Um."

I snuggled closer to him, laid my head on his chest and toyed with his flaccid dick, flopping it back and forth. "Don't take it back. Don't explain it. Just . . . let it stand."

"Okay."

"So did we just agree that you're moving in with me?" I asked after a few minutes of contented silence.

"I think we did."

I wasn't looking at him, but I could hear the smile in his voice.

The room phone rang, and Puck answered it. "Yo . . . oh, hey boss. Yeah, we'll come down . . . news, huh? What kind of news? Fine, fine, be that way. Yeah, give us a few minutes. There's still grub? Sweet. Yeah, see you." He hung up, and I waited for the explanation. "We gotta head downstairs. Harris is gathering everyone for a team breakfast slash debriefing slash news update."

"But he wouldn't say what the news was?"

"Nope. Asshole. Said he didn't feel like repeating himself half a dozen times, so he was calling a war council."

That made my heart skip a few beats. "War council? Does that mean it's not over?"

He shrugged and then stood up. "Nah, not necessarily. But he didn't sound worried."

"Oh."

There was a knock at the door, and Puck wrapped a towel around his waist to answer it. I stayed hidden in the bedroom as he spoke to whoever it was, and then I heard the door close again. Puck appeared with a stack of parcels wrapped in tissue paper and tied off with twine.

"Apparently Roth had his people get some clothes for us, since neither of us have shit. The majordomo or whatever that cat's title is said these should fit, but they could only guess at our sizes."

He set down the two packages, handing one to me. It had my name written on the tissue paper in neat, precise handwriting. I opened it and found a new set of clothes from the skin out, everything with the tags still on. Bra and panties in a matching set, a cream knee-length sweater-dress with a wide green belt, and a pair of Toms flats in a matching shade of green. Whoever it was that chose the clothes had pretty damn amazing taste, I had to say. Puck's clothes weren't exactly what I'd consider his natural style—fitted, faded jeans with a bit of stretch to the denim, and a green polo shirt, with a brown belt, and new boot socks. Not his style, probably, being far too preppy/pretty boy for his taste, but I thought he looked amazing.

"I don't think I've worn a shirt with a collar since I left the FBI," he remarked, tugging the shirt on. "Don't miss it."

"You probably had to wear business casual when you worked for the Bureau, huh?" I asked, donning my own clothes.

He nodded. "Dress slacks, a button down, and a tie. I fucking hated it."

I buttoned the three buttons of his polo for him. "Well, maybe not your style, but you look nice."

He eyed me as I buckled the belt high around my waist. "You look positively edible."

I swept past him toward the bathroom, winking at him. "You've already eaten me, remember?"

"Yeah, well, I'm feeling a bit peckish again."

I found a brush in one of the drawers and tugged it through my hair. "War council, remember?"

"Yeah, yeah. And breakfast."

I emerged from the bathroom and took his hand,

and we exited the room together. "So, war council and breakfast, then we go for a ride or a drive out in the countryside, and then we come back here and fuck each other's brains out." I bumped him with my shoulder. "Sound like a plan?"

"Yeah, except you forgot one part."

"What's that?"

"We go for a drive out in the countryside, and we fuck each other's brains out in the grass somewhere, and then we come back here and fuck each other's brains out again."

"Oh," I said, laughing. "That's a lot of fucking. We might need a picnic in that case. To keep our strength up."

Colbie and I found the dining room after more than a few wrong turns, and we were very obviously the last ones there. Most everyone was nearly done eating already, although it looked like no one had gotten any more sleep than Colbie and I had, and for the same reasons.

With all the fucking happening under this roof last night, it's a wonder the whole place didn't just collapse.

We'd barely sat down when two staff members brought plates piled high with food and set them in front of us, and then returned to pour us each coffee.

There were plates of bacon, plates of pancakes, plates of scrambled eggs, English muffins, toast, bagels, fruit . . . a shitload of food.

While we were eating, Harris stood up, tossed back the last of his coffee, and then set it on the table. "Listen up, y'all. I've been in contact with Lear and Anselm. Our boy Cain is in the wind again. Lear tracked him down to a high-rise in Belgrade, but by the time Anselm could get there with his rifle, Cain was gone, and now he's gone dark. Anselm and Ivar collaborated with Interpol and tracked down what was left of his trafficking setup. There was a warehouse in Marseilles full of women, another in Istanbul, and a third in Marrakech. There were a good three or four hundred women between the three locations, and the capture of the assholes running the warehouses led to hits on various other smaller depots and safe houses. His shit is shut down for now. That's the good news."

"What's the bad news, then?" Duke asked.

"Cain is still out there," Harris said with a shrug. "Gone to ground for the time being, and I don't think there's any immediate chance of him popping up, since between us and Interpol we've taken down most of his high-ranking payroll members and freed all his so-called merchandise. But . . . he's still alive, and we know he doesn't forget."

"So is it back to business as normal?" Thresh asked.

"Pretty much. We'll keep our ears open and stay

sharp, because that's just how you stay alive in this business, but I think we're in the clear. I know Ivar and Anselm both have a serious hard-on for taking Cain out, so I'm pretty sure between them, if that fucker can be found, they'll find him and put a slug in his skull."

He cast his gaze from person to person around the table. "Doesn't mean go lax on the personal security measures, boys. You know that, but I feel compelled to remind you. Especially now that most of us have women to protect, just make sure you're staying sharp. But I think, for now, we can put this whole stupid business behind us."

"I wouldn't exactly call it stupid," Layla pointed out. "If I were y'all, I'd almost thank Cain—thank him, and then kill him, but still thank him."

"Thank his ass for what?" I demanded.

She smirked and pointed at Colbie, who was practically on my lap, and then at Temple and Lola, who were both pretty much straddling their respective men. "All of y'all. Thresh got Lola out of this whole thing, Duke got Temple, and you got Colbie. Sounds like a win all around, since all of us walked away intact."

Duke, his arm in sling, snorted. "Speak for yourself."

Thresh laughed. "I second that."

Layla rolled her eyes. "Oh, whatever. Don't be pussies. You'll both be back to deadlifting

Volkswagens in no time."

I acceded her point with a tilt of my head. "She has a point, fellas."

Both Duke and Thresh glanced at me, at each other, and then at the women on their laps, and then at Layla.

"Yeah, well, still. I may be thankful, but the only thanks I'm gonna give Cain is a potshot," Duke said.

"Leave that to someone else," Temple said. "I'm taking you home with me to Beverly Hills. Mom is gonna flip when she meets you."

Duke frowned. "You do realize I'll fit in like a pit bull at a cat shelter in Beverly Hills, right?"

Temple just laughed. "That's what I'm looking forward to." She stroked his ridiculously chiseled jaw-line. "I won't be surprised if you get offers to model or act or both."

I laughed. "That'd be the funniest shit in the world, if you get a gig moonlighting as an underwear model."

Temple laughed. "It wouldn't be underwear he'd be modeling," she murmured under her breath, and then dissolved into giggles.

Which set off the rest of the women, and left us men staring at them like the slack-jawed mouth-breathers we all were.

"I feel like we missed a joke, Duke," Thresh said.

Duke was suddenly studious about adding cream to his coffee, even though the dumb-shit took his coffee black, the only real way to drink coffee. "Speak for yourself," he mumbled, shooting a grin at Temple.

The penny dropped, and Thresh just stared. "Dick models? Is that really a thing?" He eyed his own crotch dubiously. "I could probably do that."

Lola choked on her orange juice, and once she recovered, patted him on the chest. "Yeah, you'd break the internet if you did that. Maybe leave that to men with something to prove."

Duke glared at her. "What exactly do you think I have to prove, woman?"

Thresh's voice rumbled threateningly. "Don't call her woman, jackass."

"Don't call me jackass, jackass."

Temple and Lola exchanged *men are so stupid* looks as Thresh and Duke decided to resolve the matter with an arm-wrestling match, even though both of them had an arm in a sling. It was funny to watch, though.

Layla stood beside Harris's chair, leaning against him, running her fingers idly through his hair, watching the whole thing with an expression akin to a mother happily watching her grown boys horsing around.

Which wasn't far from the truth, it seemed to me. She was the boss lady, after all.

"Yo, Layla," I said, and she glanced at me. "You kicked ass out there, by the way. Not too many people in this world I'd trust to have at my back, and you're at the top of the list. "

She grinned at me. "Oh, go on," she said, waving her hand. "No, really, keep going."

I laughed. "And so humble, too."

She shrugged. "I mean, you did see that shot I took in the Rover, lying across two people, one-handed, didn't you?"

"From one moving vehicle to another moving vehicle. Yeah, I saw. Badass boss lady shit right there."

She patted herself on the shoulder. "Hey, what can I say, I was born for this shit." She glanced lovingly down at Harris. "Plus, I had a good teacher." She squeaked, jumping, and I realized Harris had pinched her ass. "Okay, okay, a perfect, amazing, wonderful, patient teacher. The *best* teacher."

Harris didn't give away much with his expression, but I saw the glint in his eye. "I think the teacher is ready for another lesson."

Layla winked at me, which was an inside joke now, after Colbie's explosion about my winking. She took Harris by the hand and led him out of the dining room.

Two by two, the rest of the team dispersed, Duke and Temple to make arrangements for a flight to LA, Thresh and Lola to go house hunting in Denver, apparently. Which left Roth and Kyrie, and Colbie and me.

"Hey, Roth," I called out. "You got a ride around here Colbie and I can borrow? We wanna go for a spin out in the countryside."

Roth had been watching the whole proceeding silently, browsing his phone now and again. He nodded at me. "Nigel can show you the garage. Take your pick."

I stood up and lifted Colbie to her feet. "Well, thanks for the room, the Scotch, the hospitality in general, and . . . just for everything. You guys are awesome."

"It has been my privilege, I assure you," Roth said. "And if you're ever in need of a vacation, I know a rather nice place in the Caribbean."

Colbie nudged me. "I do have a lot of vacation time saved up. I've never been to the Caribbean."

I grinned at her then pointed at Roth. "Sounds like we'll be taking you up on that," I said. "We'll hit you up when we have plans made."

It was weird to be talking about *we* already, but damn if Roth hadn't nailed it on the head: when it makes sense, it just makes sense, even if it doesn't make any fucking sense.

Colbie and I made our way out of the dining room and through the maze of hallways, getting turned around more than once in our quest to find Nigel, who Roth said would be in the kitchen.

We stumbled past a courtyard at one point, just a few square meters of green space and open sky tucked into a corner created by the layout of the mansion. There was a profusion of trees, a little fountain, and a wrought-iron bench. On the bench sat Harris, his arms stretched out to either side, his head tipped back, his eyes closed. Layla was on her knees in front of him, her hands and mouth moving.

I nudged Colbie and pointed, whispering. "See, what'd I tell you?"

Colbie covered her mouth. "Oh my god! Right there in the courtyard?"

"Shameless," I said. "And relentless. Like I said, that man gets a crazy amount of head from that woman."

Layla's eyes flicked up, and she saw us as we kept moving past the courtyard. She winked over the top of Harris and returned her attention to what—or who, more accurately—she was doing.

"What would you consider a crazy amount?" Colbie asked, a few minutes later, after we'd found Nigel and had been shown the garage.

I shrugged. "Like, all time. Just about every time I see them, she's either obviously just blown him, or will after the meeting."

"Are you challenging me?" Colbie demanded.

I eyed her. "I—"

"Challenge accepted."

I blinked at her. "Um. Okay?"

She glanced around the garage, empty except for about twenty automobiles, from restored classics to utility vehicles to a brand-new Hypercar. Then she pushed me to a nook between a Wrangler kitted for heavy off-roading duty and a giant Silverado 3500 geared for heavy hauling, shoved my back against the wall, and fell to her knees.

"Oh." I watched as she undid my jeans and pulled me out. "Challenge accepted, huh?"

She had me hard in seconds. "Not really. But I should point out that when I decide I like something, I get kind of addicted."

"A-*DICK*-ted, huh?"

She smirked up at me as she jacked me. "Penis-based puns. My favorite." She leaned closer to me. "Yes, you might say I'm quickly becoming a-*DICK*-ted to your cock. Which is probably good for you, and your chances of receiving . . . how'd you put it . . . a crazy amount of head from this woman."

"I'm on board with this addiction."

"One caveat, though."

"Name it."

"Don't be shy with the cunnilingus."

I laughed. "Babe, just try and keep me away from your pussy."

"Why would I do that?"

"Good point—oh . . . *ohh*. Holy shit, babe . . . Jesus, you're gonna make me come in thirty seconds flat if you keep that up—"

Which seemed to be her goal, and one at which she succeeded.

Followed by me returning the favor, which meant we didn't end up leaving for our spin in the countryside for quite a while.

And yes, we fucked each other's brains out in the grass beneath a spreading oak tree.

And again in the car, on the side of the road.

And again when we got back.

And again in the back of Roth's private jet on the way to New York.

And again in her apartment in DUMBO, which was a gorgeous little loft full of sweetness and light and tasteful decorations.

And again, and again, and again that night.

You get the point.

EPILOGUE

I TRIED TO STIFLE MY NERVES, BUT IT WAS NO GOOD. "Yo, relax, Cole. It's fine. Harris could land this bitch in the dark in a windstorm without instruments." Puck took my hand and squeezed, speaking to me over the private channel between his headset and mine. "Don't freak."

I gulped hard as the helicopter Harris was flying swooped low over the water, nose down, skimming barely fifty feet above the waves. "Can he . . . slow down at all?"

Puck thumbed a switch that looped Harris into our headsets. "Harris, quit showing off, you asshole," I heard him say.

Harris, up front behind the controls, chuckled. "Aww, you ain't scared are you, Colbie?"

"Maybe a little," I squeaked. "You're flying like it's a fighter jet."

Puck, Harris, and Layla all laughed.

"Don't tempt him, hon," Layla said.

"Too late," Harris said.

"Shit." Puck cinched his five-point harness tighter and then reached over to cinch mine so tight I could barely breathe. "Keep your eyes open, Cole, and keep breathing."

"Ready?" Harris said.

"NO!" I shouted.

"Too late."

I watched his hands shift gently forward, and I felt a corresponding increase in pressure on my chest as we accelerated. That wasn't so bad—

And then he hauled backward on one of the controls, and our nose lifted abruptly, forcing my stomach down toward my toes. We climbed like a rocket for what felt like a full minute, though I knew it was far less, and then instead of merely leveling out, Harris tilted us to the left and tipped our nose downward, and now my heart was in my throat and threatening to pop out of my mouth, and I felt dizzy and fought darkness at the edges of my sight. We dove and dove and dove, arcing around and down in a long steep curve, and I could see water through the windscreen up front and beyond the window on my left, water rising toward us at a terrifying pace, a brilliant azure. Harris banked the helicopter over to the other side so now I was totally suspended in the air, only held in the seat by the harness Puck had tightened. I glanced to my right, and Puck was gripping his knees with white-knuckled fingers, but he had a wild grin on his face as we soared tilted sideways, nose down, toward the Caribbean.

At what seemed like the last second, he leveled out, and this time he was maybe twenty-five feet above the water, so close I could see the individual whitecap waves.

All we'd done was a rising loop, going up and around back down so we were heading in our original direction, yet it had felt like an entire airshow's worth of death-defying tricks.

I gasped for breath as Harris slowed back down. "I hate you, Nicholas Harris."

"That was nothing," Layla laughed. "You wanna really toss your cookies, go up in one of his actual vintage fighter jets. He just got his paws on a Harrier, so now he can do some really crazy shit."

"No thanks," I gulped. "I don't even like roller-coasters, much less death-defying aerial acrobatics."

"Death-defying, she says," Harris said with a sarcastic guffaw. "We can't even break the sound barrier. We're in a goddamn *helo*, for Chrissakes. You want death-defying, let me take you up in my Phantom. I can make you shit your actual pants."

"Truth," Puck said. "I went up with him in the Phantom, and I did actually poop a little."

"I'm good." My voice was, once again, a sissy squeak.

The rest of the flight was thankfully uneventful, even a little boring. It was the week before Thanksgiving, and the entire A1S family was heading down to Kyrie and Valentine's guest village. Yes, that's exactly what I meant: a entire village. Roth had gone whole-hog, as he was apparently prone to doing, and bought a tiny little island near the one their home was on, and he built a village on it. Renewable energy via wind and solar, plumbing and water reclamation, internet, a post office-slash-general store, and ten individual two-bed one-bath homes, each with its own private beach access. Fucking ridiculous, was what it was. He'd sent emails to all of us with a link to a Dropbox account, containing a hundred-plus photos of the village, with detailed descriptions of the amenities available. Of course, throughout the year he rented the homes on a week-by-week basis to tourists, but it was officially "closed" from Thanksgiving to New Year, so all of us at A1S could come down for as long as we wanted.

I'd worked my ass off and saved my vacation time throughout the year and had gotten the entire holiday season off, mainly because I'd closed on more accounts myself than any other three people combined. It's amazing what being truly happy could do for a woman, especially when that happiness was derived from regular orgasms thanks to Puck's talented fingers, tongue, and cock. I kept him happy with all the sex and blowjobs he could want and then some, and in return he made sure I rode a near-constant high from my own orgasms. It was a perfect scenario. He'd be gone for a week at a time with work, and I'd worry my tits off, and then he'd come home and we'd fuck for an entire weekend, not leaving the bed for anything except food and to use the bathroom—and to shower, but that also ended up with more sex.

He wanted to flat-out purchase my apartment, but I refused to let him, leading to our first blowout fight, because I refused to let him take over my finances, and he wanted to "take care of me," which was nice, but fucking no; I'd been taking care of myself since I was sixteen and wasn't about to let any man, even Puck, have that kind of control over my life, even if I did trust and love him without reservation. So we compromised, and he bought a penthouse suite in downtown Manhattan, thanks to a literal steal of a deal via Valentine—meaning, Roth had bought the entire upper floor of a building, renovated it, and "sold" it to Puck for a sixteenth of its actual market value. It was a breathtaking place, glorious, jaw-dropping, with floor-to-ceiling windows on all four sides, an expansive kitchen . . .

And a personal chef whenever we wanted him, a personal trainer, and a valet—which didn't just mean someone to park cars, but do our every bidding. *Perks of the condo*, Valentine had said, with a subdued laugh in his voice. And shit, it was amazing, so how could I say no? It was literally a five-minute walk from my office, and, oh yeah, did I mention the helicopter that was only a text message away, ready to take us wherever we wanted to go? Apparently, when Valentine Roth decided he wanted to thank someone with extravagant gifts, he didn't accept no for an answer.

Puck kept working for Harris, of course, and I kept working at my import-export firm, but we accepted Roth's generosity and took full advantage of it.

And now I had a month and half of vacation time, paid, and we were going to spend it in the Caribbean with the whole gang, drinking excessive amounts of alcohol, sitting on the beach around a fire, and of course, absolutely inordinate amounts of time spent naked together.

Sounded perfect.

Eventually, we landed on a helicopter pad built on one end of Roth and Kyrie's private home island; the landing was smoother than an elevator ride, with barely a bump as we touched down. Kyrie was waiting, a little girl of three or four years at her side, and a brand-new baby on her hip. Apparently she'd been pregnant when she was snatched and hadn't found out until a month later.

Layla, too, was showing a bump, which was a more recent development.

Nothing here, nor would there be any time soon, although I had noticed Puck surreptitiously browsing for engagement rings online. I'd say yes in a heartbeat, obviously, but neither of us were in any way ready for kids. Jeez, just the thought made my spine shiver. I loved babies, loved kids, they were sweet and fun and cute, and I liked to be able to give them back.

Which was why I was puzzled when Kyrie handed me her little one, and my heart melted as the adorable little tow-headed, blue-eyed boy gurgled up at me and yanked my hair in a slobbery fist, and I found myself thinking maybe it wouldn't be so bad.

Also weird was that I carried Cal, the baby, all the way from the helipad to the house, and continued holding him as the gang all gathered on the deck and started the usual bullshitting, teasing, joking banter. I didn't give him back until Kyrie needed to feed him.

Puck noticed.

We were sitting in a deep, comfortable chair near a fire on the beach, me on his lap, his hands in my hair.

"You ain't gettin' any ideas, are you?" he murmured.

Why not test him? Stupid and bound to backfire in some way, but fuck it, right?

"Umm . . ." I shrugged, as if unsure. "I mean, no. Right? No. That's a stupid idea." I didn't sound like I believed it.

And the dumbest part of the whole thing was . . . I wasn't entirely sure I was testing him, or myself. OR that I wasn't actually speaking the truth.

"Cole, honey. You for real?" He shifted sideways

so he could look into my face.

"I wasn't at first, but for some reason, it doesn't sound too terribly crazy. Does it?"

Puck didn't answer for a very long time, sipping his Scotch and staring up at the stars. "I'm a wild man, Cole. I don't know the first fuckin' thing about kids."

"You're not so wild," I said. "And I don't know anything about kids either. But . . . why not?"

"Why not doesn't seem like a valid reason to have kids."

"I know. But, I'm not saying we *should*, just that maybe it's not a crazy idea, and it's worth talking about."

He sighed slowly, heavily. "Between you and me, sweet thing, the idea scares the shit outta me."

I searched his face. "Why?"

"Because . . . my old man was a piece of shit."

"But he didn't raise a piece of shit," I told him, cupping his face. "You're an amazing man, Puck. A *good* man. You've got some rough edges, but then hell, so do I. So does Layla. And Harris, and Duke, and Thresh, and Lola. Not Temple, but she's a freak like that."

He laughed. "Yeah, she's kind of absurdly perfect, in an annoying way."

Duke was sitting near us. "She farts in her sleep and doesn't know the first thing about taking care of herself. She's as helpless as a kitten by herself. Can't even boil water. She tried to make me plain ol' Kraft

Mac 'n Cheese once, and nearly burned down the fuckin' condo." He grinned at us. "She ain't perfect. Nobody's perfect, bro. Not even me, if you'll believe it."

"You? *Nooooo*," Puck drawled sarcastically. "Why, I'll bet you shit roses and fart rainbows."

"Nope, just kittens and puppies."

I laughed. "Not even mac 'n cheese? For real?"

Duke chortled. "She put all the ingredients in at once, right at the beginning, and then turned on the heat. When it wouldn't cook right, she put it in the fuckin' oven, pot and all."

"And you just watched this happening?" I demanded.

"Hell yeah, I did!" Duke said, laughing. "Also, she told me to shut up and let her do it, even if she was doing it wrong. Hell, I even told her to follow the directions on the damn box."

Temple came up as Duke was finishing. "Shut *up!*" she shrieked, whacking his arm. "You are *not* telling that story, you colossal dick."

"It was relevant," Duke said.

"To what?" Temple demanded.

"To the fact that our boy Puck here is scared to have a kid because he's worried he ain't perfect."

"That's not—" Puck started.

"Oh my god! You guys are having a baby too?" Temple said it loudly enough that the whole group heard.

I covered my face in embarrassment as everyone turned toward Puck and me, beginning to offer congratulations. "No, no, no. We were just . . . discussing the possibility."

Temple saw my mortification and looked chagrined. "Oh. Um, shit. Sorry, Colbie."

I waved her off. "It's fine. Just a misunderstanding."

Layla waddled over and plopped down on the chair on our other side, hands over her belly. "Hey, I'm a perpetual fuck-up, and Nick is a grouchy asshole, and all of us do dangerous shit for a living. Yet here I am, fat as a goddamn whale, about to have a kid, and I'm no way ready for this. I wake up at night in a panic, because I'm absolutely certain I'm gonna fuck this kid up."

Roth, who had Kyrie perched on one leg and Cal on the other, spoke up for the first time. "I was a high-level arms dealer. I ran in a circle with the most dangerous men and women on the planet. My father was a cold, hard, unforgiving, unloving bastard, and my mother was a simpering pet who did whatever she was told." He kissed Kyrie's temple, and then Cal's hair, and Cal reached up and poked at Roth's eyeball. "Yes, buddy, that's my eye, thanks," he chuckled. "I'd say I'm a pretty good father, all things considered. Point is, if I can do this, any of you can do this."

Kyrie nuzzled his cheek. "You're an *amazing* daddy, Valentine." To the rest of us, "And he's right. Obviously, it's not easy, and it's scary, especially at first, but give them your love and your attention and just try to give them everything none of us had as a kid; they'll be fine."

The conversation then shifted to our childhoods, and all the crazy fucked-up shit we'd all been through, which turned into a bizarre competition for who was the most fucked up, but it was a competition no one person seemed to have a lock on, as we were all equally fucked up in different ways.

Later that night, after Roth's smaller yacht dropped us all off at the guest island and Puck and I were in bed, naked and sweating and still gasping, he cradled me against his chest and kissed my cheek.

"You're serious about all that?" he asked.

I didn't have to ask to know what he was referring to. "Only about it being worth discussing. In a more private setting, though."

"Like this one?"

I stroked my fingers through the hair on his chest. "Doesn't have to be now, Puck. I guess I'm just more curious as to whether you're even willing to consider the possibility, or hell, if *I* am."

He caressed my ass, thinking before responding. "It's no crazier of an idea than us jumping headfirst into a relationship less than forty-eight hours after meeting, and having it actually last."

"You see this lasting, then?"

He spanked my butt in a sharp swat. "You're not getting rid of me, Cole. You're stuck with me, now.

Too late to back out."

I tugged on his beard. "Good."

He reached over, slid open the drawer of the nightstand, and came back with a small black box. "We could make it official."

I stopped breathing as he opened the top to reveal a two-carat princess cut diamond solitaire. "Puck?"

"Marry me, Cole."

I kissed him, slowly, deeply. "Yes, Puck. Yes. A thousand times yes."

He slid the ring onto my finger, and I felt myself crying, but I didn't bother trying to stop them. Puck himself seemed . . . choked up as we watched the dimmed lights glint off the diamond.

I palmed his cheek. "I do have one small condition for marrying you."

He frowned down at me. "Okay . . .?"

"Your name."

He sighed, chuckling. "It would be that, wouldn't it?" Puck yanked on his beard, which told me he really didn't want to tell me, but I waited silently, and eventually he spoke. "Okay, well my name really is truly and legally Puck. No middle name, just Puck Lawson. But it wasn't always. I turned eighteen just after I'd finished boot camp. I'd hated my name my whole life and had been going by Puck since I was thirteen."

"Why Puck?"

He shrugged. "When I was thirteen, my

seventh-grade literature teacher took our whole class to Little Rock for a performance of *A Midsummer Night's Dream*. I thought Puck was the coolest guy in the whole play. All the other kids were going on about Titania and Oberon and whoever, but I was all about Puck. The way the actor played him was as a trickster, a sneak, a practical joker, the kind of guy who could annoy you to death as easily as charm your pants off, and sometimes both at the same time. I just . . . loved the character. I went home and read the play myself, and I didn't understand shit, but I loved all of Puck's lines. And since I hated my name, and had hated my name since I was old enough to hate anything, I decided to start going by Puck. Annoyed the fuck outta my dad, because I was adamant about it. Just wouldn't answer, acted like I didn't hear him or my teachers unless they called me Puck. The old man even tried to beat me out of it, but I was back at it as soon as I could move my jaw again."

"Jesus, Puck."

He waved a hand. "Bah, that was twenty-five years ago."

"So what was your birth name?"

He blew out a raspberry. "You don't wanna know."

"Yes, I do."

"Well, I don't wanna tell you."

"How about if I suck you off? Would that help?"

"No hands."

"Deal," I said, kissing his chest.

I slid down his body and used my lips and tongue and mouth to play him into erection. He watched and waited until I was ready to start really going down on him, and then he finally sighed yet again, heavier than ever.

"You cannot tell fucking anyone. I mean *anyone*. Ever."

His voice was hard enough that I knew he wasn't even remotely joking. "Jesus, Puck, it must be really bad. Of course, baby, you have my promise I won't ever tell."

He closed his eyes as I took him into my mouth. "Bartholomew Bucephalus."

I had to back off so I didn't choke on him as I laughed. "Holy shit, that *is* bad."

He laughed with me, thankfully. "No shit. Do I seem like fucking Bart to you? That's what everyone called me. Bart.

"Dear god, why would anyone saddle a poor innocent child with a name like that?" I asked.

"My grandfather and his father were both Bart. My dad was Bucephalus, went by Buck."

"And you chose the name Puck, when your dad was Buck?"

He chuckled. "I got him off my back by telling him I'd picked it to sound like his name, which was a dirty lie, but he went with it, and I went by Puck from then on. Soon as I turned eighteen, I changed my name legally to Puck."

"I'm glad you did. Your name fits you perfectly."

"You know what fits perfectly?" he asked, a smirk on his lips.

"Your big cock in my mouth?"

"Exactly." He moaned as I resumed fulfilling my promise, taking as much of his cock into my mouth as I could. "Although that wasn't what I was gonna say."

I glanced up to communicate the question my mouth was too occupied to verbalize.

He groaned, watching me. "You marry me, take my name, you'll be Colbie Lawson."

I brought him to the edge and took him over, swallowing every last drop as he grunted and groaned and fisted my hair. "I love the sound of Colbie Lawson." He hauled me up his body and kissed me. "And I love the thought of being your Colbie Lawson even more."

We lay together, drifting off to sleep.

I woke in the predawn gray to Puck's mouth between my legs. "Good morning, my love."

"Good morning, future Mrs. Puck Lawson."

I sat up enough to watch him, holding onto his head. And then, as he brought me to a swift, shuddering orgasm, I had an idea. He finished licking me through my aftershocks and then crawled up my body.

"Puck, baby?"

He groaned as I welcomed him into me, bare.

"Yeah, love."

"I have a really crazy idea."

"I don't put a condom on?"

"I'm on the pill, silly. I don't want you to put one on anyway—this feels too good." I clung to him, arms around his shoulders, legs around his ass. "What if—oh god, oh god, *Puck*—what if I become Mrs. Lawson while we're down here?"

He faltered. "What? Really?"

I nodded. "Really. Why wait? Everyone we care about is already here, and I know I want this, I know you want this, so why not?"

"You're sure?"

"As sure as I'm sure I'm gonna come in about four seconds."

"For real, Cole. Like, now?"

"Maybe next week. Enough time to get some flowers and an off-the-rack beach dress or something. Doesn't have to be fancy or elaborate. Just you, me, and the Alpha One Security family."

He moved faster, and faster, and faster, and I clung to him through it, breathing my love in his ear, and then I bit his shoulder as I came, and my orgasm triggered his, my pussy clamping down around him and throwing him over the edge, and he came bare inside me for the first time.

A week later, on Roth and Kyrie's beach, we were married. I wore an off-the shoulder, off-the-rack dress, and Puck wore a tux barefoot. The rest of the gang were all there, and it was simple and fun and cute and romantic, and I didn't wear any underwear, and I was relatively certain Puck impregnated me during the reception, since we'd agreed I'd stop taking birth control and see what happened.

Crazy, right?

Nah. Crazy isn't so crazy when it just makes sense.

THE END

Visit me at my website: **www.jasindawilder.com**
Email me: **jasindawilder@gmail.com**

If you enjoyed this book, you can help others enjoy it as well by recommending it to friends and family, or by mentioning it in reading and discussion groups and online forums. You can also review it on the site from which you purchased it. But, whether you recommend it to anyone else or not, thank you *so much* for taking the time to read my book! Your support means the world to me!

My other titles:

The Preacher's Son:
Unbound
Unleashed
Unbroken

Biker Billionaire:
Wild Ride

Big Girls Do It:
Better (#1), Wetter (#2), Wilder (#3), On Top (#4)
Married (#5)
On Christmas (#5.5)
Pregnant (#6)
Boxed Set

Rock Stars Do It:
Harder
Dirty
Forever
Boxed Set

From the world of *Big Girls* and *Rock Stars*:
Big Love Abroad

Delilah's Diary:
A Sexy Journey
La Vita Sexy
A Sexy Surrender

The Falling Series:
Falling Into You
Falling Into Us
Falling Under
Falling Away
Falling for Colton

The Ever Trilogy:
Forever & Always
After Forever
Saving Forever

The world of *Alpha*:
Alpha
Beta

Omega
Harris: Alpha One Security Book 1
Thresh: Alpha One Security Book 2
Duke: Alpha One Security Book 3

The world of Stripped:
Stripped
Trashed

The world of *Wounded*:
Wounded
Captured

The Houri Legends:
Jack and Djinn
Djinn and Tonic

The Madame X Series:
Madame X
Exposed
Exiled

Badd Brothers:
*Badd Motherf*cker*
Badd Ass

**The Black Room
(With Jade London):**
Door One

Door Two
Door Three
Door Four
Door Five
Door Six
Door Seven
Door Eight
Deleted Door

Standalone titles:
Yours

Non-Fiction titles:
Big Girls Do It Running
Big Girls Do It Stronger

Jack Wilder Titles:
The Missionary

To be informed of new releases and special offers,
sign up for
Jasinda's email newsletter.